# Good Night, Oregon

## The Lutheran Ladies Series

*B.K. Froman writing as Kris Knorr*

Plucking One String
Through the Knothole
Thanks for Leaving
Melody Markett's Crash Course on Life

## The Two Pan Series

*B.K. Froman*

Mornings in Two Pan
The Lights of Two Pan
Women and Thieves of Two Pan

## Hope and Hometown Series

*B.K. Froman*

Good Night, Oregon

# GOOD NIGHT, OREGON

B.K. Froman

Morning West Publishing

Good Night, Oregon
B.K. Froman

Morning West Publishing

Printed in the United States of America.

Good Night, Oregon by B.K. Froman
ISBN: 978-1-938531-30-9
1.Family Relationships—Fiction. 2.Humor—Fiction 3.Education—Fiction 4.Oregon—Fiction

To Ken.
And for all of us, who at some time or another feel we don't fit in. Don't you hate that???
Well, you're not alone.

*By improving yourself the world is made better. Be not afraid of growing too slowly. Only be afraid of standing still.*
~Ben Franklin

## 1. 1997

I ADMIT IT looks suspicious to push a broom along an unlit hallway. Luckily, no one is around. If they were, they'd joke about what a poor custodian I am, sweeping in the dark. I'd tell them I'm done for the night and too tired to fly it home. We'd have a laugh. Then I'd be forced to attempt this on a different night.

But tonight the hall is empty. I rest the broom against the wall, unlock the door, take a last glance around, then slip inside.

Country music plays so low, it's barely noticeable. The anteroom is half-lit. I pass through another set of doors and sit at "the board." Red and yellow lights glow among the buttons and dials. I should stop now.

But this is my courageous risk-thing for today.

A rocker switch turns on the reading spotlight. I snug headphones over my ears, pull folded papers from my back pocket, and open them. My hand freezes above the red switch.

"You've got this," I whisper. "You've repaired most of this equipment. Confidence coefficient—ninety-eight percent."

I don't wait for the song that's playing to finish. I flip the lever. The twangy boot-shufflin' music cuts off mid-note. The "On Air" sign hanging from the ceiling turns neon red.

I'm alone. Alone in the studio. The only ears are the ones at the far reach of the radio waves. Dead air drops through the speakers. Some women like to talk. Not me. My mouth feels like I've eaten cotton balls.

I swallow and lean in to the microphone.

# 2. 1997

## ON AIR

GREETINGS. THIS IS The Navigator.

Sorry to interrupt your music. The thin hours of the night are always the worst, aren't they? Are you working or studying right now? Maybe you're driving with the windows down, radio blaring, trying to stay awake on that long stretch of I-5. Maybe you can't sleep, reliving memories or lost in the world of I-wish-I-could-do-that-over. You toss and wrestle with the bedsheets—the alarm clock ticks toward morning.

Listen, I'm going to tell you a secret. Maybe it'll help. This is insight they don't teach at school. Instructions left out of life's operating manual.

This is a story about confidence. Why it runs off and abandons you. How to lure it back.

I smooth my papers flat. The rustling travels over the airwaves. I take a deep breath, letting it out slowly.

# 3. Piggy Ankles

## ON AIR

IN 1979, I was eight years old, sure of who I was, where I lived, and ready to take on each new day. My Dad said I was "plucky like a rooster."

That was just before I saw Lily die. I wasn't so sure of the world after that.

While Mama and Daddy were at work, my Gramoo corralled my sister and me, making sure we didn't kill each other or set the farm on fire. Being the older sister, I was free to wander our twenty Oregon acres, but that wasn't as much fun as sneaking pears from the McClellan place a mile away.

I wormed through a slit in the row of thorny Bois d'arc trees hiding their orchard from the road. One of their pears was a good climbing tree. I made it to the top, sat on a limb, and ate, watching butterflies and wasps gnaw holes in a few overripe pears. Sweet juice ran down my chin and covered my fingers.

The *snap* of a stick froze my jaw in mid-bite. I'd been oh-so-careful not to make a sound and bring Mr. McClellan down his long driveway. But it was a girl my size who came through the trees and walked up from the road. Spotting me, she asked, "Can I have some pears?"

A too-small t-shirt showed a strip of her belly over cut-offs. A pillowcase trailed from her hand. "How old are you?" I asked.

"Eight."

Well, at least she wasn't older than me. I didn't know her. Her braids were longer than mine, tied with pink rubber bands that had butterflies on them.

I decided I didn't like her. "No. You're trespassing."

She began climbing my tree anyway.

"Get down! Get away!" I threw my half-eaten pear; it glanced off her neck, spattering her with juice. She kept coming even though she wasn't a good climber and slipped once, scraping the skin off her elbow.

"I just need a few." She stopped a couple feet below me, out of breath. "If I don't get some, Troy will make me haul water."

"Why? Do you have cows?"

"No, silly. We haul it to camp to drink." She yanked on a pear. It wouldn't come loose, so she twisted it, corkscrewing the stem.

"You're the stupid one. It won't break because it's not ripe. They ripen starting at the top of the tree." I plucked one beside me. "Don't you know that? Where'd you go to school?"

"I don't. Mom and Troy teach me. We're on the road."

"What road?"

"The road to Ashland. We live in our van."

"All of you?"

"When we get to Ashland, Mom says I'll get my own bed. And I can have a cat." The twisted pear broke loose causing her to slip backward. She yelped and grabbed a limb, catching herself.

"Shut up!" I hissed. "We're not supposed to be here."

"So these aren't *your* pears." With that, she climbed higher and lodged herself next to me. "A fella at the campground told us about this place. Mom says land belongs to no one. Nature and its bounty is a gift to all people." With a hard tug, she snapped a yellow fruit off the branch, stuffed it in the pillow case, and continued picking.

"You don't have a house or go to school?"

"Nope. We're free as birds. Go where we want, when we want. It's righteous."

I wondered what she meant as I eyed the bag on her lap getting bigger. "You're taking too many. Only take one or two so the McClellans don't know." But she kept picking. "You're gonna have a hard time getting that down the tree," I said.

"Mom and Troy are waiting on the road. They'll help. People don't hurt kids when they catch—" She violently fanned her hand past her ear.

"Don't hit it." I hissed, watching the wasp dart around her. "Stay still. It'll go away." But she ducked, twisted, squealed, and batted at it. The bag fell from her lap, fruit tumbling out as it hit the ground.

"I think it got me." She grabbed her neck.

"Lemme see. I don't think so. It's a little red, but maybe that's where I hit you with a pear."

"It hurts." She pawed her throat, starting to cry. "It burns."

"Don't scratch. You're making it puff up."

She turned clumsily, grabbing the trunk, her legs dangling, toeing the limb below her. She slid to a lower branch, her face red, breath wheezing. "I've never been ... stung. My mom's allergic ... to bees."

"That was a wasp." I frowned, watching her grab her chest and bend forward. For a second she teetered on the branch, then tumbled, hitting several limbs as she fell.

The wet *thud* sounded like a watermelon splitting. I quickly climbed down. She was lying on her pears, not moving. I shook her, but her eyes didn't open.

A red rash was turning her forearms pink. I stepped one way then the other, unsure whether to run to the McClellans' or find her mama. Finally I rushed toward the road, yelling, "Help! Wasps!"

A woman appeared in the gap of the Bois d'arcs and came running, shouting over her shoulder, "Get the epi-pen, Troy!" When she reached the girl, the man was right behind her.

"I didn't buy the epinephrine." He leaned over the girl.

"Whaddayou mean?" the woman shrieked, staring at him. "You've always gotta keep one around for me."

"It was that or gas." He scooped the girl off the ground.

Seeing blood on the pillowcase, the mother shrieked again. "Her head! She's bleeding." She dumped the rest of the pears from the bag, screaming at me, "Where's a pharmacy?"

My mouth opened, but nothing came out. I felt like I was in class with the teacher grilling me. I focused on the bloody cloth in her hands.

"A hospital!" the man shouted. "She's dying. Where's the nearest hospital?"

"Eugene, I think." At eight years old, I didn't know things like that. I'd never been to a hospital. They were the adults here. They were supposed to know what to do.

He took off running, the woman kept pace beside him, trying to hold the pillow case against the girl's head. "Lily," she wailed. "Oh, Lily. Oh, Lily."

In less than a minute they were gone.

Mama was making supper when I banged through the screen door. I came in and leaned against her, wanting to feel safe inside my house, next to an adult who was doing something normal like preparing to feed me. "Mama, what happens when you get stung by a wasp and you're allergic?"

"You're not allergic. If you got stung, rub ice on it, then wash the spinach in the sink."

"Don Thorton was allergic," Gramoo said as she showed my five-year-old sis where to place the flatware. Root, who seemed to only understand the language spoken on Mars, stuck each spoon in a water glass. Gramoo didn't correct her, continuing her story, "He bloated like a toad. Throat closed up. Turned red. Flopped down and suffocated right there in the paint section of the hardware store. Stings are serious business."

Mama gave her mother a shut-up look.

"I think I saw a girl die today."

Mama stopped peeling zucchini and surveyed my face. "Where?"

It took a second to spin up a lie so I wouldn't be whipped for going off our land. "Down where the creek crosses the road." I told them about the girl, the wasp sting, falling out of a tree, and the blood. I didn't mention pears.

"Oh, Stiks, I'm sure she's all right," Mama said. "I didn't hear anything at the grocery store about it. Who were these people?"

"I don't know. The guy had a ponytail. They live in their car and—"

"Hippies. Oh, well, they'll be all right. Hippies use a lot of natural remedies."

"But the girl looked dead. When the man carried her, her arms and legs flopped like they weren't hooked to anything. They were taking her to a hospital. How far is it?"

"I'm sure they made it. Now wash the spinach." Mama cast another dark look at Gramoo, who later filled me in with better details of death by bee stinging.

Over the next week, I asked Mama if she'd heard anything. She said no, but I figured she was lying. Mama's way of dealing with calamity was pretending it never happened.

As time passed I came to believe that Lily had most likely died and I'd helped. I'd smacked her with a pear, making her smell juicy. I didn't help her climb down, even though I could see she was having trouble. I wasn't able to spit out directions to a pharmacy because I didn't know it was the same thing as our drug store. The one thing I got right was the closest hospital, but how to get there was a mystery.

The most eye-opening revelation was that the world could kill me. And adults weren't particularly helpful in stopping it. This was not a safe place to be. Suddenly, I wasn't so sure of anything or anybody, especially myself. If a wasp could cause this much trouble, why trust in anything? Why believe cars will stay on their side of the road? That dogs won't take a bite out of you? That the sun won't go out like a candle?

I stayed that way for two years, scared I couldn't take what might come along.

Then one evening in 1981, my confidence changed again.

My family entered my fourth-grade room. Dad stared, mumbling, "Ho-ly donkey crap!"

Mama screwed her elbow into his ribs so hard he grabbed his side with an *uff*. He'd been warned. Before we'd entered Montgomery Elementary School on open house night, Mama had set clear rules. "No cussing. No jokes. And don't raise your voice louder than a whisper."

My classroom was filled with parents and kids, but still smelled of the typical school droppings: eraser rubbings, lunches left in desks, and art projects stowed in corners along with chalk dust. Usually, Dad didn't come to school conferences because he was at the mill or cutting site. And when he was at home, he'd declare, "Why would I spend time with a buncha eraser lickers? I've got the smartest girl in class right here." He'd pull me to his chest, his fingers circling the base of my ponytail, twitching it back and forth as I'd try to pry loose. If he hadn't had a chance to shower, I'd hold my breath against his musk of grease, sweat, and sawdust.

Tonight, I smelled his Hai Karate cologne as he leaned his head next to mine. "Sweetie, you don't have to look at that ol' gal after lunch, do you?"

My eyes flitted from my teacher, Miss Gardner, to my black sneakers that looked like Keds, but weren't. Mama had said if I was going to climb trees, she wasn't spending money on expensive shoes. I knew it was an excuse. The only leather shoes in our house were Dad's work boots, so I wouldn't be giving up climbing trees any time soon.

Melinda Kutcher was staring at us. She had dark hair, dark eyes, and a pixie nose whose primary function was to make her look cute.

The biggest problem was—she was smart. And that was my realm. It was all I had going for me. When the teacher asked a question, Melinda's hand and mine shot up like rockets. Often she was first because I was daydreaming "like a blue-eyed fly" as Dad would say. "A thousand thoughts seeing different worlds." It didn't matter. Miss Gardner usually called on Melinda. I figured it had to do with her just-right-everything.

My parents and I stood in a loose line of people, waiting to talk to my teacher. "That is one ugly woman," Dad whispered. "And I've seen some biddies who could, honest to Pete, scare the bark off trees. But your teacher ..."

I laughed, my hand quickly covering my mouth. When I saw people looking at me, my attention flicked back to the floor tiles the custodian had polished to a gleam.

Ignoring Mama's scowl, Dad leaned closer, wearing a lopsided grin. "You only see hair like that on a poodle-dog."

"Tonk ..." The tone of Mama's voice prickled with layers of past lectures. She didn't have to worry. I knew what Dad was doing. He was king of busting up solemn occasions and best behaviors.

Dad took Mama's arm, snugging it under his. "Hon, no wonder Stiks has stomach problems, if she has to watch this permed Bigfoot after lunch."

Melinda's father turned and looked at my dad. He stood a head taller. His purple-collared knit shirt had a logo over his heart, Cumbria Investments. He wore real leather shoes with thin laces. He didn't say anything. Just looked at Dad.

The corner of Dad's mouth kicked even higher, but his smile didn't touch his eyes. He began telling Mama one of his stories, yet his focus stuck on Melinda's father. "Did I tell ya I recently met a woman who had an eyeball that spun like a merry-go-round?"

"Tonk." My mother stepped in front of him, her voice full of thorns. "Why don't you go sit until it's our turn." She shifted her measured look to me. "Take your father to your desk. Show him your artwork."

I didn't have anything artsy in my desk except doodles on math papers and broken crayons, but leaving sounded like a great idea. I tugged Dad's arm.

"Okay. Back in a minute." He gave a nod that landed beyond Mama and onto Melinda's father.

Dad pulled out the molded-plastic chair at my desk and sat, one leg stretched out, resting on its booted heel. "What's the story there?" He leaned forward, studying a small drawing of a sharp-toothed, angry-eyed pig taped to the desk next to mine.

"Eden Matheson drew it. It's me. She calls me Piggy."

"You don't have a flat nose." Lines creased his forehead as he peeled the picture from the desk, rolled it into a ball, and flicked it across the room.

"Eden says I have 'big pig ankles, pig eyes ...'" The words glubbed in my throat. "Piggy hair."

"Good grief, Stiks. You look in the mirror every day. Not one part of you looks piggy. Geez! Don't cry. Maybe that's why she picks on you. There's always gonna be jerks. They were around when I went here. I hated this place. You like school?"

"I like math." I swallowed as I pulled my pencil from my desk, and tapped it against my palm, easing my antsy feelings. "Everything else is boring. Miss Gardner makes subjects really simple so she doesn't confuse Henry." I pointed at a nearby desk. "He spends most of his time chewing the yellow paint off his pencils."

"Sounds like a winner. Oh, rats. Now your mother's waving at us."

I glanced at Mama, who was beckoning with quick fingers. She didn't believe in holding people up. She also didn't like to call across the room like those families at D-Sacks Grocery who yelled down the aisles for the entire store to hear, discussing their choices for chips and soda pop.

Dad frowned, watching me blink and try to act tougher. He frowned at Mama. He stood up, giving my head a couple of rough pats and grunting, "Stay here."

I watched him stroll up the aisle toward the teacher. A chill began in my stomach. Melinda and her family had left. At least that was a relief. I knuckled my eye to clear the film I'd blinked into it. I'm not sure why I felt like crawling under my chair.

Dad's words didn't carry to my desk, but his low tone filled the room. Mom patted his arm. Miss Gardner's eyebrows rose toward her hairline. Parents, waiting to speak to her, stared. With a thin smile, my teacher fanned her hand at the door, suggesting the discussion move into the hallway. Dad shook his head and continued.

Mama turned away, calling to me, "Let's go!" She hurried through the doorway, her face dark as a thundercloud.

I followed, but loitered at the door, not wanting to completely abandon Dad, whose voice was still growling like a late-winter wind.

When he finished, he joined me. Neither of us spoke as our footsteps clapped down the corridor. At the corner stairwell, Mama's hand grabbed him, pulling him into the off-limits area under the risers.

She froze me with a stare. "You stay right there." She herded Dad farther into the dark, cramped space. "*What* is the matter with you?"

"Geez, Grace, you're the one who insisted I come. Stiks says there's a kid picking on her. You complain they're not teaching her anything, then you snap your twigs when I point these things out to the teacher. It was the gospel truth, wasn't it? Nothin's gonna change if somebody doesn't speak up."

"These aren't lumberjacks and whistle punks on your crew. You don't need to beat them with unvarnished facts. Stiks has to face that teacher tomorrow. Your other daughter goes to school here, too. The parents in that room come through my grocery line. Have faith in the teacher and the school system. Stiks will learn what she needs."

"If you say so." His gaze lowered to the floor as he shook his head. "Okay, who do we see next? The P.E. teacher? I'm gonna suggest more dodgeball. I'll teach Stiks how to bean her bully."

Mama groaned. She turned and breezed past me with a "C'mon!" The metal release bar clanked as she hit the door to the parking lot and pushed through without stopping. I watched it close.

Dad slipped an arm around me. "Well ... I guess this means we're skipping the rest of the tour. You okay with that?"

I stared at the door.

He turned me to face him. "Look. You're no pig. And sometimes you gotta put up with crap-talk, but you sure don't have to take it from another ten-year-old. Got it?"

I nodded. A whirlwind of voices, footsteps, and colors buzzed in my head. I began counting floor tiles to escape the noise and thoughts bombarding me.

"Shug, look at me. Focus." Dad tapped the tip of my nose. "That ugly broomtail you've got for a teacher ... she thinks you're lazy instead of bored. So you see, she doesn't know squat about you. Still ... as your mama says, you're gonna have to put up with her nonsense. Personally, I don't think you need fourth grade. I told her you oughta skip on to fifth or sixth grade where they might actually teach you somethin'." He paused, letting his words soak in. "Hey, look at me."

I lifted my head. My dad had bent his six-foot frame level with my face.

"As far as school goes, you got this whipped. I believe in you." He gave a nod and a thumbs-up. "Now let's find your mama, and we'll all cool off with a cone from Rainbow Drive-In."

It's just a sliver of a memory. One that has stayed with me for years. It's become my salve for not-so-great moments. It marched into my heart the day my prom date dumped me. And years later when I was far from home, lost, not knowing what to do, the memory of Dad came back to me. "You've got this whipped. I believe in you."

It's a powerful tonic to have someone put stock in you. It's like priming the pump that lets you believe in yourself, no matter your past mistakes.

Immediately after that fourth-grade conference, I realized I wasn't lazy or a daydreamer or a pig. And Dad was right. I was able to skip two grades. In some ways, it made my life at school even harder. But that's another story. The takeaway was that I was able to quit worrying about disasters that *might* happen and instead imagine what could come true because a cussing lumberjack believed in me and cared enough to tell me so for sixteen years.

Sometimes that's all that's necessary to help a person edge through the rest of their life. I lost my grit when Lily died. It bloomed again at that open house. Confidence lives in our minds. It's a tool to predict outcomes—and it's often faulty because we use wrong data. We remember negative experiences more than the positive.

Confidence isn't trusting that the world is a safe place, but believing you'll find a way to handle whatever happens. It took a long time to figure that out. Probably because I didn't trust the wisdom of a backwoods, uneducated father telling me, "You got this."

So in the wee hours of this morning, I'm asking you to remember it doesn't matter if you're a custodian, a clerk, or a kid. Believe in somebody—then tell them. Years from now, those words might be the salve that gets them through a difficult time. You'll probably never know, but you might change the world because you did it.

Take a risk once a day. Show compassion every day.

Good night, Mama. Good night, Oregon.

# 4. 1997

A FLIP OF the switch, makes the ON AIR sign goes black. Country music wings through the speakers again, starting where I cut it off.

Standing, I push the chair in, making sure everything is like I found it. I fold my papers and slide them into my back pocket. The broom is still next to the door in the empty hallway. After stowing it in the janitor's closet, I go to the lobby downstairs.

It's dark outside the plate-glass windows. The lamp on the street corner nets the bushes with patchy shadows.

Sitting on a thinly upholstered bench, I gaze through the windows. My mind tells me to throw these stories away. Nobody cares. Look what I'm risking.

I sit.

I wait, letting the voices within the story fade like children busting down hallways, hurrying toward recess and freedom. When all is quiet in my mind, I search the dark street again.

Security should show up any minute now.

# 5. 1997

THREE BUILDINGS CREATE Valley State University's Science Complex. Physics, Engineering, and Chemistry Departments, join together in a 'T'. I sit in the shared-lobby calculating the number of floor tiles in the entry. They pay me to check equipment, log power readings, and clean six floors of physics rooms rising above me.

I give the money back, paying them tuition and fees.

Tonight, before the broadcast, I wiped down the few whiteboards that permitted erasing. Each classroom has boards on all four walls. Hand-written numbers and symbols parade across them. Red-marker lines corral some equations, labeling them with exclamation points: **DO NOT ERASE!!!! EVER!!!**

But the third floor is different. There's always something to erase in "Flippers' Corner." The two rooms are jokingly called that because student disc jockeys flip radio switches with no clue how or why the devices work.

Each evening after logging amperage of the almighty transmitter, I wipe down the Flippers' whiteboard.

*USE AN EXCITED VOICE FOR ANNOUNCEMENTS AS THOUGH YOUR HAIR IS ON FIRE.

*MAKE YOUR BROADCAST AS EASY TO LISTEN TO AS A LARGE-PRINT TOM CLANCY NOVEL!!!

If there are instructions on the board. I leave those.

*KURT, NOBODY WANTS TO LISTEN TO YOU BROADCAST BIRDCALLS.

*KURT, STOP SUGGESTING A PROTEST RALLY WHENEVER SOMETHING UPSETS YOU.

*KURT=ASSHAT, DID YOU EAT THE MAPLE BAR I LEFT ON THE CONSOLE?

A decade ago Dr. Slompka, dean of physics, ignoring protests from other departments, moved the campus radio station out of the Liberal Arts Building into his own empire. He said the delicate broadcast equipment required too much maintenance each day to leave in the hands of nonprofessionals.

Then he required physics students taking classes in instrumentation and electrical systems to get hands-on experience cleaning soda pop out of consoles, unsticking switches gunked with donut frosting, and rebuilding microphones. "Good for your resume," he promised.

The Physics Department only babysits the equipment and makes thankless repairs. The talent comes from the School of Communications. The broadcasters are kids with big personalities whose main skill is jabbering. They hope to turn pro doing it. This annoys physics students whose logic dictates elegance, and ideas be expressed in the fewest, most accurate words possible.

I'm a little more forgiving, although physics students call me The Crank. The sign on my door reads, "Technician/Maintenance." I'm asked to help with many strange tasks, especially in the middle of the night which is the time students look for me because faculty and staff aren't around.

Earlier this evening, a freshman stopped me in the hallway, saying, "I was told I needed to find Sophia Bolton. Is that you?" When I gave him a squinty look he added, "The copier isn't working."

"What's your name?" I asked.

"Jason."

"Have you checked the paper? Toner? Jams? No? Well, Jason, this is the moment you decide if you're a scientist or if you're a marketing major. Come find me when you've figured out what's not working on the machine."

"I thought that was your job."

"No, keeping the world running is everyone's job."

My hope is by the time they're seniors, they'll have learned to troubleshoot their own problems. These students may be smart, but they don't know how to fix what really matters. It's not covered in our education system. But it should be. We need lessons in how to pick ourselves up and keep climbing the hill.

Now, I look at the 1,457 tiles I estimate cover the lobby floor and tell myself that waiting for Security is the honorable thing to do. I broke the rules; I should wait for justice.

But my dad's voice floats through my head. "Aw hell, you don't know what you can get away with until you try." My confidence coefficient in my dad's advice is fifty percent. Good enough.

I stand. The street is still empty. Country music continues to lull through the speakers. I should stay busy while waiting for justice, and if they don't find me, I'll broadcast again in a few days.

The adrenalin of hijacking a radio station is kicking in. I take the steps upstairs two at a time.

# 6. Gravity For Traitors

## ON AIR

WELCOME. THIS IS the Navigator. I'm not a regularly scheduled program, but a late-night "filler," so thanks for listening. Last week I talked about confidence, but tonight I'll tell the story of how I became a traitor. I used to blame my downfall on gravity, but eventually I realized it was because I threw like a girl.

First of all, you need to know you were born to notice the world around you. This is so your frontal lobe can make predictions. It's supposed to help you make better decisions.

It's probably no surprise that teenagers' frontal lobes aren't well connected to the rest of their brains. Those neural networks grow later in life. Our brains don't fully mature until our early thirties. So we can expect to make some really stupid decisions in our youth.

When your thirteen-year-old eats an eraser on a $5 dare, spends two days in the hospital, and you yell, "What were you thinking?" please understand they *weren't* thinking. Their frontal lobes were barely firing.

In 1981, even at ten years old, I thought Finley, a kid on my school bus, made bad decisions. I wondered if he would live to adulthood.

I'd known him since first grade, and both of us had plenty of opportunities to put kid-muscle on our arms and legs, but by the fourth grade, he still gandered around with a just-hatched look. Not because he was ill. His DNA gave him a big-head, all-ears look. His hair was burred, which made his neck appear scrawny. His bony body was always bagged in overalls with brass hooks and buttons. Kids called him "Tin Pants," from the heavy clothes loggers wore. Finley never unhooked a shoulder clasp, showing off a Star Wars or Nintendo t-shirt. He was always firmly buttoned up.

When the bus pulled up to his long dirt driveway, we'd strain to see his house way back from the road. You could tell a lot about a family by their broken-slatted porch swings, tubs to catch rain, and clutter of machines they kept around. Old cars without wheels meant someone kept the relics for parts and was handy at repairs. Wild-eyed cats darting under the porch meant the animals were on their own and had to mouse for what they ate. Fat old hounds flopping their tails when you waved at them meant someone was kind enough to keep an animal past its prime.

There were no clues about Finley. No dogs followed him down his long driveway. When the bus pulled to a stop, he was always standing there—never late. In the fall, dust flumed forward, fogging over him. He'd climb the steps, rubbing grit out of his eyes.

In the winter, he boarded the bus wearing a coat two sizes too big and a stocking cap that slid over his forehead and Dumbo-sized ears.

Throughout the year he wore lace-up work boots, clomping to the back of the bus. He'd learned not to sit with anyone, but it didn't protect him. "Hey, Finley! You steal that coat from your mama?" yelled Kyle Griel, the lead jerk. "Looks like it'd fit an elephant."

The jokes weren't clever, but the razzing would stop if Finley didn't answer. Usually, he'd sit, thin-lipped and tight-jawed. A flush would begin on his neck working upward, until bright red skin showed beneath the stubble of his hair. It was like watching lightning strike and a wisp of smoke curl into the air. We hoped it would burst into flames and put on a show.

There weren't many rules about bullying in the '80s. It was fashionable for the older kids to make fun of others. The younger kids' salvation arrived when sophomores, one by one, abandoned the bus as soon as they got their driver's licenses. Being caged in a school bus honed the rule of survival: Find a friend and ignore everyone else.

Finley had no friends. Sometimes he sat behind Loretta and me. A few times I tried to advise him. One ten-year-old giving another pointers. "Act like you don't hear them," I'd whisper. But he sat hump-shouldered, staring out the window, pretending he couldn't hear *me*.

Late fall, he surprised me, reaching over the seat and tapping my shoulder. "Why're they picking on me?"

Loretta and I exchanged a glance. It was a stupid question. Finley was a walking invitation to be pestered: the way he dressed, his out-of-date ideas, the obvious grudge that surfaced in his words. He was like a garter snake, harmless, but when poked, he'd hiss, trying to be bigger than he really was. And why would he think he was the only target? Didn't he hear the insults hurled at girls who wore whale-spout ponytails on top of their heads or had curls locked down with hairspray? Kyle Griel swore he had to keep his bus window open because the smell of Aqua Net made his eyes cross.

Trying not to be seen, I whispered back to Finley, "You don't fit in. Why don'tcha grow your hair out?"

"What's wrong with it? Grandpa's been cutting it this way since the first grade."

"You see anybody else wearing their hair like that?" I wondered if he ever looked in a mirror.

The next day, after Evie Winnel got on the bus, one of the cool guys gave a fake scream as she sat in front of him. "Aaaaeeeh, Evie! Did they take you to the hospital after you stuck your finger in the socket?" He waved his hands around her fuzzy hairdo.

"Whatever! Shut up! It's called crimping. It's French, you corn chip."

"Makes you look like the butt-ugly sister of the bride of Frankenstein," Kyle Griel said and everyone laughed.

Mike, the bus driver, glanced at the rectangle mirror reflecting the kids behind him. He was a mellow guy and only had three rules: No standing while the bus was moving. No hitting. No throwing. None of that was happening so his focus went back to the road.

When catcalls about Evie simmered down, Finley tapped my shoulder, his voice testy. "Nothin's wrong with my hair." He pawed his skull like he was washing it. "Clean-shaven is easy to take care of."

Mama had told me he lived with his grandparents, so I was sure those were his Grandpa's words. When others weren't looking, I explained what was wrong with his wardrobe. I thought I was helpful, but each morning after that, he got on the bus angrier than the day before.

A week later he sat behind me and poked me hard. "You're an idiot." I didn't turn around. "There's nothing wrong with the way I dress. These are Herter's work boots." He lifted his foot holding it next to my seat. I batted it away. "They're leather. I only need one pair of shoes a year. And they're a lot more expensive than your sneakers."

I looked at my fake Keds. I only got one pair of shoes a year, too. Finley's were holding up better. A hole had started over my big toe, but I'd patched it on the inside with duct tape.

"So why pick on me? Why not you?" he said.

"I don't wear overalls. You look like a goof."

"These have room. Cool in the summer. Warm in the winter. Adjustable straps. Let 'em out as I grow." His voice was starting to squeak as he tucked a thumb under the brass shoulder hook and pushed it out on display.

"Yeah," I rolled my eyes. "My grandpa used to wear 'em. Doesn't mean I do."

His fists clenched. "I get new clothes the beginning of each school year ... well ... 'cept my coat. It's gotta last two–three years. Doesn't make sense to spend money on the latest foo-foo that'll change. That's stupid."

"Okay. Okay." I hissed, holding up my hands and peeking over the seat. "Look ... when you call the high school guys 'poopheads' or 'evildoers,' your voice gets squeaky, and they think it's funny. You're just asking to be badgered. Stop getting all mad. Don't talk to them."

"Other people sass 'em back."

"Other people know how to cuss. You don't. Ignore 'em. When I'm upset, I do math in my head. Why don't you try remembering state capitols or humming so you don't hear 'em?"

It was the last of our talks, and I felt relieved. Days passed and Finley didn't say a word when he was razzed, but I could tell he'd changed. Anybody who took a good look at him could see his face carried an ill-tempered edge.

I wondered if it was my fault. Maybe I'd destroyed both his worlds—school and home. It was clear he'd never fit in at Montgomery Elementary, but now I might've poisoned his mind against his grandparents—the only folks who loved him. The only place he actually fit in.

Over Christmas holidays, I didn't give him much thought, but the first school day after New Year's, he got on the bus wearing a green and white stocking cap. Its long tail trailed down his back and ended with a fat red pompom.

"Holy elf crap!" Kyle Griel yelled as Finley came down the bus aisle. "What fairy tale did you walk out of?"

Finley sat down hard in the seat across from Kyle. There were empty seats farther away, but Finley had claimed his territory, his eyes drilling into the loudmouth. The rest of us watched, sensing a wisp smoke rising between them.

"Oooh. Is that your evil look? I'm so afraid." Kyle wiggled his fingers and rolled his eyes. "It'd work much better without your barf-me-out hat. I'm surprised your giant ears fit under it."

Still giving Kyle a hot-eyed glare, Finley opened his mouth. "Oh my darlin', oh my darlin'..."

Kyle's eyes widened, his eyebrows rising into question marks. He leaned forward, yelling into Finley's face, "You fugly little dweeb-o-rama!"

Finley looked away and sang, "Oh my darlin' Clementine ..."

Kyle stared for a moment, and then he began to sing, too. "Oh my darlin'..." he howled. His friends joined in, adding mock yodels and fake sobs at the line "lost and gone forever." Soon everyone on the bus was bellowing and singing.

A corner of Finley's mouth smiled. It was probably the first time he'd been in a spectacle that began with him then shifted to anyone other than himself.

After the second chorus, Mike, the bus driver, stared in the mirror and shouted, "All right. That's enough. Be quiet!" When a few people continued, he tapped the brakes. The singers stopped. Laughter faded into the hum of an everyday ride, and the bus picked up speed.

Finley looked at me. I gave him an okay sign.

The peace lasted ten seconds. Kyle snatched the stocking cap off Finley's head.

"Give it back!" Finley lunged.

With one hand, Kyle pushed him away. The other hand dangled the hat out the window. "Ooooooooh. Watch out. Watch out. Better not hit me. I might accidentally drop it."

"Give it to me, you ... you ... *dipshit*!"

Kyle's mouth gaped. He covered it with one of his big paws, frowning and huffing, "Little Tin Pants cussed. Oh no." A collective gasp came from the high school group, followed by suggestions of more swear words Finley could try.

"Shut up, you farts. Gimme my hat!" With his face mottled red, Finley swung his fists.

Kyle shoved him away. "Damn! You little dickweed. You barely missed my nose. Here's your crappy turban." He tossed the hat. It arced toward Finley, but another high schooler nabbed it out of the air.

"Gimme!" Finley yelled, but the hat flew to another person.

Standing in the aisle, hands reaching, Finley lunged, crashing into people, struggling for an intercept. The passes picked up speed, like a game of hot-potato, flying from person to person. Even little kids got in on the game of keep-away.

"SIT DOWN!" Mike hollered when he saw Finley standing.

"They got my hat!"

"Get your butt in a seat! We'll sort it out before anybody gets off."

Finley slowly sat, glaring at the traitors on the bus. Mike turned his focus back to the road.

Three rows in front of Finley, Evie Winnel peeked over her shoulder. She held the hat's red pompom next to her big hair like a bow, waggling it and calling, "Looks good on me. I think I'll keep it."

Maybe Finley thought he could he could wrestle it from her because she was a girl. Whatever his reasoning, he bolted toward Evie. She squawked and heaved the hat like it was a snake. It hit me in the chest.

Now here's where my memory of the event gets strange. In slow motion, step by step, I can see it clearly, but I can't recall what was going through my head.

Finley and I locked eyes for a second. Relief passed over his face. He walked toward me, his hand out.

Balling up the cap, I turned and winged it to Kyle Griel.

I've replayed the scene many times and none of my conclusions make me look good. I'm sure my frontal lobes weren't connected to the rest of my brain. It's one of those childhood do-over moments I wish I could get back.

As I threw it, I watched Finley's face harden. I expected to hear laughter from others about the fake-out I'd made. But there was only silence, except Evie Winnel's tiny gasp. Not even the evil Kyle Griel had expected me to throw. The hat had whizzed right past him and out the open window.

"Stop!" Finley screamed and ran toward the front. "Stop the bus!" By the time he'd gibbered out his catastrophe and got Mike to turn around, we' d traveled at least a half mile. Mike drove back slowly. Every face was plastered against the windows on the left side of the bus, yelling, "I think it was here" or "No, stupid, it was farther."

Finally the driver parked on the dirt road, both hands resting over the top of the steering wheel, commanding, "Finley, Kyle, get your butts out there and find it quick. You, too." He pointed at me. "Finley says you chucked it."

"But everybody else ..." I began.

"Get out there. If you don't find it, you're gettin' him a new hat."

Finley clomped down the steps, his voice angry with hate. "You can't buy one. My grandma made it."

As we walked alongside the bus, Kyle shoved me into the ditch. "What's th' matter with you? Girls can't throw."

Kids watched and yelled. We spread out down the road, poking weeds, and flushing quail from the buckbrush. A woman in a truck stopped to see if the bus had broken down. She talked to Mike, her voice loud, hands waving. Maybe she complained he shouldn't have kids strung along the road like a work gang because as soon as she left, he called us back to the bus.

Finley wouldn't get on. Crimson-faced and cussing, he yelled that he was "gonna stay" until he found his cap. Mike grabbed him by the collar and hoisted him up the steps. Finley's over-sized coat tented above his head. Only his eyes peeked out as he kicked the driver.

"You earned suspension for that." Mike shoved him into the first seat. The one reserved for kids who needed watching. "Shut up and sit there. You understand?"

The air went out of Finley. His body shrank, his shoulders rounded. He stared at the floor.

Mumbling, Mike sat down and slammed through the gears. The rest of the ride was quiet. Kids stared at the floor and occasionally glanced at Finley. His chin was on his chest. He rubbed his eyes.

When I got to the house that night, Dad happened to be home from the mill. I told him the whole long story. I'd learned it was better to tell on myself than have him talk to the principal. And this way, I could make my part more innocent than it was. "So ... could you drive me over to Fork's Road so I can look for the hat?" I asked.

"Nope. You got yourself into this. You trot over there and find it."

"Kinda late. Gets dark early."

"You shoulda thought of that when you decided to play Judas."

"But all the other kids ..."

"I don't give a damn what those other bean-brains were doin'. You're supposed to watch out for a weaker fella. You wouldn't kick a dog when he's hurt, would you?"

"No sir."

"Then do the same for another kid. You've got my family's blood. That's what we do. I don't care how squirrely the kid is. Now git walkin'."

Cutting across woods and pastures shortened my trek to two miles instead of four. And maybe Dad could see the benefits of walking this far. Searching, and finding it would make me a hero. It'd wipe out my mistake.

It shouldn't have been hard to spot that stupid red pompom, but dusk had turned the weeds and ditches gray by the time I got there. I searched way past dark, using my hands, feeling for soft lumps among the brush and dried hawkweed. I didn't find the hat. It was as though God himself had snatched it up to keep his ears warm.

It took longer to walk back home. I stumbled over gopher mounds and rutted cow paths. Stickers needled through my jeans. A cold north breeze buffed my ears numb, but I figured that was fair. Finley didn't have a hat either. Several times I wished Dad would've just pulled off his belt and whupped me. I would've felt better about the whole thing.

The porch light was on, and I could see Mama, bundled up, sitting on the steps. My feet slowed, and I considered cutting through the fruit trees and going in the side door so I wouldn't have to face her.

When she heard my footsteps on the gravel, she shined a light in my eyes. "I was worried sick. Why your dad sent you out in the dark, I don't know. Next time, wait and talk to me. I'd have taken you over there."

I shrugged. "I've walked pastures before. No big deal. I didn't find the hat. Maybe somebody came across it."

She shook her head. "I called Finley's grandparents. They looked for it, too. I can't knit, so I told her I'd get her yarn so she can make a new one. What were you thinking?"

"I don't know." I shook my head, knowing the yarn would come out of the grocery money.

"Finley's been suspended for two days for kicking the bus driver." She cupped her hands over my ears, trying to warm them. "Your Dad says you're going to bed without supper, but I left a sandwich in your room. He's in a mood, griping how he came home to relax, but all he's heard about is a stocking cap, so don't sass or say a word."

I shook her hands off my head. "How's any of this fair? The hat was ugly. It was just kids messing with each other."

She sighed, looking into the darkness. "That's the way it is in a crapstorm. Everybody gets dirty."

I never saw Finley again. Not on the bus. Not at school. Not even when we went to his grandparents' house so I could apologize and deliver the yarn. When I asked Mama about it, she said he was living with another relative, and she hoped I'd learned a lesson. I wasn't sure what I'd learned, except don't wear overalls or talk sassy, but I already knew that.

Through the years, I've replayed the Finley incident, trying to make it turn out different. At eleven, I wanted to believe it was the wind that had sucked the hat out the window. When I thought about it at thirteen, I convinced myself it was Finley's fault for being goosy and getting upset at the slightest provocation. At eighteen, I moved on to blaming Kyle Griel, but that was because I was dealing with other idiots in my life. I'd discovered there were lots of people who enjoyed causing crapstorms so they could make others feel small.

Now I'm twenty-six, and I admit I was part of the problem that day. Like firecrackers tied in a row, we'd set each other off. If only one of us would have done what was right, we could've stopped the powder trail of events. It wouldn't have erased what came before, but it would've slowed down what happened to the kid who wore a bull's-eye on his self-esteem.

If Finley had been born thirty years earlier or later, his shaved head, stocking cap, leather lace-ups, and overalls would've been in style. Today his bullies would've been kicked off the bus and out of school.

I often wonder what became of him. I can't remember his last name to look him up. I hope his relatives were able to fill him with positive experiences and offset the sharp-tongued taunts from mean-spirited kids with partially-connected brains.

I hope he became owner of a hardware store in a small town in Ohio or Oregon with a fat, happy dog flopping its tail to greet customers. I can see him leaning over the counter, telling a joke, going bald naturally now. I hope he found his sense of humor.

And I hope he still wears boots so he can kick ass.

Good night, Mama. It took seventeen years, but I finally learned something. Thanks for the sandwich. Good night, Finley, wherever you are. Please know I'm sorry.

And to everyone listening, take a risk and use compassion every day.

Good night, Mama.

Good night, Oregon.

# 7. 1997

I LOOK AT my watch as I push the broom along the fourth floor of the building. Twelve-thirty a.m. A new day is born. So far I haven't seen any faculty around. It's been five days since my last broadcast. Perhaps I could do one tonight.

The lights are on in the machine shop. Peeking through the narrow glass in the door, I spot a teaching assistant working on a project. No problem. He'll be occupied for a while.

"Sophia Bolton!" a voice calls as I pass the physics lab. "We've got a waves problem."

I stick my head in the door. Four undergraduates stand at different whiteboards, pondering calculations.

As soon as I step inside, Craig speaks fast. He knows I won't stay long. "A microwave detector sits on a lake. A radio star rises, emitting a coherent microwave signal. It begins at zero, increases to maximum then—"

"Yeah, yeah." I ignore him, reading the problem above his diagram. "What exactly are you trying to calculate?"

"The local maximum between the incident angle of the radiating star and the reflected light off the lake," says Joe.

I look at each one's work, waving them quiet when they try to explain. "Well, okay. You need to recall that any maxima and minima are critical points." They stare at their diagrams, my words clicking through their brains. I tap an equation. "So the derivative is zero. That'll get you started. Of course, there are other ways to solve it, but I think that's the most elegant."

"Thanks," Craig says as I move toward the door. "How's your dissertation going?"

I grab the broom I'd left in the hallway, and one of the students gives me a quizzical look. I nod to him. "I study gravity, including the stuff that falls on the floor." I turn to Craig. "*I* believe I'm done with the research. *My committee* thinks it needs expansion. What can I do?" I shrug and leave.

A voice leaks from the room, "*She's* the custodian?"

"You want on her good side," Craig says. "She's a grad student, and when you're stuck at two in the morning, she's a miracle worker. But you'd better have considered the problem from all perspectives before you bother her."

"She looks like she's my age ..."

I smile to myself and push on.

Three students are in the computer lab. One asleep. Two guys I hadn't seen before are drinking beer.

"Out." I stand in the doorway, thumbing behind me.

"We're waiting for our simulation to finish," whines one of the drinkers.

"Don't care. I'm not fixing equipment from spilled drinks. The rules are no open containers. You'll have to take it somewhere else."

They stare at me. I'm short. No makeup. I'm not sure if I remembered to brush my hair today. Obviously I'm not imposing enough to scare them. "I haven't seen you guys around. You must be new. What class is this for?"

They gather their stuff. "If we leave the building, we can't get back in."

"Nope, you can't."

They head for the door. "But we've got papers due."

"So does he." I point to the guy, head on the table, sleeping in front of the monitor. I hate simulations. My program has so many variables, it takes thirteen hours to run. If it crashes twelve hours in, I have to troubleshoot, recode, and start it again.

I watch them leave. If they're smart, they'll find one of the many nooks in the building. I know all the hiding spots, but as long as they're quiet and not making a mess, I don't bother students.

Usually, the same people are here past midnight, but there seem to be more tonight. A classic sign the term is winding to a close. There's a comforting camaraderie in being around others who are burning their brains cells at such a late hour. Some will work through the night. Twisted Toppings Pizza stays open twenty-four hours and delivery guys will bang on the lobby doors. If I have to answer it, everyone knows I get some of the pizza.

The heavy metal blast doors of the Research Lab are locked. I enter and ensure the heater blocks, instruments, and vacuum pumps are off and sign the verification sheet. On the third floor, I log a transmitter output reading in the radio room.

On the fifth floor, I find the newbies' empties. Lazy louts. Couldn't even haul them to the recycling bin.

Along with the beer, there's a canning jar. I smell it and am jolted into being nine-years old examining a similar container.

The jar was in the barn and looked innocent as water, but somehow I knew it wasn't. A twist of my wrist made it swirl like a whirlpool hiding its snakes. Even trapped in glass it had a dangerous aura.

The container hid behind cans of paint thinner and kerosene, but it wasn't dusty. I sniffed it, recognizing the sharp scent sometimes came from Dad. He probably thought Mama wouldn't find his stash there.

Alcohol was one of the bandages of our family's life like mud for mosquito bites, udder salve for scrapes, and duct tape for everything else. The jar was labeled Snapping Turtle Juice, and it turned my Daddy's blues into different hues.

Recently, I've questioned the personalities in our household. As a kid, I often wished I'd been born into someone else's family—some normal folks who had indoor toilets.

Mama was two people. At home, she wore frayed, mismatched clothes. She always donned a wide-brimmed hat and gloves for outside jobs like hoeing or plucking chicken feathers.

But Monday through Friday, work days, her brown hair was swept up and pinned to the back of her head. She said it made her look more professional. "It's important to dress above your station."

Dad laughed saying, "Who cares what a grocery clerk looks like?" But Mama worried what people thought. She was always presentable when she left the house.

Gramoo was one person. What you saw was what you got. A thin, knobby-jointed old woman who wore dresses and peppered her talk with "sugar pea" and "dammit to hell." She was eternally ticked off, excusing herself with, "It's easy to be testy when you're as old as I am." It was years before I learned there were pleasant old people who walked into their golden years without kicking everybody traveling with them.

Dad ... I'm not sure how many people he was. Sometimes I wished he was someone else. Most of the time he was away working, but on the occasions he was home, we never knew what to expect.

I strongly suspected the Snapping Turtle Juice had something to do with that. Mama would sigh, saying, "He needs to keep busy."

Sometimes he was happy. Sometimes angrier than a bag of wild cats. But the worst was when he'd sit on the porch, staring at the horizon, not talking. I felt it was my job to draw him out. "Dad, is there a time limit on fortune cookie predictions?" or

"When lightning strikes the ocean, does it kill fish?" or "If you died with braces on your teeth, would they take them off?"

Sometimes he'd continue staring as though he hadn't heard me. Other times, he'd make up wild stories for answers. Dad made me laugh more than Mama did.

Me ... I know who I am. I'm one person, though students would say I'm two. Sophia, the Late Night Fixer. But right now The Crank is taking these empties to the computer lab for a discussion with a couple of slobs.

When I step through the door, the newbies aren't there. I predict they'll be asking for extensions on their papers. The other student is still sleeping. I wake up his monitor and check his program. The values on the screen look correct. The program is running. If it were stuck in an infinite loop, I'd wake him. Instead, I turn off the lights as I leave the room.

"Sophia! Join us!" Craig passes me, carrying boxes. "Pizza!"

"You want to eat on the roof? I'll unlock the sixth floor stairwell." My compassionate deed for the day.

"That'll be easier than hauling everything up the fire escape like we were planning to do." He yells into the lab for his companions to bring chairs and hurries on. The scent of pepperoni and salami trails after him.

I toss the empties in the recycle bin and stop at the soda machine long enough to smack it 47 centimeters from the base and 24 centimeters from the back. A student who'd graduated gave me the coordinates as a parting gift for helping him with his paper. A Dr. Pepper rolls out.

I can broadcast later. Now I grab a small telescope from the equipment room. Never miss an opportunity to observe stars and trade ideas with intelligent minds. Who knows, tonight we might even figure out questions Dad and I couldn't solve: When you sit in a movie theater, which armrest is yours? And why can't donuts be square?

# 8. Cleaving

## ON AIR

HELLO. THIS IS your early morning navigator. This is the story of how I woke up and climbed out of a dark, soul-crushing moment. To understand this, we need to talk about cleaving—the act of splitting an object into parts. It's used a lot in science. We split crystals to create semi-conductors. We split the nucleus of an atom to release energy. In basic biology, an organism divides into new organisms. Cleaving often creates something new.

We'll begin tonight's story with a humble observation I made in 1982. I was eleven and thought my Gramoo washed dishes in a weird way. After a meal, she wiped plates with a slice of bread, then she ate the bread or gave it to our birds. Chickens will eat almost anything, including dog crap. Ducks are more discerning. This bit of knowledge has affected my menu choices right into adulthood, but that has nothing to do with cleaving.

So, Gramoo swabbed dishes in a beat-up aluminum pan along with a squirt of soap and a little water. She'd pile them into another pan, where they'd be baptized with scalding water from the tea kettle. Finally they were laid to rest on tea towels to air dry.

It was different with Mama; we had to massage the plates a lot. She insisted we scrub both backs and fronts with a soapy sponge, rub them under running water, then polish them dry.

You'll notice we use a lot more water and plate-petting with this method. I'd complain, "Gramoo doesn't do it like this."

Mama would say, "That's just your grandma."

This was baffling. I thought something as simple as cleaning dishes would have universal rules. Thus began my initiation into the world of there-is-more-than-one-way-to-skin anything.

All washing techniques had one thing in common: when we were done, the water was hauled to the garden. Bathwater was carted out. The washing machine drained into buckets so we could lug them to vegetables. "Why can't we use the well and a hose?" I whined.

Mama would grouch, "Your dad says we'll run the well dry." We had a bajillion tubs and barrels surrounding our house to catch rain. Mama said rainwater made our hair softer, but there was no science to prove that. Dad said "save-it," so we did. And Mama would pretend it didn't bother her, sighing, "That's just your father."

We used the phrase a lot. Four words of family code squeezing past history into ongoing frustrations. It was delivered in a voice that said the other person would never change—so stop arguing about it.

Except, I didn't stop.

Sixth grade was a banner year for me. I discovered a lot of differences between me and the town kids on asphalt streets seven miles away. My classmates played in water. They ran through sprinklers that didn't soak tomatoes or corn. They filled balloons with it and heaved them at one another. "Why?" I asked, unable to imagine wasting water or a good balloon. Eden Matheson, my enemy, looked at me like I was one of those crap-eating chickens. "Because it's fun, stupid."

As soon as I got off the bus that afternoon, I decided to have a little citified fun. I poked holes in a plastic bottle I'd found, duct-taped it to the end of a hose, and turned the spigot full blast. It was delightful. Now I understood the luxuries and appeal of living in town, even if you couldn't shoot a gun or pop firecrackers in city limits. My little sis joined me, slipping in the mud, squealing, spraying ourselves clean. It was grand—until the well went dry. And Mama came home. Then Dad.

I suppose I should've assessed his crappy work day from the scowl on his face and the number of cusswords he used as he got out of the truck. But I was brimming with urban worldliness, and I didn't give a whiff the dinner beans weren't picked, or Dad was covered with grease and sawdust and couldn't clean up, or the pump needed to be primed.

"What the hell happened here?" He looked at the hose-contraption and muddy weeds.

I don't remember what I said. But it must've been a doozy about how poor and deprived we were.

Dad had a classic move. Holding me with a glare, he'd unbuckle his belt and yank it off, making it *pop* the air with a warning: *All ye children who disobey, a big whupping is coming upon thy little butts.*

That was the moment my little sister and I usually started wailing, "I'm sorry. I'm sorry." But I'd been thinking about this ritual. Growing up, we'd been spanked with hair brushes, fly swatters, wooden spoons, green switches, and belts. The first lick stung a little, but if we squealed misery and regrets, our parents were satisfied, and there were no more licks.

I changed the moment.

I decided right then I was too old to be spanked anymore. And when Dad doubled his belt in half, growling, "You and your smart mouth get over here," I stared at him, wondering why, for all these years, I had dutifully presented myself to be whacked. It was illogical. "C'mere!" he said louder.

I shook my head.

Now he was forced to walk to me. I ran.

I was surprised to see him chasing me. He was ancient. Over thirty years old and tired all the time. He never ran. It wasn't hard to outpace him. I circled around, listening to him huff behind me. My young bones would outlast his, but then what? I'd have to hide outside all night. And I'd get whupped in the morning anyway. I might as well get it over with. I stopped and prepped myself for the sting.

The belt lashed down hard across my hip. Searing white heat burned along the strike line. I screamed, falling to the ground, hugging my knees to my chest. In that moment—everything changed. It wasn't supposed to happen like this. Spankings were supposed to be a few easy licks and a mumbled, "I'm sorry." Shock buzzed my brain, making my vision foggy.

Another full-arm swing of leather slapped my skin. I heard my own screams, stupefied and sharp. Four more lashes needled my back and bottom. I shrieked, surprised I couldn't stop howling or at the pain ripping down my butt and legs.

Then I was alone. Lying in our yard. I shook, sobbing, thinking Mama or my sister would come help me. See if I was okay. But they had disappeared. The strikes burned hot. It wasn't fair. If I'd known whippings were going to change, I would've kept running.

I pushed to my feet. Under my shorts, six long red welts were swelling and purple blotches beginning to bloom. It was hard to walk. My leg wouldn't fully straighten. When I limped into the house, I couldn't sit. Mama inspected my welts and gave me ice in a tea towel, but all she said was, "You shouldn't have run. You know better." Instead of eating supper, I drew a picture of a donkey kicking Dad in the head and taped it to the living room wall. Mama took it down.

When I went to school, I wore long pants and kept the bruises covered, but at home I wore shorts, putting the purple stripes on display. If Dad walked into a room, I left. I ate supper early or late, and when ordered to eat with the family, I went to the barn and read instead. There was no punishment.

Dad tried to joke with me like he used to. I could tell he was sorry. But he never apologized. He'd say nice things to me. I'd stare at him.

A week later, Mama sat on my bed as I did homework. "Your dad feels bad. Real bad." She touched the yellow inch-wide marks across my thigh. "I was hoping somebody at school would see this and do something."

I gave her the hateful scowl perfected by preteens. "Why didn't *you* do something?"

"He'd had a bad day. That's just your father." She shook her head. Her voice ran out, so her final words ghosted into a whisper. "I don't know ..." And that was the last breath of the situation.

Years passed. Every so often I re-examined the memory. I finally understood sometimes Mama felt trapped and helpless. And there were times Dad felt the world conspired to crap all over him. I'm not making excuses for them. In no way am I condoning hitting. That was their situation. Dad drank. Mom forgot.

But here's the point of my tale. The blackest moment was also my brightest. Lying on the ground, after that belting, I had one moment of shining clarity. If I wanted to get off the ground ... it was up to me to pick myself up. No one was coming to save me.

If I wanted to get off that farm to a place that didn't have rags stuffed under the doors to keep out the cold, it was up to me; I wasn't going to inherit an estate. If I wanted indoor plumbing or food that wasn't shot out of a tree or raised in our chicken coop, I'd need to get my own house—one where I could dance in the sprinklers.

For that, I'd need a salary—a good one. And for that, I'd need an education. Mama and Dad would be of little help in these things. I'd have to figure out how to get them on my own.

Perhaps every child has a moment of cleaving—a time when they realize a parent or a friend can't, or won't, come to the rescue. Could be you're far from home and your car breaks down. Maybe you're lost on a mountain with your foot trapped under a boulder. Maybe it's a dark waking-up moment when you realize if you're going to get out of your mess, then it's up to you. A pulling-up-of-your-bootstraps. A lighting of your inner fire. A straightening of your spine and bracing it with determination. The dawn of becoming you.

Cleaving—it often creates something new. There's more than one way to become an adult. And sometimes it is the worst event that births the brightest moments that follow.

Take a risk. Show compassion each day.

Good night, Mama.

Good night, Oregon.

# 9. 1997

I'M LAMENTING MY present life as I sweep a second-floor classroom, and what do I find in the back row? A little pile of toenail clippings. GAAK. What kind of person does this? And how boring does a class have to be to clip your toes? Not even *I* am that socially ill-bred.

I brush the pieces into the dustpan, inspecting them, guessing if they're male or female. Usually men do this sort of thing. Dad did. When the loping notes from the TV show *Dallas* played, Dad got out his clippers.

Root and I groaned, but he pulled off his socks, revealing big, wide toenails and wiggled them. "Beauties, huh?"

Mama's eyes stayed on the TV. "Your toes are your best feature, Tonk."

He'd smugly reply, "If you don't take care of your feet, you're not going anywhere."

What Mama was really saying was, "Do you have to do that here? Now?" And what he was replying was, "Yep."

Years of heated arguments had distilled their nitpicks into coded, but more civil, conversation.

*Click. Click. Click.* In my mind, I still see a semi-circle of nail somersault into the air. Toenails lay around his feet on our braided rug. Then the real assault and cussing began. His big toe. It was thick and ornery because "Too many jerks needed a good ass-kicking."

After he was done, he'd say, "C'mere, shug. Let's trim your hooves." I'd shake my head so fast, I could feel my brain jiggle against my skull.

I liked my toenails long. Mama complained they poked holes in my socks. I didn't care. She had a last-straw fit when my big toenails scratched holes in the tops of my fake Keds. "Those had to last all year. You either trim those toes like a young lady should, or I'll sit on you and your Dad will do it."

Dad grinned, one eyebrow cocking up as he shook the clippers like a silent tambourine. I grew to hate the *Dallas* theme song or anything to do with the show.

Unfortunately, toe-memories always include Eden Matheson, my arch enemy. To this day, I still wonder what I did to merit Eden's foul attention. I can see her broad face and her big-boned hand appearing next to me, giving a wad of my skin a hard pinch, then slinking away. In the first grade it was irritating, but by the sixth grade she'd added a twist to her vice grip, and any part of my body was up for grabs. I always carried a pencil and poked her with it if I saw her coming.

Mama gave me words to say: "Stop it. I don't like it when you ... blah, blah." Eden laughed when I used them. When Mama saw the bruises on my arms, I begged her not to get involved, but she talked to the teacher, and sure enough, what I expected, happened.

Out of nowhere, when walking to the cafeteria or standing in the library line, I'd be pushed into a wall as Eden slipped past. At lunch, whenever my milk carton spilled, it was Eden. I spent most recesses mopping up. I sure didn't tell Mama because *that* had turned out so swell.

I told Dad. He showed me how to make a fist. A tight one so the knuckles would stand out. "Aim right for the tip of her nose." His voice lowered. "Just pop her good once. That'll stop that act." I practiced on the hay in the barn. It scratched up my knuckles, but I figured I wouldn't actually have to hit her if I looked like I knew how to smack her around.

The next day I carried my lunch sack and milk through the cafeteria and Eden tripped me. The memory plays out in slow motion. I bumble into a table, pulling Del Reeth's tray off. It dumps down the front of my jeans as I land gape-mouthed, sprawled on the floor. Kids laugh. The duty aide shrills her whistle twice and everyone shuts up.

"Don't worry." The cafeteria lady showed up with a sponge and towels. "You'll grow out of your klutziness."

At that moment, I hated my bonehead life. My mind gloomed over. Voices faded. I dived into a funk, realizing I had six more years of school-misery with Eden. By the time I tramped outside in my damp, corn-stained jeans, recess was almost over. I walked past the playground to the baseball field where I could be alone. We weren't supposed to be there, but the duties were worthless. They gabbed next to the recycle bins and only looked up to blow their whistles when it was time to go inside.

I was past home plate when footsteps thundered behind me. Eden's thick-bodied bulk knocked me into the dirt.

I lay there, a sense of clarity and purpose overtaking me. No pain. No anger. Only the steel-driven certainty she didn't get to hurt me anymore. I balled my fist like Dad had shown me, but she stepped on my arm, pinning it to the ground. She bent over, her face puckered, calling me names. Mama's words snapped into my mind: "Ask her why she's doing this."

Sorry, Mama.

I kicked—as hard as I could. My toe drove into Eden's shoulder, snagging for a half-second before she tumbled backward into the dirt.

In a moment, she was screaming, "You coulda killed me!" She stared at the edge of the concrete dugout next to her head. "My skull woulda cracked open!"

I stared. The sickening wet *thud* of Lily's fall surged through my ears. I hadn't thought ahead. I hadn't looked around. I'd just kicked. By an inch, Eden was still alive. It would've been bad. So bad.

Eden ran off. The duties were blowing the whistles—but not at us. Time to go in. I walked, swallowing down my queasy stomach.

The afternoon was a dull fog of replaying my blunder and wondering what was squishy inside my shoe. I didn't look; I waited for them to frog-march me to the principal's office, but the summons never came.

When I got home, Mama was frying dinner. I waited on the porch for Dad. As soon as he drove in, I met him at his truck and led him to the barn, spilling my story.

"Well, baby girl, what've you learned?" He took off my shoe.

"I hate my life and I'm awful."

"No. You're not bad. You were pushed to the limit, but you acted without putting your brain in gear. It happens when you're down. Many a man has been snakebit for jumping without thinking. This time, the price you paid was small. You busted it loose." He hinged my long flappy toenail up and down, making me wince.

"The good news is, this'll grow back. Eden Matheson's head wouldn't." He popped off his belt.

I closed my eyes. I'd take the punishment.

"Put this in your mouth and bite down." He handed me the belt. It tasted like old boot laces and sweat. This was the same belt he'd lashed me with a couple of weeks ago. Now, here we were, partners in not telling Mama I'd kicked the daylights out of a girl.

He took his first aid kit out of his lunchbox. Then in one tug and one squeal, he pulled the toenail free. The belt dropped out of my mouth. "I wanna see it," I gasped, but he'd already flicked the nail behind him and had started wrapping my toe with a bandage.

"Don't wrap it so big. I need to wear shoes. I don't want Eden to know I lost a toenail over her."

"You gotta give up something to get something." Dad tied it off and stood, threading his belt back through his loops. "Your next nail will be thicker. But that's okay. It means you can kick bigger jerks." He leveled his finger at me. "You may feel down now, but happiness and sadness change. Just remember to turn on your brain before doing anything about it. And if your Mama finds out, I don't know jack squat about any of this."

The toenail grew back. But the strange thing was my confidence grew too. Eden never ratted me out. She also never touched or spoke to me the rest of sixth grade or middle school. Then one day, in high school, in the hallway between second and third period, she said, "Hi."

Just like that ... she was nice from then on.

It was a mystery why I had been her target. Maybe because I was smaller and had been advanced two grades. But why had she suddenly stopped? Dad said it was because I stood up for myself. I wasn't sure. For some reason as I got older, I trusted his wisdom less and less.

Now I keep my toenails trimmed and remember Dad was right about emotions changing. Happiness will grow back. If I forget, I look at my big toenail. It's thick. And it's a beauty.

# 10. Eyes Still Open

## ON AIR

GREETINGS FROM THE Navigator. This is a story of why I went to the forbidden land.

In 1982, I wasn't supposed to be in the woods, but I'd already explored everything worth poking a stick into around our place. At eleven years old, I needed to expand my world. Gum Creek was calling me. Crossing it was forbidden.

The concept of limits had always seemed iffy to me. When I asked why I couldn't pet strange dogs or run down the aisles of the grocery store, Mama's answer was, "Because I said so." It simply wasn't logical.

And then on a rare family vacation, Gramoo accidentally explained why rules were so dicey. Dad drove our black '71 Chevy Biscayne across country with Mom in the front. Root, my eight-year-old sister, and I sat in the back with Gramoo, who refused to sit between us. So Root and I elbowed each other past miles of dirt, fence posts, and occasionally, white butts of antelope bouncing across fields.

We looped through California, so Dad could apply for an oilfield job. The lumber mills in Oregon had begun closing. The supply of logs and his work were looking chancy. We continued through more ugly country and finally piled out of the car at a place called Four Corners. A skinny guy was already there, reading a lengthy plaque.

Root glanced at it, asking, "Whatzit say, Stiks?" Long ago, she'd twisted my name with the switches I liked to poke and swat things with.

"Read it yourself." I thumped the top of her head and left her whining.

Dad asked the man to take our family's picture. Gramoo stood like a bent fence post, cussing the big historical sign. "Why don't they just say, 'X marks the spot'? Damn gov'ment. Wordy as a chapter of Leviticus."

"Well, Moo ..." Dad guided Gramoo to the photo area. "Maybe folks don't know which four states come together here. The sign tells 'em."

"Oh law! If a fool don't know where he's at, he deserves to be left in the middle of this godforsaken nothin'."

I followed them to the metal plate on the ground and stood on the crosshairs so I could be in all four states at once. Root jammed her shoulder into my gut, trying to push me out of the way. "Mama! Stiks is hogging all the states!"

Giving her a squinty smile, I slid my foot over a couple of inches. She immediately tromped her tennis-shoe next to mine, thinking she'd easily won the battle.

Dad put Gramoo in Arizona, suggesting, "If you start walking southwest, you could make it to Mexico in a month." Mama elbowed him and took her place in the Utah quadrant. Dad grinned at the camera from Colorado, their hands linked across state lines.

"Everybody smile," the man said.

"How do they know this is the spot?" I stared down at the perpendicular lines extending in four directions.

"Gov'ment don't know a damn thing. Just made-up lines in the dirt," Gramoo said.

This explained a lot. Somebody was simply making up borders and rules. It also seemed like a good a time to shove Root out of my boundaries. Then the camera clicked.

I received a whack on the back of the head for my creative thinking. The stranger offered to snap the photo again, but Dad thanked him, took the little Nikon F2, and announced he was heading to the car to take medicine for a future snapping turtle bite.

In the fifteen years since the photo was taken, I've looked at it several times. It's always made me smile. My parents are squinting into bright sunshine, pained expressions on their faces, while Gramoo and I are staring at the invisible state lines. Open-mouthed and screaming as usual, Root is stumbling into New Mexico.

The interesting thing was that technology in global positioning proved Gramoo was right. The Four Corners Monument was off from original state surveys by 1,800 feet. That wasn't a lot considering the equipment the surveyor worked with in 1875. But once a monument had been accepted as "the spot," it became *the official spot*. Issues of legality trumped scientific details.

Back then, I took Gramoo's words to heart. Boundaries, fences, and lines in the dirt were ideas to be questioned.

So was the crossing of Gum Creek.

That was my name for it. Dad called it that "skeeter jungle" up north. He'd warned me not to go there. These were his woods. As a boy, he'd hunted and wandered miles from the family homestead. "There's nothin' up there that concerns you. A pack of wild dogs will leave pieces of you layin' around. Stay closer to home. The only thing dangerous here is Gramoo."

My gray-haired granny, sitting at the table, snapping green beans, nailed him with a dried-up look. She knew his six-week shift in the oilfield was an enjoyable way to escape her company. It had become her mission in life to bedevil Dad and remind him hard times were always coming. She stayed with us, even though she hated being called "Gramoo." I supposed she'd become like that government monument; once she'd accepted the name and the "spot," she became stuck in it.

Listening in on our kitchen conversation, Gramoo asked Dad, "Where's Stiks wanna go?" She usually took any opinion opposite of his. For an instant, hope flickered. I might have an ally.

"Crawford place."

"Oh." Gramoo went back to her beans. Silence fell over the kitchen, except for the *clink* of a spoon as Dad scooped blackberry cobbler into a bowl.

"Why can't I go there?" I picked up several fat bean pods and broke off their tips. "I've never heard any wild dogs howling. What's so dangerous over there?"

"Olin Crawford." Dad pulled out a chrome-legged chair and sat across the table from us.

I grabbed another handful of beans, trying to sound uninterested. "You've never talked about him. Why's that?"

"He's a mean old angry son-of-a-buck. Never leaves the place. You don't cross his land—he won't bother you. Once killed a man."

My eyes grew round, but before I could speak Gramoo muttered, "Some men need killin'." Her stare locked onto Dad, her mouth straight as a steel seam. *Snap, snap, snap*. The backs of beans broke and thudded into the bowl.

"You're kidding!" I ran my hands through my bangs, making them stand straight up. "Why hasn't anyone told me this before?"

"You were too young," Dad said. "Now that you're older, you're ranging farther. Go east or west, but *don't* cross his place. And don't say anything to RuthAna. She'll be squalling about the boogey man."

Dad always used my sister's full name, probably because she was christened in honor of his mother. But he was right about Root being a titsy-fritzel. She was scared of bats, worms, mice, and every animal common to a farm. No need to worry about her straying far from the back door. If we would've had neighbors closer than a mile, they could've heard her screams each time the geese chased her around the yard.

"And don't tell your mama." Dad said it to me, but his stare was aimed at Gramoo.

"It was self-defense." Gramoo smacked bean pieces into the yellow crockery so hard one skipped out.

"That's not the way I heard it. Olin Crawford started the whole ruckus," Dad said.

"And what would you know about it? You were still in short britches when it happened."

Slowly I scooched down in my chair. These were the usual opening notes of a set-to between Dad and Gramoo. If I was quiet and didn't fish-stare—bug-eyed and open-mouthed—I learned secrets. I'm not sure why they fascinated me, except it always shocked me that my parents lived before I was around.

Dad pointed with his spoon. "I know what my pop told me. And he should know since we've shared a property line with the Crawfords for ninety years."

"And you traipsed all over their land, stealin' walnuts, fishin' their ponds, an' lookin' for arrowheads, didn't you? When did it get too dangerous to be there?"

"After Olly chopped off Curtis Bilyeau's right hand."

I swallowed and sank lower.

"Oh well," she said, "Ratcrap Bilyeau shouldn'ta been usin' his fists on his wife. The jackass was prob'ly getting a snootful so he could beat her again."

"It's a hell of a thing to wake up with a hangover and missing a hand."

"If he was so snockered, the amputation didn't hurt a bit."

"Remind me not to drink around you. It doesn't take Sherlock Holmes to figure who did it. Who else would have taken revenge for beating his sister?"

"We'll never know because Sheriff Goans sold out. I remember when that Ratcrap-Bilyeau shot the Methodist minister's hogs. Said they was keepin' him awake afternoons. The reverend marched his pudgy self—you know how his collar always looked like it was chokin' him—probably from too much bacon.

"Anyway, the preacher went to the sheriff and filed charges. The next thing we knew, the reverend had moved to Snakebum, Arizona or some such mysterious place. The church was closed. Folks who actually knew what was goin' on, instead of guessing"—she gave Dad an impatient glare—"knew Bilyeau had paid the sheriff to look the other way while he ran off the reverend."

"I don't wanna hear about some pork-lovin' pastor." Dad's voice hitched up a notch. "Just tell me ... why did Olly Crawford go to the pen if he wasn't guilty?"

Gramoo's words matched his decibel. "Because the jury was rigged! Ratcrap-Bilyeau had the indecency to die from infection, makin' it manslaughter. His daddy was the mayor and thought somebody should pay."

"Oh hell," Dad snorted. "You mean my pop and everybody else has been mistaken all these years, and Crawford didn't do no wrong? I swear, Moo, every day another one of your marbles jiggles loose."

Gramoo's eyes narrowed, her face tightened, making her cheekbones sharp. Her voice hissed like it could slice flesh. "You tell me this, Ray, what d'ya think would happen if Stiks marries a guy who knocks out a couple of her teeth and her cheeks swell up till she can't open her eyes or eat for two weeks? And that's only what he's done to the outside of her. You tell me, what d'ya you think you'd do?"

My eyes flicked to Dad. Waves of anger washed over his face, drawing down the corners of his mouth. His jaw clenched and Adam's apple bobbed as he swallowed.

Gramoo leaned forward, her voice still sharp. "Yeah. I thought so." She nodded. "You'd cut off more than a hand."

The screen door creaked as Mama stepped inside, catching the tail end of hawkeyed looks disappearing over the table. "What's going on?" She sat a bucket of shucked corn in the sink.

Gramoo shrugged, her face softening, her voice becoming sing-songy, "Breakin' beans."

Dad stood, mumbling as he walked away, "Breakin' balls is more like it. I'm goin' out to push RuthAna." The screen door creaked its usual complaint as he opened it and paused. "Shug ..." He waited until I looked at him. "Go east or west. Leave north alone. Don't cross the creek." He left and the door banged shut behind him.

Mama frowned as his footsteps thumped down the stairs. "What was that about?"

Gramoo used the side of her hand to scrape up the stems and bean tips that had missed the chicken-feed bowl. "Oh ... nothin'. Just talkin' 'bout places we used to wander." She gave me a wink. I stared at her, white-eyed with surprise.

"Like where?" Mama added lard to a skillet and lit a flame under it.

Granmoo pointed at Dad's bowl smeared with cobbler juice. "Wander that over to the sink, Stiks. And when you grow up, remember it's your husband's job to clear his own dishes."

"Yes, ma'am." Confused, I stood and reached for the bowl. The stories, the stares, the wink that said something. I didn't understand any of it.

She clamped my wrist to the table, putting her head close to mine, whispering, "I 'spect you'll cross that crick sometime. If the dogs don't eat you, mention Winnie Lee."

My face wrinkled with questions, but she let go, shooing me with the flick of her hand. I continued to stare. Finally she swatted me to get me moving. It was the end of whatever moment we'd had. If I asked what she'd meant, she'd say it never happened.

Dad and Gramoo often spit nails at each other, but they'd never talked about killing. When I was younger, I used to sneak out of bed at night and hide under tables or around corners to listen to adult conversations. But this was different; I was part of this one. I'd stuck a toe into the inky pool of adult talk.

I'd crossed a boundary Dad and Gramoo had thought I was ready for, but they'd also silently agreed not to let Mama know they'd tainted the innocence of her oldest baby.

I felt both giddy and anxious. Before now, it was easy to learn limits; somebody set them for me.

In this new world—their adult world—the limits varied. Gramoo's borders were different than Dad's, which were different than Mama's.

For the first time I understood why adults were so confused. Each person set their own boundaries.

Maybe there were a few basic rules like "thou shall not kill"—but maybe not. I'd seen the protestors on TV at school, raging about nuclear weapons and the Cold War, arguing whether it was right or wrong. Not even death was clear. This was like standing on the edge of a cliff, looking down into the confusing freefall of adulthood. I wanted to take a step back.

I went outside and sat on the porch step. Dad was pushing Root high on the swing. At the top of each arc, her body paused in the air, then slack left the rope; she'd drop a few inches before swinging the other way. "Open your eyes!" Dad yelled, and she squealed each time her stomach tried to decide if it was going forward or backward.

Mama was busy frying chicken and didn't hear the squeals, or she would've been on the porch yelling, "Stop pushing her so high."

But that was Dad. He took delight in prodding folks past what was accepted. He reveled in it. He acted as though it were a God-given requirement to nudge himself, his kids, and anyone around him beyond what made them comfortable.

Except crossing Gum Creek.

*That* made him uneasy ... this man who'd survived two explosions at the mill. Now he was climbing oil rigs, hanging off platforms, and fitting big pipes. Maybe he understood the unseen dangers that lurked behind blackberry bushes more than I did. For the moment, I decided to honor his boundary.

"Don't close your eyes!" Dad yelled. "And don't let go!" My chicken-little sister yowled, but kept swaying back and forth, testing the limits. I jumped off the steps to join her.

Through the years, I've discovered life is like those events in my childhood. Each day—testing the limits. A ride of ups and downs with a lot of pauses and squeals in-between. I've followed Dad's advice, "Open your eyes and hang on."

And I followed it the year I finally crossed Gum Creek, but that's a story for another night.

Thanks, Dad, for teaching me how to expand my borders. Eyes still open. Still hanging on.

Risk and compassion every day.

Good night, Mama.

Good night, Oregon.

# 11. 1997

"PLEASE, MINA, WHEN is the very next opening in Dr. Slompka's schedule?" My voice sounds beggarly. I don't care. I'm tired and willing to ask for favors. The most important people in an organization are the administrative assistant and the custodian. A lot of back-channel progress can be made with those two.

Mina flips pages back and forth, comparing them to a calendar on her computer screen. "He'll return from the astrophysics conference in Florida on Wednesday. I know you're up most of the night and usually sleep till noon, but there's a Thursday morning opening. Ten a.m.?"

"If it's my earliest chance, so be it."

"You look tired, but would you mind helping me take these packages to the post office? I need to talk to you about something."

My stomach clenches. She's probably overheard faculty discussing my dissertation. This can't be good. We both tuck a couple of boxes under our arms and walk. She begins by chattering about food. I listen as though I'm interested. Halfway across campus she says, "You've got to tell me the truth. I won't be mad. Do you think I could keep up in college classes? I mean, am I too stupid?"

I give her a wild look. "Is that what you wanted to talk about?" She nods. A relieved breath escapes me as I look at the sky. "Why would you *ever* ask such a thing?"

"Because everybody here is so smart."

"Yeah—geniuses. The department head can't check his calendar and notify me he'll miss our meeting. I would've loved more than four hours sleep this morning."

"Actually, that was my fault. I'm sorry. I was supposed to call everyone, but couldn't read the names he'd written. See ... I'm not smart. Yesterday, I asked a grad student for his phone number for the files. He handed it to me written in Roman numerals. Thought it was hilarious."

I laugh out loud.

"It's not funny. I looked up the numerals, but don't know if I got 'em right. Numbers give me anxiety."

"Sorry. It's math humor. You should've told him, 'I don't read Latin. I guess I won't call you when there's a meeting.'"

"I didn't want to admit I couldn't understand it."

"*Pfft*. That has nothing to do with intelligence. That's assertiveness. To answer your question, yes, you should take classes. You'd be crazy not to take advantage of the staff discount. What do you want to learn?"

"I'm not sure ..."

Ahead of us, students are waving pictures of penguins, polar bears, and exotic animals. As we thread between them, a girl sticks a brochure in my face. "Help us save—"

"I hate tigers." I push past her.

Mina gasps, as though I've dumped ice water over her. "What about your radio spiel of 'practice compassion every day'?"

I grab her, pulling her off the sidewalk onto the grass. "What're you talking about?"

She shrugged. "A week ago, I couldn't sleep. I dialed around on the radio, and heard you telling a story. It was you, wasn't it?"

"Not me."

She gave me a doubtful stare. "I'm pretty sure it was. Why didn't you tell me they gave you a program? Don't be so humble."

"You didn't mention this to anyone, did you? Do others know?" I squeezed her arm.

"I don't think so. Nobody's said anything." She stares, her face slowly changing as realization sets in. "You don't have permission, do you? Are you crazy? You could lose—why don't you get it okayed?"

"Because I'd have to take broadcasting classes—which I don't have money or time for. And because I want to tell my stories uncensored. But mostly, I do it because secretly spilling my guts in the middle of the night is satisfying."

She's quiet for a moment, then nods. "Okay. I get that. But I hate to tell you the station doesn't have much of a listening audience, especially that late at night. I've seen the stats. It's there mostly to teach students how to broadcast, so you're probably safe. I can understand why you want to tell stories, but I don't get why you hate tigers."

My shoulders slump. "I only said that so I didn't have to engage in mindless chatter."

I can see the cogs turning in her head, wondering if I consider this conversation nitwitted. I hold up a finger. "Wait here." I trek to the animal activists, apologize, and return waving a brochure. "This was my compassionate act for the day. Are you going to report my undercover radio operations?"

"No. I like secrets." Her eyes flash wide. "And that's *my* compassionate deed for the day."

I give her a weak smile and rub my stomach. I don't feel so good. Either because I'm hungry or lack sleep. Or maybe because I now have to stop broadcasting or trust a woman who's afraid of Roman numerals.

# 12. Meeting the Devil

## ON AIR

HELLO. I'M THE Navigator, bringing you another tale in the thin hours of the morning. This is the story of how I met the devil and earned glory. No fame, just glory.

In 1984, my big adventure began on the west edge of our property. I was feeling smug because I was good at secret operations—for a thirteen year old.

Sweat sheened my forehead, ran down my neck, and glued my t-shirt to my back. It was hot and this was stupid. But that wasn't a good enough reason to quit. I had wanted to cross Gum Creek since the fourth grade, and I'd carefully gathered a survival pack: a canteen, leather gloves, long pants, weapons, and cow pee in a plastic Mountain Dew bottle.

A half-mile away, back at the house, Gramoo and my little sister were napping with a big box fan pushing a hot breeze over them. They wouldn't miss me till at least 4:00.

Above me, the blue sky looked tired and washed-out in the 100-plus heat. A jet silently crossed from south to north, too high for the noise to punch through the muggy Oregon air to reach me.

The drought had dried the creek; now I faced a wall of blackberries. Again, I slashed with an old corn knife, *whap, whap, whap,* then paused to listen. No sounds. Not even the birds were singing. I heaved the cut scrub out of the way. Thorns scratched my arms. I swung the corn knife again.

*Crack!* The blade hit something and stuck. I didn't move for a long moment, waiting for—I didn't have a clue what to expect on this adventure, except it was dangerous and I wasn't supposed to be doing it.

It would be twenty years and much schooling later that I learned a kid is a sucker for snooping where she's not supposed to go. Humans are wired to investigate. It's part of our survival. It's why Lewis and Clark went west, and why we send satellites beyond our solar system. An inner drive pesters us, and the body adds a squirt of dopamine, making us feel good—excited.

I didn't know any of that at the time. I'd only heard tales of a crazy murderer and his pack of bloodthirsty hounds. I had to see for myself.

My corn knife protruded from the bushes like a sword buried to its hilt in a wall. Heat waves beat down, making vines appear to give a rubbery dance.

I pulled my baseball bat from the pack, reminding myself to work quietly. If Crawford was human, he'd be resting like a sane man. But if he were "Satan, himself," as my friend Loretta Parker said, then the King of Hell would be out, probably naked, sunning himself in the hottest part of the day.

Niggling my bat into the thorns, I pried vines apart. A skull stared back at me. My corn knife stuck in the top of it.

I jumped, stepping on my pack and squashing the plastic bottle of pee. A second passed before my brain registered it wasn't a human skull, but a narrow-nosed animal with yellowed canines curving into an overbite. A spike ran through the bones, pinning them on top of gnarled wood.

I forgot the heat. My scratches stopped burning. Itchy spider bites faded away. What kind of creep nailed skulls to posts? And why?

Torquing the handle back and forth, I pulled the knife from the bone. The twisted post beneath it was Bois D'arc. Farmers had planted groves of the non-native trees to use for fencing. The wood was so hard they were called poor man's iron. I hated their long thorns.

Pushing more vines aside, I found rusty barbwire. My legs weren't long enough to crotch over the top of the fence, so I threaded through the strands, a barb ripping my shirt.

Swinging the blade, I gapped a slit through the stickers in front of me. After a while, a white fuzz floated in my head. I bent over. I needed water and shade. Briers fine-combed my body as I wiggled back through the cut and through the fence. As soon as the canteen was in my hands, I poured water down my throat, telling myself to go home.

*Oh c'mon*, my brain whispered. *You scouted the property line. This was the easiest spot. And you can't do this at night. If there really are man-eating dogs, they're not gonna run after you in the belly of the day. Right now, they wouldn't chase a steak if it trotted in front of them.*

I nodded, confirming my own intelligence report. I'd planned. I'd prepared. This was my quest. Now was my time. I could do this.

As I drank, I forced the bat along the fence line and found another toothy animal skull spiked onto a  thorny post.

Dad's voice cautioned my thoughts. "He murdered a man,"

"They never proved it." Gramoo had snapped back.

I looked at my ball bat. I was definitely going to need more water and weapons.

Tomorrow. Tomorrow would be the day I conquered my fears. I'd disobey two years of warnings and boogeyman stories. Tomorrow I'd cross Gum Creek and explore Crawford's hidden fields.

I checked my watch. Besides ... it was almost 4:00. I gathered my stuff, except for the smushed liter of cow pee. I left that in the weeds.

As I trudged across the pasture to the house, a few cicadas sang. Not a leaf stirred. My arm ached. Stickers had worked through my leather gloves, welting my fingers. And there were still more briars to cut. It reminded me of a poster from sixth grade. A rock climber hung from a ledge by her fingertips, dangling in air. The words read, *The greater the obstacle, the more glory in overcoming it—Mollière.*

I'd have glory all right. Enough bragging rights to get through middle school. I'd pry one of those skulls off a post and show Loretta and the older kids on the bus. Show anybody who called me a liar.

And I'd forget about Dad, who on Parents' Night, squinted at the poster saying, "Who in the heck would hang off a mountain to have their picture taken? At least when I dangle off a derrick, I get paid for it. Screw glory. Glory don't pay the electric bill. Gimme a paycheck."

Before reaching the house, I hid my tools in a ditch. When Gramoo saw the scratches lining my arms, she called from the porch. "Mercy sakes, whatta you been doin'?"

"Messin' and wanderin' around." I sat on the porch steps.

"Heaven help you if you turn out to be rambler like your father. You finish that hoeing?"

"Almost."

"Well, get back out there and finish. And pick some squash for supper."

"Yes ma'am." With a sigh I pushed to my feet and plodded toward the west acre, dragging a hoe behind me. Tomorrow. Tomorrow I'd go adventuring. Tomorrow there'd be glory.

The sun beat my back, assuring me it would be there, too, spotlighting my achievements. With every footstep, a puff of dirt ballooned around my fake Keds, reminding me I was anchored to this farm and this small life.

It was a day before I could get back to my grand quest because Gramoo insisted we make blackberry jelly. So, instead of cutting a path to the unknown world, my squirrelly sister and I worked in a hot kitchen. But the next morning, I globbed jam on toast and was out the door before Gramoo thought up any chores.

By nine, it was already eighty degrees. I'd been chopping for a half hour when my corn knife sliced a tiny opening through tangled vines. I ogled the gap, staring as though it were a peephole into the boy's bathroom.

It was shady on the other side. Safe and pleasant-looking. I wriggled back through the vines to the smushed liter of pee. Pouring it on the ground, I tromped in it. If the stories about crazy dogs were true, I hoped this would keep them from tracking me.

I put on my pack, glad to have the ball bat, pocket knife, extra water, along with duct tape. Three of the Apollo space missions had used duct tape to get out of jams, so I considered it indispensable.

Back in the bushes, three more slashes made the vines pry open like a door. I hated to leave the corn knife here, but it would cut up my pack, and I already received enough insults at school about looking like a hobo. So I held the bat in front of me and stepped through. The vines folded back into place, conveniently hiding my entrance.

I was in a fine grove of walnut trees. The lower branches had been trimmed way above my head. Dead limbs had been picked up and stacked into miniature tepees here and there.

The ground was bare as though it had been swept. Even the wormy nuts that had dropped early were gone.

Slipping from tree to tree, I worked my way to a hedge, unlatched a sturdy gate and entered a garden with neat rows of spiked-leaf plants.

I stowed my bat in my pack and tore off a narrow leaf, smelled it, then tasted it, my nose wrinkling at its dank stink. I spit like Gramoo had taught us in case it was poison. A bitter, moldy aftertaste rode my tongue. I couldn't identify any of the fusty greens.

There wasn't anything to see here, so I scuffed the soil, covering my footprints and latched the gate behind me. In a crouch, I duck-stepped through the tall grass, tracing a hose. I'd gone twenty feet when a heavy grunt sounded behind me.

Whipping around, I froze."

I'd seen this on a vacation in South Dakota. Dad had stopped the Biscayne so Gramoo could hang her old box camera out the window and take a picture. He got out of the car, so I got out, too, glad to escape Root and the backseat. Mama yelled, "Get back here!" but Dad and I moved to the front bumper, surveying the animals.

I pulled in a lungful of air, hooking my thumbs in my shorts pockets. Just me and Dad. Mama was shouting, "Tonk, you proved your point. You and Stiks get back in."

Dad strolled several feet up the road, tapping a cigarette on his pack of Pall Malls. "Damn." He shook his head. "With the racket coming outta that car, I'm surprised every animal in the park isn't runnin' for the hills."

Five bison stood twenty feet away, heads down, ignoring us. The hairy brown humps floated in a sea of prairie grass. I jumped in the air several times, thinking it would help me see more of them. One bison looked up, but the tall grass hid its face. Discovering how to get its attention, I jumped on one foot, kicking a leg in the air and na-nahing my fingers in my ears.

"Stop it." Dad blew a long trail of smoke. I lurched out of his reach as he tried to grab me. On one foot then the other, I jigged around, waggling my rear like a rodeo clown. One of my leaps landed on the edge of the pavement. I flapped, circling my arms, trying to regain balance. All five bison looked up. I lost the fight with gravity and rolled down the ditch onto their field. Three of the brown mountains stepped toward us.

"Shit!" Dad tossed his cigarette, grabbed my foot, and yanked me through weeds, up the embankment, and onto the pavement. I couldn't see what was happening, but heard Mama and Gramoo yelling. When Dad continued dragging me along the asphalt, I started yelling too. After a few yards, he clawed a fistful of my shirt, heaved me off the road, and ran with my legs dangling between his. Throwing the driver's car door open, he launched me like a Mercury rocket into the front seat. I banged into Mama who was shrieking. Gramoo was slapping the back of the seat, yelling, "Go! Go!" Root was strangely quiet, which proved she was weird.

Pulling my head from Mama's armpit, I yelled, "They stopped!" But Dad was leaving a trail of smoke and rubber behind. I floundered over Mama's lap, desperate to behold the creatures that had walked with saber-toothed tigers and woolly mammoths. In a brown blur, they passed from my sight. Mama smacked my head. "What were you thinking?"

"I wanted a close look at their faces."

"Oh, good grief." She pushed me off her lap and sighted a glare at Dad. "And you—"

For the next ten miles she railed about the stupidity of our risky act, then she included stunts that had happened yesterday and the day before on the trip. When I tried to defend our bravery, Dad elbowed me. "Shut up. Take the medicine. Get it over with." I nodded and tuned out Mama's voice, imagining cavalry men hiding in clumps of grass as Sioux women ordered bison to stomp on Custer and any soldier they found.

Mama finally fell silent. We rode a few miles with everybody lost in their thoughts. I glanced at Dad and he winked at me. That's when Gramoo asked him, "That cigarette you were smoking ... you snuff it out?"

He gave her a half-lidded look in the rear view mirror. For the rest of the trip, wherever we stopped, Gramoo enjoyed asking people if Custer State Park had burned up. She'd give Dad a pointed look, adding, "I heard some ignoramus tossed out a lit cigarette there."

I was disappointed I didn't get to see a bison's face that day, but now I was close enough to see the fly crawling into the behemoth's black nostril. It gave a grunt and shook its head, black horns curving up just like the devil's. Slowly, I stood, backing away.

It watched me retreat twenty feet, then with a huff, its ropey tail jerked straight in the air. It charged.

I turned and ran, the bat in my pack banging my head. I had a lead, but the hoofbeat behind me was growing louder. With fists pumping and the bat beating me, I raced for the next band of trees, even though they were Bois D'arcs.

Halfway there, I glanced over my shoulder. The bison had slid to a stop, its head down, front legs wide as it wheezed and coughed. I trotted backward, watching until I stumbled and fell splay-legged in tall grass.

The bison didn't notice. It continued snorting and hacking, its sides heaving in and out. Suddenly it raised its head and looked east. I followed its gaze. I hadn't noticed cattle in the pasture—and now five small animals bounded through the high grass between the cows. They moved strangely and fast like—dogs! I pushed to my feet and took off running again.

There was no barking no baying, just brown-backed animals diving through the feathergrass. Targeting the Bois D'arcs, I shucked my pack so I could run faster without getting a concussion. For a moment, I considered staying on the ground and kicking the hounds rather than ape up a tree limbed with thorns, but in a split second, I decided to climb.

My first handhold missed any spikes; after that I didn't have time to look. Swinging into the fork, four feet off the ground, I clambered upward, hearing the snap of teeth behind me. I kept my arms around the trunk, where no thorns grew, and scooched higher.

Within seconds, five brown-black speckled hounds surrounded the tree. Two put their paws on the trunk. Another one kept springing into the air as though it were on a trampoline. The other two circled. They were eerily silent except for a grayish one. A low *grrrr* gargled in its throat, and it wore a perpetual grin, showing its teeth. Not a bark, yip, or howl came from them. I looked for something to throw.

An hour passed. My feet, wedged in the tree at weird angles, ached, but I couldn't sit on a branch without a thorn gouging me. I spit at the dogs. Nailed one over the eye; he walked around with the big goober stringing across his face like it didn't bother him. I used all the cuss words I knew on the dogs and on myself for being so stupid.

"Get the hell up." A man kicked a dog that was lying down. I hadn't seen him approach. He'd simply stepped from behind a tree and snapped his fingers. The dogs slunk over to him. He eyed me. I hawk-eyed him right back.

He was tall and skinny like you'd expect Lucifer to be, but his nose was round and tipped-up. His gray beard hid his mouth, neck, and part of his chest. A sweat-stained straw cowboy hat topped his head and overalls covered his body. He inspected me a few moments, then turned and strode toward the bison.

"Hey," I yelled, "could ya call off your dogs?"

He kept walking. The hounds circled me, the gray one still grinning.

From my bird's-eye view, the big animal seemed to be breathing more easily now. The man ran his hand over its withers and down its legs. Its big black tongue snaked out and licked the old fella several times. After a while, the man came back and stood, burning me with his eyes. "You about killed Gordon, ya little shit."

"I'm sorry. I didn't mean to. How old is—"

"How'd you get this far back in the pasture?"

"Cut through the blackberries. I live over—"

"So you're a neighbor brat, huh? Well, you look like your dad. He was a little shit, too."

I looked away, unsure whether sassing back would make him madder, so I nodded. "Gramoo would agree with you."

"Who the hell is Gra-*mooo*?" He drew out the last bit, like a cow, but then his face changed as though he'd been kicked by a new idea. He took a step closer, squinting up at me.

My brain sparked with a memory. Nodding fast I said, "She told me if ever came over here, I should say, 'Winnie Lee.'"

The man stared toward our property, and I guessed he was looking into the past when he said, "Gra*moo*, huh? Serves her right. Your grandpa was a muttonhead."

I kept quiet, letting whatever film playing in the old coot's mind spool to the end. I hated this community. Everybody had a story about somebody else. Only half of it was true, but nobody knew which half. And all of the blab took place before I was born, which made it boring. Now I understood why Dad preferred the excitement of the oil patch to the slump of this place.

My left foot tingled with numbness. I shifted, easing the weight off it, but my right foot slipped through the fork. I grabbed a branch as I fell.

For a second, I dangled in the air like the rock climber in the poster, then gave an inglorious screech and let go. As soon as I piled on the ground, the grinning dog sunk his teeth in my ankle.

"Here, git back!" The old man kicked the mutt. I barely noticed. I was busy howling and staring at the black, two-inch thorn broken off in my palm.

"Pull it with your teeth." The old man clacked his choppers together like a Halloween skeleton. "Th' longer you leave it, th' more poison'll get in."

"I know what to do." I gave him a go-to-hell look. This was his fault. And his damn dogs too. Putting my palm to my mouth, I sucked and bit, then spit the long slender spike on the ground. One of the dogs rushed over to smell it, but the man backhanded the mongrel out of the way, picked up the thorn, and inspected it.

"Piece of the tip may still be in there. C'mon." He walked away.

The wound was already throbbing. Thinking he may have some herbal concoction for Bois d'arc punctures, I followed. Besides, he was headed toward the blackberries and the way out.

When we reached the walnut grove, he pointed to the ground. "Sit. Wait here."

I gave him the evil eye developed through years of public schooling and remained standing, slouching against a tree. "Why's there skulls on your posts?"

"Suit yerself." He snapped his fingers twice as he walked off, and the dogs plopped on their haunches, pink tongues panting in the heat. In a few minutes he returned, carrying a two-gallon can. "Hold out yer hand."

"Is that kerosene?" My voice came out high like Root's.

"The puncture's sealed up. Startin' to swell. Ya need to make a slit to get to it." He pulled out his pocket knife.

"I've got my own knife." My voice cracked. A couple of fingers had gone numb and the throbbing had moved up my arm. I really didn't want anything to do with kerosene or cutting. I only agreed so I could get my knife out and make my getaway. It was a good plan, except my blade was in my right pocket. My hand was too swollen to get it out, and I couldn't reach it with my left.

"Here. Hold still." He snatched my wrist. I didn't yank it back, figuring this was a take-my-medicine punishment. The old guy cut a shallow X on the puncture wound. "You want somethin' to grab onto?"

I shook my head and in the next instant shrieked so loud the dogs ran several yards away. Tears sheeted from my eyes. When I finally blinked them clear, I was surprised I was hanging onto the codger's shoulder. My hand still throbbed, but it was bearable. He pulled a wadded bandanna from his overalls, splashed it with kerosene, and tied it over the wound. "Keep that on. Stick out yer foot." Mindlessly, I held out my ankle and hardly noticed the lightning shooting up my leg when he sopped the dog bite with fuel.

He screwed the top on the can. "Stop yer tears. You'll live. Ya done as good as yer dad." He offered his hand. "I'm Olly Crawford."

I hesitated, looking at his bony paw, surprised Satan would shake with a kid, but Dad had strict rules about the honor of handshakes. I gave him a you're-lucky-to-meet-me look and tried to grip him with numb fingers dripping with fuel. "I'm Stiks."

Olly's stare bore through me like a prospector assaying dirt. When he dropped my hand, he wiped his on his overalls, I could see he'd come to some sort of conclusion. Good or bad, I couldn't tell. I swallowed and looked at my feet. Dad's etiquette only covered "Don't give weak-assed handshakes." I had no idea what to do next, so I asked, "When did you doctor my dad?"

"None of yer damn business." He leaned forward, staring like a coyote tracking a rabbit. "Now git outta here, and if you tell anybody, I'll come find you."

"You want your bandanna back?" I held up my hand.

"Dammit. Be smart. Solve your own damn problems."

He watched me as I poked blackberries with a stick to find where I'd entered. I pried vines back and stepped into the slit, pausing. "Why don't your dogs bark? That's not natural."

"I tore out their tongues. Don't come nosin' around again. I'm lettin' you off once 'cause of yer grandma. You used up your favors."

"But why—"

He made a smooching sound, adding, "Sic 'im." The dogs ran at me. I let the vines drop over the opening and tore through the narrow channel.

I thought I heard him say, "... Epsom salts ... thorn out." But when I finally stopped on my side of the fence to listen, all was silent. I was alone.

Now, you may ask, "Was it worth it?" Nobody but the risk-taker can figure that out. On that day, the center of my palm puffed up like a goose egg. I cradled it next to my chest as I trudged home, cross-eyed with pain. So this was what glory felt like.

It hurt.

But … I'd met an inmate, been chased by a bison, outran dogs, and discovered Gramoo and my Dad had secrets. So far it had been the most exciting adventure of my life.

And I planned on going back.

As your routine days unfold one after another, may you take the first stubborn strides in stepping over whatever scares you, then do it again. Take a risk. Do something compassionate each day.

'Night, Mama.

Good night, Oregon.

# 13. 1997

THE YELLOW NOTICE flaps on the door of my apartment. I was expecting it. The official wording reminds me to sign a new lease or vacate by the first of June. It's only one room above a garage, but I get to use the washer and dryer downstairs. I've talked to the landlady about renting by the month, but she won't hear of it. She wants a contract for a year, and we both know she won't have any trouble getting it in a college town.

My savings balance isn't healthy enough for a hotel. The custodial job and freelance work help, but it's a differential equation: more outflow than income.

Only a few more weeks—that's all I need. I don't live large; most everything I own can be stored in five medium-size boxes. And this whole problem would be moot if my committee would quit making changes and stop arguing among themselves. I need to graduate and get on with whatever's next.

I've got seven days to find housing. I suppose I could ask friends for a bed, but it's embarrassing and who wants a guest who works all night and needs silence during the day?

I carry a glass of lemonade downstairs into the backyard. As soon as I sit down I feel ashamed. If my friend Dez were here he'd say, "Lookit you. Sippin' a cool drink. Sittin' on a lawn chair with your feet up. What're you complainin' about?"

Dezmond LaBlu—the most optimistic human ever born. Four years ago, eavesdropping in the hardware store had allowed me to meet him. Back then I was working on my Masters, had a lovely two-room apartment, and my biggest problem was needing a tiny wrench to adjust my car's ignition points.

I walked the store's aisles but only found big honkin' tools, so I waited to ask where the small gadgets were. The black man in front of me was taking an inordinate amount of time, asking for a variety of nuts and bolts. Someone had smashed his bike-cart. He'd already found second-hand wheels. The bolts were for the frame.

"That's gonna make it heavy," said the hardware man.

"I don't mind. My bike and carrier have more patches than a quilt. No," he shook his head, "it's what they did to my campsite while I was at school that's the tragedy."

"You camp and take classes?" I asked, forgetting to apologize for being snoopy.

In pieces, he told of living outside of town in a tent for the last three school years and biking to campus.

"Good grief! What about winter?" I asked.

"Oh, there's only about two weeks of really cold weather. The rest is just rain and nuisance." He existed by showering in the gym, doing laundry at a dorm, and studying in the Business Building. It had worked until some jerk saw his tent and vandalized his stuff while he was in class.

The store owner gifted him the hardware and wished him luck. When I left with my wrench, Dez was on the sidewalk, working on his ragtail bike.

"You want a ride? It's an ancient car, but it starts—sometimes." Back then I had a VW, and he wedged his bike behind the bumper. It stayed in place for the five miles to his campsite.

He had sugar-coated his catastrophe. The tent lay in strips; water jugs were punctured; clothes thrown in trees; pages had been ripped from his textbooks. His cookstove, lantern, and equipment—gone.

Dez slept on my couch the rest of his senior year. He kept assuring me he'd pay me back because after he graduated he was destined to inherit his uncle's painting company. That was why he wanted a business degree.

I told him he'd already paid me—every day. If I moped about my family or money or spending nine hours on one physics problem, he'd make a show of sticking his finger under the kitchen faucet. "Hot water out of the tap! This is livin'. You don't know how good you've got it."

If it were chilly or rainy, he'd announce, "You know what we don't have to do? Cut wood, haul it, and build a fire in the rain and try to keep it burning." He'd nudge the thermostat, then rub his hands, saying, "Instant heat! Thank you, Lord. We've got health, some grub, and a roof. We're good.

I poke the ice floating in my lemonade and feel ashamed. A degree was so important to Dez, he'd make any sacrifice to get it. How important is my PhD? Am I willing to live in the woods so I can finish it?

If he were here, he wouldn't condemn me. He'd simply say, "Make do with what you find." Then he'd look at my drink and exclaim, "Ice! Oh, man, in the woods, I missed ice most of all."

Several minutes pass before the right side of my brain sparks an interesting thought. I pull keys from my pocket and look at them. I have a better place to camp than a forest. The Physics Building of the Science Complex.

I can move into the custodian's closet on the fourth floor. No one goes in there but me. It'll be small, but I only need to sleep and change clothes. There's enough room on one of the shelves to roll out the lucky sleeping bag. A few cleaning supplies will need to be shifted to other closets. Something I could start prepping tonight.

No one needs to know.

# 14. How To Deliver Jam

## ON AIR

GOOD MORNING. I'M The Navigator. And this is a story of how I saved a person. I saved a life for about twenty minutes—after that I learned the world could rescue *me*.

Being interested in science most of my life, I didn't pay attention to social rules because they didn't make sense. For instance, it's considered impolite to comment on items in other people's shopping carts. Or you shouldn't take a person's photo without their consent. And even though it's an efficient use of time, it's considered improper to carry on a conversation between bathroom stalls. That rule can be broken if you're out of toilet paper.

These unspoken guidelines are called soft skills—which change depending on the country you're in. The only way to learn them is by having someone mentor you or by making embarrassing mistakes.

I'm going to help you learn the proper way to deliver jam.

It begins in 1984 with the correct way to hang laundry. I was thirteen, and we still dried our clothes outside. I wiped the steel line with a damp rag to remove the dust, bird poop, and black oxidation. Gramoo's voice followed me, droning, "... people get older, but they don't lose all the other persons they've been."

This was what I got for telling Gramoo my secret. I shared my run-in with Olin Crawford with her because I didn't think she'd blab. Now I was rooky-doo'd into helping her with chores. And I had to listen to her tell me stuff that was supposed to mean something.

"When Olly was a kid, he was shy as a secret. He's had reasons to grow into a skittish man." She handed me the end of a damp white sheet.

I took it with my good hand. Mama had bandaged my other hand, after I'd lied about how I'd gotten a thorn in it. "*Pfffffft.*" I made a face. "He's a mean ol' fart."

"You shouldn't have been tresspassin'. Your dad told you to stay off his place." We draped the sheet over the wire and she clipped a couple of clothespins on top.

I wiped the second clothesline as Gramoo flapped a plaid shirt, snapping out the wrinkles. She hung it upside down by the hem, quietly saying, "When I was young, he called on me several times."

"I bet that was a bag of fun. What'd he do, let you watch him run around with a board smacking butterflies?"

She clipped a dishtowel next to the shirt so one clothespin held corners of both. "He was very polite. Too polite compared to the barn bums around here. They picked on him somethin' terrible. He was sort of a weird duck."

"No kidding."

"He kept a hive of bees in a gallon jar. It was fascinating. You could see those little boogers climbing over each other, makin' honey. He was whip-smart about bugs and plants. Once, his mama complained how the peaches and the green beans had to be canned in the same week. It wore her out. So he grafted several kinds of peaches onto one tree. They ripened at different times and spread out the canning season. 'Course, he coulda helped with the work, but that's not the way a man's mind operates."

"He's got a buncha strange plants over there right now." I wiped down the third clothesline. "I don't know what they are."

"I'm not surprised. He created a tomato vine that stood up to hunnerd-degree days."

"So why didn't he sell it and get rich?"

"People thought he was a little off. He learned the hard way to keep his creations to hisself. He was just smart and quiet, that's all. But maybe his troubles have changed him."

"You mean prison?"

The sound of the screen door interrupted her answer. My little sister wandered across the porch and down the steps. She always ruined everything.

"RuthAna, come help us!" Gramoo called. Slower than a possum, Root dawdled. With the childlike wonder my parents thought was so adorable, she broke off a milkweed and watched the sap ooze into a sticky white bead.

"Get over here, prissyboots!" I yelled.

"Get to hanging. Both of you!" Gramoo commanded.

My sister stuffed her pockets with clothespins. Using only her fingertips, she sorted through the damp clothes until she found a pair of her pink underwear.

When she started to pin it next to the shirts, Gramoo flicked her away with, "Uh-uh. You know better. Help Stiks get the other sheet on the outer line." I waggled my bandaged hand at her.

"You know unmentionables are strung between the sheets," Gramoo said. I rolled my eyes at Root. Yes, we'd heard it a thousand times, but because of my sister's airheadedness, we'd have to hear it again. "Laundry on the line is like gossip," Gramoo said. "Everybody can tell who's sick, or if there's visitors, or who came into money and got new clothes, or how raggedy poor you are. It's nobody's business. Remember that."

"This is stupid. Hanging bakes our clothes into boards. Why can't we get a dryer?" Root whined.

"Why don't you get a job and pay the 'lectric bill?" Gramoo said.

"In the winter, Suze Reynolds puts her pajamas in the dryer to heat them up for a few minutes before she puts them on. When I grow up, I'm gonna marry a guy who can afford electric heat instead of a wood stove, and I'll leave the lights on anytime I want."

Gramoo stopped working and stared at her.

Normally I'd punch Root for bringing on another lecture, but I enjoyed watching her get chewed out.

Gramoo's eyes sparked with fire. "Well I'm sorry, Princess Grace, but I'm not lettin' you grow up expectin' a man to take care of you. Look where that got me! When your grandpa died, he left a rickety house and dog. There shoulda been money in the bank to pay property taxes, but there wasn't. Women couldn't have bank accounts back then." She jammed a clothespin onto the toe of a sock. "Gone! He'd invested in a radio converter. Supposedly all you had to do to get television on your radio was plug a special adapter in the back. The man was an idiot. Tryin' to get rich without doin' the work. If somebody had said they had a gizmo that converted a bicycle into a car, he'd have bought it. I woulda put a screechin' halt to his nonsense if I coulda gotten control of our bank account."

"Well, women can have their own accounts now. Mama does." Root's tone hinted it was Gramoo's fault for being born in the wrong era. "Besides, Daddy has a good job. He takes care of us."

"Your papa's a reckless knucklehead," Gramoo huffed. "RuthAna, you're gonna get an education and a job and learn to stand on your own feet. I know women who are only forty, and they're scrapin' by because they thought someone would take care of them. Where's their men now? You never know what's gonna happen next."

It seemed a tad early for me to jump into the conversation, but I was impatient. "You mean like Mr. Crawford? Did he go to prison and leave his wife penniless?"

"Who?" Root scowled.

Gramoo skewered me with narrowed eyes. "He never married." She wasn't buying into where I was steering the conversation, but I could fix that. I blurted out the biggest whopper I could think of, knowing she'd grind her teeth to correct it. "It's our neighbor," I told Root. "When he was young, he beat a girl to death."

"He did not!" Gramoo's voice notched up. She gave me a black look as Root's eyes widened.

"Olly found—"

"Who's Olly?" Root asked.

"The neighbor." I elbowed her. "Shut up."

"Olly found his sister in the byway. It's grown-over now, but there used to be a path cutting through pastures so's folks around here could walk to town. Della, his sister, was layin' in the byway. She was tryin' to get to her folks' house. She'd collapsed, one eye swollen shut, the skin on her cheek the color of liver, her lip busted, blood dripping down her front. That was the outside damage. She was married to a big-fisted man whose hobby was whiskey."

Root waggled a dishtowel emphasizing her words. "Well, I would never marry a drunk."

"Nobody *plans* to marry a drunk, missy. It didn't start that way. Usually doesn't." Gramoo gave a disgusted snort. "Your grandad didn't start out stupid. He got desperate the more he failed. And do you think your mama dreamed she'd be checking groceries at D-Sacks? She thought she was in high cotton when she married a logger. Then the mill closed. Well, let me tell you, oil fields boom and bust, too. Trouble and tornadoes come out of nowhere to drop on you."

I sighed. Root could pull any conversation off topic faster than a politician. "So why'd Olly get in trouble instead of the wife-beater?"

"Because the beater-husband was the mayor's son. Della thought she'd taken a step up in the world when she married him. I coulda told her he was no-good, but she didn't ask. You young things think a man is the solution to all your problems. It was bad enough Della was laid up in the hospital after getting knocked around, but they brought in her ratcrapper husband to share her room after he'd passed out drinking and somebody had whacked off his hand. *Hmmph!* Then it got infected and he died."

Gramoo looked at me. "Olly didn't do it. He was at Looper's Auction, but the mayor and his mucky-mucks lied and stirred folks up. Olly went to jail five years before they got the ruling overturned. His pa and ma died while he was in there. Since he got out, nobody sees him. He stays to hisself. I feel sorry for him."

"An axe-killer next door? I'm *never* sleeping on the porch again," Root declared.

"Oh hush. You mix everything up." Gramoo hung a towel, shaking her head. "He's lived over there since you were born, and you didn't even know it. People live with all kinds of histories and don't have a clue until some gossip points it out. You are goin' to learn to fend for yourself. Now go in and start frying meatloaf patties for supper. I'll finish here. And don't go blabbin' this little talk to your mama—or anybody else for that matter. I don't want her yapping at me for getting you worried about nothin'."

Gramoo and I gave each other looks worn by the doomed. We both knew Root couldn't keep a secret. She'd blackmail both of us the next time she wanted something. Some family members you simply could not trust.

"What about Stiks?" Root whined as she walked off. "Why aren't you making her promise to shut up and learn to take care of herself?"

"Because I'm smarter than you, prissyboots."

"But you're ugly. If you put your face by a door, nobody would ever come in, blockhead."

"Girls!" Gramoo yelled. "Root, go start supper."

I tried to make a quick escape too, but Gramoo's voice, quiet and low, cut through the socks hanging between us. "How'd Olly seem? Was he well?"

I turned to look at her. She kept her eyes on the panties she was pinning to the wire.

That afternoon I carried a baseball bat in one hand and a jar of blackberry preserves in the other as I walked to crabby ol' Crawford's place. Gramoo insisted I walk the roads instead of sneaking through the blackberries "like some hillbilly."

His mailbox leaned at a lazy angle next to his gate. I looked in it. There was a baby-blue envelope, the size of a store-bought card. Normally, I'd carry mail to the house—a common courtesy when you know folks—but I left it. I climbed over the gate and trekked the quarter-mile driveway. Pasture fronted the road; his house squatted in the back. With each footstep I expected his hell hounds to bound out like wolves on the hunt. I was ready with my bat.

I made it all the way to his yard without seeing a dog—which seemed pretty strange. The one-story house had a tin roof which also covered the porch. At one time, the home may have been green, but faded patches of paint clinging to wood was all that was left of happier days. A garage and empty chicken pen huddled nearby. At the corners of each building, washtubs and rain barrels clustered on tall platforms with a network of plastic pipes running into troughs of lush cucumbers, tomatoes, and squash.

The porch was sturdy. A couple of new boards had been fit in among the gray ones to make repairs. I knocked and waited. No answer. He was probably in the back acres with Gordon, his bison. The proper thing to do was to stow the jam on the porch and get out of there.

But I sat on the step, considering my options. If he was gone, when would I ever have a better opportunity to look in a convict's bathroom or see what oddities a jailbird kept in his fridge?

I got up and pounded the door again—just a courtesy. I tried to open it, but it wouldn't budge—Crawford probably had it barricaded.

That wasn't odd. Most folks only opened a front door to get a breeze through the rooms. No one actually used it.

Besides, I was imagining the look on Loretta's face when I told her what our local ex-prisoner kept under his bed. I jumped off the porch and headed around the house toward the back.

Wary of those nasty dogs, I was looking behind me, around me, and everywhere except where I was going. I almost tripped over a pair of legs sticking out of the crawl space under the house.

The skinny body was belly down, clad in dirty jeans. The booted toes rested on the hardpan, not moving. I glanced around. So this was where he hid people. I wondered if that severed hand was under there, too. I backed away, hugging the jam jar to my chest.

Scuffling and thudding came from under the house, along with the throaty *grrr-rrr* of his creepy dog that always wore a grin. A low *uuungh* followed.

I neared again and poked the boot with my bat. "That you, Mr. Crawford?"

"Whaa-t? Somebody there?" The voice sounded strained and faraway, but maybe it was because of the bumping, thumping, coughing, and cussing. "Be still, you sonsabitches!"

"It's me, the neighbor kid, Stiks," I yelled. "You okay?"

"No. No I'm not. Can't move. Pull me out!"

I stood for a while, considering his demand. Leaving him would be good payback for the dog bite, thorn in my hand, and running me off his land.

His voice was quieter, tired-sounding when he said, "Been in here five hours."

I guessed that was about enough torture, so I put down the jam and the bat, grabbed his boots, and tugged. He let out a scream of holy agony, causing me to drop his legs. When his toes banged the ground, he hollered again. Frantic bumping and stirrings came from the crawl space. It sounded like all the hell hounds were trying to get out at the same time. His swearing grew louder.

"I'm goin' for help," I yelled, picking up the jam and my bat.

"No ... don't ... leave me." Pain punctuated each word.

Day after day I had wished I was a grown-up, and now that I had a chance to act like an adult and rescue somebody, I wasn't big enough or strong enough. Truth was, I was afraid of the dogs, of him, and of not knowing what to do. I wanted someone else to take over.

"You there?" His voice was faint.

Several long moments passed before I squatted next to him, my hand hovering. Finally, I patted the side of his leg. "I'm here. Are you stuck in the little opening?"

"No. As I was crawling in, something popped in my back. Muscles went into spasms. I can't dig my toes in to drag myself back out." He let out a stuttering groan. "Thought ... it'd ... ease up."

"Your dogs. Why're they under there?"

"Went in after a possum. Damnit, pull me out."

I was silent. If I left and got somebody, there'd be nothing he could do about it. This was an adult's job.

"Please. Help." His words were barely a whisper, but carried a sadness that filled the black crawl space, the tired house above it, and the whole ancient farm.

I let out a long sigh. I knew what Dad would say, "Take care of the small guy, the one who needs rescuing."

Crap. I put down the jam. "Okay. I'll give it one more try." I took my position, sitting on the ground behind his feet. Keeping one hand on the bat and one on his boot, I scooted backward. He yelled, but he'd moved a couple of inches.

"Grab ... both ...boots," he panted.

"No way. I don't trust your dogs. I'm keeping a grip on this baseball bat. Ready?"

Switching from one foot to the other, I tugged. When his shoulders cleared, dog snouts snuffled around him. He snapped his fingers several times and the hounds lay down. By inches, I got him out. The mutts stayed put, their heads poking from of the crawlspace, watching me.

Mr. Crawford was chalky white, except for the dirt crusted on his cheeks.

The only first aid I could think of was, "Let's roll you over." So, I turned him onto his back.

That's when I saw something I'd never seen before. This mean ol' coot who poured kerosene on wounds and sicced dogs on kids was knuckling tears out of his eyes, his voice cracking. "Peed while I was under there. Nobody's been on this place in years. Didn't think I'd get out." The tears ran faster, dripping off his cheeks into the dirt.

I was confused before, but now I was utterly lost. What to do for a crying adult? It was as though all the demons of his life had ganged up and visited him while he was in that black hole.

I patted his shoulder. "Gramoo sent me over with some jam." I held up the jar. A broken smile crossed his mouth, but his tears still dripped. "Listen," I said, "you can't lie here, and I can't lift you by myself. I'm gonna go get Gramoo. You can trust her."

To my surprise, he nodded. We plotted out a strategy to trap the dogs. I got in the chicken pen, he let the dogs rush me, and I jumped off the hen house, over the fence, pulling a rope to close the gate behind the hounds. They leaped against the fencing, staring in that hair-raising way they do without ever barking.

"Can you drive?" Mr. Crawford rasped.

I nodded, feeling like I could do anything after outwitting a pack of wild dingos. "Dad lets me practice when Mama's not with us."

"Get yer grandma. Truck keys are on a nail next to the sink."

The air inside his house smelled like stale crackers, but I didn't look around, just snatched the keys and ran back out. Before I left, I brought him water and fixed a couple of chairs and a blanket to shield him from the sun. "I'll be back. I promise." He didn't say anything.

His old Ford started on the second crank of the key. Sweat grew under my arms as I went down the driveway. I kept mumbling to myself, "Don't wreck a rescue mission." Dad's voice rang in my head, "Keep both hands on the wheel! You can drive with one hand when you become a bootlegger." I concentrated on the road, but from time to time glanced at myself in the mirror, grinning ear to ear. This was what it felt like to be a hero, as though some part of the world counted on me to make sure it ran right.

I began honking about a quarter mile from the house. It drew Gramoo and Root onto the porch so they could see my grand entrance. Gramoo was shocked when I told her what happened. "Get over!" She shooed me across the seat. "RuthAna, you come, too."

Within a few minutes we were back on the road and my hotshot feelings had withered. When Gramoo got out of the truck at the farm, Mr. Crawford called, "Sorry, I can't get up to greet you, Winnifred. I apologize for the bother."

"Oh, don't you worry about that." Gramoo waved his words away, talking like this was an everyday visit. She took over, like adults always do, ordering Root and me to fetch this and do that. I felt sorry for Mr. Crawford and his pee spot, so I covered him with a blanket, and we rolled him onto a board and toted him inside. Gramoo ignored his protests, and she and I got him undressed. The blanket was handy for that, too.

When he was finally in bed, a few silent tears slid down his cheek. Gramoo shooed me outside where Root was roaming around. I wondered if Mr. Crawford was crying for himself or at seeing Gramoo or maybe he was overwhelmed by three people in a house that hadn't heard more than him breathe for years.

"Hey!" I noticed Root. "Get away from those dogs. They'll take your hand off."

"No they won't." With doe-like trust, she was running a finger over a snout sticking through the fence.

By the time I'd grabbed her shirt and yanked her away, Gramoo had appeared at the door. She called to Mr. Crawford, "I'll be back in a coupla hours to check on you." To us she said, "Quit makin' a racket. Let's go."

"He needs to go to a hospital," Root said. "Is that man the killer?"

Gramoo scowled as she got in and started the engine. "You have no idea what they'd do to him in a hospital. When you're old and alone, you don't get out of those places."

"Why? Whadda they do?" Root said as she hopped in. I followed, shoving her into Gramoo. Root frogged my thigh with her fist. The truck spewed gravel as we took off, and we jerked against the seat, ending our fight.

"Those money-grubbing doctors will run tests and keep finding something wrong," Gramoo said. "They'll poke and prod till you catch somethin' somebody else has. And if Olly manages to get out, he'll be in worse shape than when he went in. 'Cause he's alone, some gov'ment worker will snoop around his house. They'll declare it old and unsafe if he doesn't have ramps and handrails, and he can't go back there unless there's somebody to look after him. They'll stick him in a care center, say they've done their job, and forget all about him. It'll eat up what little money he has, and he will *never* see his farm again. One day you're sittin' on your porch and *whoops,* the next day you lose it all."

Her voice had grown angrier with each word. Hard lines etched her face. Her wrinkled skin was even more well-creased and papery-looking than ever. Blue veins stuck up on the back of her hands as she gripped the steering wheel. When had she gotten so old?

She lived with a son-in-law she didn't like, a daughter who worked and barely talked to her, and two grandkids who fought most of the time. She did the chores, keeping a house together like she'd done all her life. I wondered why she'd put up with it.

Years later, it struck me that her quirky, bawdy family were all she had between a home and being forgotten like Olly.

Maybe she didn't trust Dad's recklessness and Mama's forgetfulness, and she'd made it her purpose to help Root and me through the hard and soft skills of life. She didn't celebrate the giddy moments of joy or do dangerous, new things. Mostly she talked about the rules that came with the slow, repetitive motion of getting banged around simply by living. Then there was the terror of losing it all, which had made a rock-hard old man cry.

That should've been enough to make me stay childish like Root, but I ached to grow up, even with the terror of ending up alone and forgotten.

I looked forward to being an adult because I'd witnessed something else that day. One of life's generous surprises.

Sometimes it sends someone to find you and drag you out of your darkness. It gives second chances. New journeys can begin.

And that's how you deliver jam.

Practice grace on everyone, my friends. Every time.

Take a risk. Show compassion. Every day.

Good night, Mama.

Good night, Oregon.

## 15. 1997

"WHOT YEAR IS your Cortina?" asks a male voice. There's a hint of Brit in the vowels. I assume that's why he has recognized my Ford clunker. It was manufactured solely in the UK.

"Sixty-five," I answer. I can't see him. I'm lying under my car in a parking lot. The toolbox I lugged from the Physics lab isn't within reach, so I waggle my hand. "Would you mind handing me a wrench ... uh ... a spanner?" Several moments pass before I hear the guy rummage through the tools. He's probably getting over the surprise that the coveralls protruding from the undercarriage belong to a woman.

"Whot size you need?"

"Something big. I'm using it as a hammer."

"Hold on a minute. Whot're you doing?"

"Changing oil. The filter won't come off."

He offers to "give it a go." I crawl from beneath the car to see a short thirty-something with wavy hair to his shoulders. I give him a smile and a nod. He takes my place on the cardboard I'd laid on the asphalt.

"I grew up with a car like this," he says. "Ours was a Mark Two." He grunts as he strains and pulls, but he can't budge the filter. I knew he wouldn't be able to.

I scooch back under with a pipe wrench and a ten-inch drift punch. "We'll use physics, or as my Dad would say, 'We need a little more leverage.'" Several hard hits with the wrench drives the punch crosswise through the filter. "Let it drain, then we'll wrestle it off." I rest my head on the pavement, watching warm oil stream into a plastic tub.

It's been a long time since I've worked on a car with someone. Dad and I used to lie in gravel, an oil pan between us, staring at the bottom of his truck and sorting out life.

My helper interrupts my thoughts with, "Did you know Ford named this auto after an Italian ski resort? For a publicity stunt, they drove several Cortinas down the bobsled run. It was quite memorable. My old man was always cleaning the breather tube on our Mark Two. He loved that car." Oil drips as he shares more car-memories, finally asking, "How did you come to own this one?"

"Bought it from a professor. It was cheap, and I needed something simple I could work on." I whack one end of the drift punch, knocking the filter into a grudgingly slow twist.

"I'll finish up," he offers, "if you'll hand me the new filter." He seems happy to do it, so I crawl out, pass it to him, then clean tools and pour used oil into plastic jugs.

"Where'd you learn to work on this?" he asks, sliding from under the car.

"My dad started me out changing spark plugs and antifreeze. Then we moved to ignition points, adjusting brakes and bleeding the lines. He was what Brits would call an off-the-wall-mechanic. You're from the UK, aren't you?"

"Manchester." He wipes his hands on a rag. "Working on my dissertation here. Biology."

I look at him. "Say, I have a great idea. Why don't you buy this fine automobile? Obviously, you know how to work on it." I run my hand across the shabby fender trim. "A few of the stitches have pulled from the seats, and there's corrosion around the headlights and doors, but it's gotten me where I needed to go."

"It's a classic. You can't sell this."

"I need the money. I want it to go to a good home."

He shakes his head, patting the hood. "Sorry, wish I could. I'm afraid it's not in the budget. But these are brilliant cars. As long as the timing chain isn't rattling and it's not smoking, you should get more service from it."

"I'm Sophia Bolton. Thanks for your help." I extend my hand and he shakes it.

"Bretton Thwaite. If you ever want an extra spanner working on it, I'd be glad to assist."

"I might take you up on that. I thought I'd be leaving soon, but Dr. Eaves, the engineer on my committee, gave me a list of suggested revisions this morning. This will be the seventh time I've edited the procedure and results sections. I should be working on it right now, but I'm going crazy. I had to get out of the theoretical world and do something real with my hands. So I'm changing oil."

He laughs and nods knowingly. We exchange stories about graduate miseries. "Care for a beer?" he offers.

I hesitate a little too long because he says, "Another time?"

"Sorry, most of the faculty are gone, and I have a project to do tonight. I can get a lot done without people around."

He scribbles his number and hands me the paper, giving me a "Cheers."

I watch him walk away.

Sitting on the hood, I pat the car. "Maybe skipping a beer was stupid, huh, Buckminster? I don't *have to* broadcast tonight." I squint down the street, but Bretton Thwaite has turned a corner. The street is empty. The parking lot is empty.

I stay a while longer, cleaning the breathing tube on old Buckminster.

## 16. Chesterfield the Bull

### ON AIR

WELCOME TO THE small hours of the morning. I'm your Navigator. This is the story of how a visiting brother at a women's convent helped me deal with conflict.

As you know, the natural world is filled with opposition. Two electrons push each other away. Same with protons. Light rivals dark. Fire conquers ice. Loft escapes gravity. You get the idea.

Within my life, two ideas are in a constant duel. Stubbornness and forgiveness. They travel with me, locked arm in arm, pummeling each other.

For example, in 1986, my family helped the old codger living next to our farm. Gramoo put in the most effort. She was sweet on him from her childhood days. At fifteen, I was curious about his coyote skulls and the weird way he lived. Even after all of our attempts, he preferred to stay on the fringe of friendship, turning down Thanksgiving, Christmas, and Easter dinner invitations. Leftovers he accepted.

He didn't venture into the community, but had a land-line phone, ordered the few necessities he needed from D-Sacks grocery, and only dealt with one person who left supplies in a wooden crate at his gate in exchange for cash he'd leave in a blue envelope glued in the box.

Because Mama worked at the grocery, he allowed her to haul his home-grown vegetables to sell at the store and supplement his income. “Don’t say where this stuff comes from!” he warned.

“These are wonderful.” Mama held up a fat orange heirloom tomato. “If I don’t say where I got them, people will think something’s wrong, like they’re tainted.”

“I don’t want people comin’out here, pesterin’ me. Tell ’em Winnifred grew ’em.”

At first, Gramoo was uncomfortable about the lie, but Olly was right. Folks showed up at our farm, asking for seeds. Gramoo became known for her gardening skills and people *oohed* and *aaahed* and asked how she did it. “I feel like a snake oil salesman,” she’d grumble.

Dad thought her moral predicament was hilarious. He’d tell folks she used coyote pee to grow big plants. “She’s shy about it because she doesn’t want anyone to know she squeezes the varmint’s dong.” That added more ammunition to their in-law battles.

Gramoo eventually settled into her green-thumb role, hinting she had fertilizer concoctions—secrets from the Santiam tribe—or that her potatoes were giant because she hand-pollinated blooms during a full moon.

At least once a week, she walked the path through our pasture to Olly’s house, taking him a casserole or a pie. He’d send her home with gardening tips and herbal tinctures to ease her arthritis. Gramoo swore the remedies worked, and Olly could make more money peddling his cures than the vegetables. He made her promise she wouldn’t tell anyone about them. Dad usually stole the little bottles of stinky oil, using the lotion to ease his neck and shoulder pain—which caused more explosive battles between them.

While this hubbub was going on at our house, Olly worked on his farm, content in his unmarried, no-family, no-bother life.

That's why late one October afternoon, when I went to help him cut saplings, I was shocked to see him sitting on his front porch with a woman. Her body was wrapped in a colorful wooly sweater which clashed with her stocking cap.

"This is Sister Minnie, from the con ... convent," Olly stuttered.

Staring, I assessed the scene. I didn't like it. The nun looked too comfortable rocking in his chair, a cup of tea in her hand. And where were Olly's evil dogs? Why weren't they eyeballing her bony frame like she was a spare rib?

On the table between them lay a green hand-knit sweater tied with a ribbon and a sprig of dried flowers.

"Yeah, everybody knows the Sister." My voice carried more disapproval than I meant to let out. I glanced at her red Angus bull tied to a fence post. "She's always walking the road, looking for that animal."

"I am." She gave a single nod, proud as an evangelist preacher. "Praise God for Chesterfield and the blessings he bestows."

I didn't have the wit to spar with a nun, so I simply stared at her and her raggedy holiness. Olly, a tenderfoot in social skills, didn't say anything.

No one around town talked much about Our Lady of Sorrows. It was before World War II the Benedictine Order of Germans had set up the mission on the east edge of the town. They ministered to orphans, Dust Bowl victims, and Native Americans who endured the reservation. They survived by selling flavored honeys, beeswax candles, hand-spun yarns—and receiving donations for Chesterfield The Bull.

The sisters quietly did chores no one wanted to do. Their humility and meagerness made others feel guilty. When my school bus passed their old brick buildings, all of us gawked, hoping to catch a drive-by peek of nuns doing mysterious rituals. We referred to the place as Our Lady of the Sticks, and for Saturday night laughs, high schoolers sneaked male-nudie magazines and rubbers into the convent mailbox.

The nuns didn't wear habits, but most went about in various types of gray sack-gowns and flat hats. They were unnoticeable, except Sister Minnie, who dressed in colors like a cleaning lady going to Mardi Gras. Today, in addition to her raggedy red sweater, her headgear was wrong.

"Where'd you get that stocking hat?" I asked.

"*Jehovah jirah.*" She smiled patiently as though I were slow and had asked where rain came from. "God provides."

"Well, that hat belongs to Finley, a kid who rode my bus. His grandma knitted it. It got thrown out the window some time ago. A bunch of us went looking for it."

"Though many seek, they do not find. And yet, it was revealed to *me* as I was searching for Chesterfield. 'Twas a bit of red, nesting in a thicket."

"You must've picked it up right after it was thrown out."

"It required a few repairs ..." She pulled the green and white stocking hat off her head, inspecting the long tail ending in a red pompom. "The blackberries were unkind."

I was surprised to see she had hair. Loretta Parker had told me nuns shaved their heads bald as Cabbage Patch dolls.

"My mama had to buy yarn to replace that hat," I said.

"I'm sure a fine lesson was learned by all, and now, like Jesus' robe, the hat has moved on to provide new blessings." She snugged it back on her head.

I looked at Olly for help. He wore the lost look of a passerby who didn't speak English.

"Ma'am, Finley was sort of a dweeby kid. He was picked on. I know it's been six years, but if I could return it to Finley's grandparents, I think they'd be happy a wrong had been fixed."

"It sounds like *you* are the one who'd feel better about the boy losing his hat." She raised one eyebrow, giving me a knowing look. "I believe you'll find returning the hat won't help you come clean. You'll have to find another path to forgiveness."

What kind of religion was she running? She was a nun. Wasn't she supposed to give up hats and worldly junk? I promised myself the next time I went riding around with Billy Dodd, we'd cram the convent's mail box full of empty beer cans from the back of Dad's truck.

The Sister stood up, her voice sing-songy, "Well, I'll be going. Peace be to all of you. Olin, enjoy your sweater."

"Oh." He suddenly got up as though he realized he had a job to do. "Let me send something with you." He went inside, leaving me alone with her.

I crossed my arms over my chest and glared. I still wasn't going to take all the blame for that stupid hat. She was God's maidservant. It was her *job* to forgive people.

An awkward stare-off began between us. "Forgiveness is a decision," she said, her eyes deep-scanning my soul. "You'll have to decide if you want it."

I had no idea what that meant, but I could tell pretty quickly I couldn't outstare her. I broke eye-contact first. Olly tromped out of the house, poking a blue envelope into a sack of vegetables.

With a sweet "Thank you," she took the paper sack. Then nailing me with the same look the school principal usually gave me, she said, "I'm sure I'll see you again."

The bag rested on her bony hip as she strolled to the fence, untied the bull's lead, and headed toward the road. About halfway down the drive—without looking back—she raised a hand and waved, as though she knew we were still watching.

"Why"—anger spiked my words—"is she *always* on the road with that ugly bull?"

"Chesterfield needs to roam. He's gotta get out from time to time. How would you feel being the only male at the convent? Sister Minnie goes looking for him. I think she likes to roam, too."

"Dad says folks won't keep a bull as long as the convent provides free community stud service." I shook my head. "So now all your calves are gonna look like that rangy piece of leather?"

Olly slowly lowered himself onto a seat. "Sister Minnie spent time piecin' together Chesterfield's past. Talked to a lotta folks. She likes to tell the story of his divine destiny. The bull is famous ... once joined the circus. Folks give a free-will donation for his work."

I flopped into the rocking chair, the pillow still warm from the Sister's bony butt. It irritated me and fed my stubbornness. "Well, I don't like her. And that's the poorest excuse for an animal I've seen."

The brute had one horn pointing at his nose and the other pointing at his butt. He had no tail or ears—they'd frozen off years before. One hock was twisted, making him walk with a swagger, causing his one testicle to jounce on display between his legs. His back was scarred like a barroom pool table, and he was piebald with birthmarks, pink and purple and white wherever the red hair didn't grow. He looked like a dollar's worth of dog meat gone to spoil.

Olly watched the nun and bull grow smaller down the drive. "According to Sister Minnie, he wandered onto the Willis farm over in Eugene. They put him in a lot, waiting for someone to claim him—which was the right thing to do. The problem was he kept gettin' out, roamin' their farm, and within a week, he'd serviced every cow and heifer they had.

"Still, no one came to claim him, and by the next week, he was in the neighbor's pasture, plowin' there. He's as horny as an antler hat rack, and the calves come out just as good as their mommas.

"After a month, he escaped and was reported miles away, along the highway fence line, makin' tracks like he was on a mission. The Willis brothers said he was somebody else's problem now."

"I'm surprised he didn't get run over."

"According to Sister Minnie, Providence had other plans. It was about lunchtime and Stockwell's Circus was leaving Lorane, so—"

"Dad took us a couple years ago." I smiled at the memory. "Colored wagons. Trick riders. Root got a poster of 'fearsome beasts.'" I made claw hands.

Olly nodded. "Well, back then Stockwell had bought a tame mountain lion from a guy who ran a tourist trap in Colorado. The guy said there was no longer a market for photographin' wildlife in posed positions. Stockwell bought the lion and put her in a bright yellow cage and painted, 'Stay back!! Man-Killer from Borneo!' but it didn't scare nobody. So he got the cougar pleasantly drunk and horrored her up with brassy streaks and spots of white and purple. I guess she looked like hell. He was pretty pleased.

"One of the flunkies helping move the circus was that addle-brained Daniel Dekes. He was drivin' the cat-truck down old Territorial Highway, daydreamin' and lollygaggin' a quarter mile behind the rest of the caravan. The road wasn't used much after they put in the cutoff on Hamm Lane.

"So the circus was heading south, and as fate had it, old Clara Koot was too. She was on the backroads, drivin' twenty-five miles an hour with her poodle in her lap, tailgatin' Daniel's truck.

"And then there was Chesterfield, standing in the tall grass, chewin' his cud, and watching the circus vehicles parade by. When he saw a gap in the caravan, he probably thought the grass looked greener on the other side. He crossed the road.

"Daniel stomped the brakes. The truck headed for the ditch. As a wheel dropped off the asphalt, the cage toppled. There was a crash, a yowl, and the sound of breaking timbers. The cougar must've thought that was no way to treat a feline, and this would be a good time to 'go and see the elephant.' So she climbed outta the broken cage."

"I don't remember any elephants in that circus," I said.

"That's not what it means." Olly's eyebrows bunched up. "Don't they teach anything in school anymore? Go look it up."

I'd never heard him talk this lively or this much. I clammed up, hoping he wouldn't stop.

He stared down the road, but the nun and bull had disappeared. After a few moments he went on. "When the truck slid off the road, Clara had to stop, too. She was craning her neck for a look-see, and *thud*! *S*omething landed on the roof of her little Jetta. Her dog started yappin' and skippin' across the seats. The big mountain lion walked down the windshield to the hood, eyeballing them through the glass. Clara froze. The dog kept yippin'.

"The cat showed his fangs. Hissed that dog into silence. Then it sprung away into the tall grass.

"Clara's shakin' like a shirt in a hurricane and waving through the closed passenger window, trying to signal Daniel who'd got out to inspect the damage. 'Get back in your truck! A tiger here! It's the end times.' The poodle was tremblin' and sittin' in its own pee.

"It was the loud snuffling behind her head that made her turn to stare into a red monstrous face, horns goin' every direction, hot breath fogging the window. Clara screamed, 'Satan!' Her tires screeched as she got the hell away, leaving Daniel on his own. Better him than her.

"She called the sheriff's office, rantin' about a wreck on the old highway and 'the devil hisself was out there with a tiger, collecting souls.' The deputy dispatched a wrecker to check it out.

"The tow truck got the cage pulled upright, and Daniel bundled it with wire he'd cut from the nearby fence. That's the way a cowboy-flunky does it—just takes what's handy. He didn't mention the big cat had escaped. Law officials were so easily excited, and anyway, it was his boss's problem. Daniel swore it was a herd of deer runnin' across the road that made him stop. And what was in the cage?

"Daniel looked around and saw the cause of all his problems twenty feet away. 'Why the Mankiller from Borneo.' He pointed at Chesterfield who was grazing and watching the entertainment. Daniel let down the cage gate and rattled a bucket. Chesterfield ambled up the ramp and inside, expecting a treat. Then Daniel latched the gate and drove off quick. All was well. One out, one in. He figured the stock count was even.

"But when Stockwell saw his wrecked wagon trussed with wire, he was speechless. The Man-Eater from Borneo was gone, and in its place was the most awful excuse for a cow God could make. He started yellin', 'Where the hell is my cat?'"

"Wait," I interrupted. "Did Sister Minnie cuss when she told you all this?"

"She tells the story a lot. It's different each time. I figure I can add my own improvements."

"I like it. Go on."

"Well, Daniel stammered and studied the dirt. Finally he said, 'The cougar's gone. So I brung this ol' bull back instead. I reckon he'll scare kids—he scared that nosy ol' biddy and her pup who was rubber-neckin' us.'

"Stockwell wouldn't hear of it. He kept yellin', 'Every farmer in this county will recognize that skag. I'm not going to jail because I don't have a bill of sale. You take him back where you found him, and get me my lion back.'

"Daniel felt sorry for the rangy-looking bull and would've liked to turn it loose where nobody but God would see him, but he drove to the next town to ask if anyone had seen a big cat.

"He stopped at the sportin' goods store downtown where Creech Walter was trying to sell a metal detector to Sister Minnie, but wasn't getting much traction.

"'Mr. Walter!' she said, 'I am not interested in treasure hunting in the convent's cemetery. I came here to ask your advice as an outdoorsman. Are sheep or goats better for keeping the grass down?'

"He said, 'Sister, you came to the right man.'" Olly made a face. "Walter always was a big blowhard. The gasbag told her, 'Your main problem is *predators*. You put woolies in your pasture and the coyotes will be singing hosannas. You'll have to watch the sheep day and night, but vigilance is scriptural, isn't it? Now I've got a fine selection of shotguns that'll help ...'

"About that time Daniel took off his hat and said, 'S'cuse me, ma'am. I know a fair bit about livestock, and what you need is a burro or a bull. Why, they can whip the scales off a dinosaur. They don't crop grass close like sheep, and you won't have to worry about the coyotes. Now, I don't have burros to sell, but I do have a fine bull to give away. He might help your cause. He's retiring from circus life and deserves a lovin' home. So if you have a grassy lot, you may be the answer to this animal's prayer.'

"Sister Minnie tugged the circus flunky outside so she could inspect the bull and get the unvarnished story out of Daniel. She's good at wrangling the truth outta folks. She took Chesterfield and promised that the sisters would pray about finding the lion. She's never told me how the cat's exodus turned out."

I gave him an unsure look. "Between you and her, how much of that story is made up?"

He stretched his legs and leaned back. "After Chesterfield gained a reputation, the Willis boys tried to reclaim him. Told the Sister they'd found him first. She didn't give him back, just like she didn't give your hat back."

"I figured that's the way she operated. You'd better check where she got that sweater before you wear it." I pointed to the bulky knit on the table.

He was quiet, his fingers petting the soft wool. Too much time passed, and I could tell I'd said something wrong. Finally, he answered, "This was hand-spun, dyed, and knitted at the convent. It's from my sister. She lives there."

"The one who—" I stopped, then mumbled. "The man who hurt her got what he deserved."

He stared across the fields. When he spoke, his voice barely carried above the breeze. "I didn't kill him."

I spoke real low too, looking in the same direction. "I know."

"Mom snuck off to see the worthless cur that Della married. She was gonna give him a piece of her mind for busting her daughter up. When she got there, he was drunk, passed out in the backyard, next to the choppin' block." He shook his head. "She axed off the hand he beat Della with. Threw it in the hog pen. She didn't figure on him getting infected and dyin'."

My eyes went wide. "You went to jail instead of your mom?"

"She wouldn'ta lasted in there. Dad wanted to take the blame, but he wouldn'ta lasted either." He was silent a long time. Finally he sighed the breath of a man who'd looked at a page for the hundredth time, but the words hadn't changed. "Turns out they didn't last anyway. Guilt got 'em."

"Weren't you angry your mama did something that ruined your life? You sacrificed your future."

"It was my choice."

"Sister Minnie says forgiveness is a decision. You have to decide if you want it."

"Sacrifice is a decision, too." He stood up, grabbed the sweater, and walked inside.

An hour passed before he joined me at the brush pile where I was cutting cedar sprouts out of the fence line. We didn't talk, only worked. I couldn't help thinking how one moment had wrecked so many lives. Two people went to an early grave and Olly went to jail. He and his sister ended up tucked away like hermits, avoiding the world.

It would be many years before I'd gain enough smarts to understand how Sister Minnie knew that seeking forgiveness would ease self-doubt or that Olly and his sister needed to forgive themselves.

But that's how it usually is, isn't it? We're more willing to extend grace to others than let up on ourselves.

We're shackled with opposition. Guilt versus pleasure. Wanderlust competes with commitment. Acceptance against complaining. It's part of our journey. Stubbornness and forgiveness locked arm in arm until finally, something outside of ourselves arrives, nudging us to seek peace.

And that's why Chesterfield the Bull is a visiting brother—in so many ways—at the convent of Our Lady of the Sticks.

Take a risk. Try something new each day. Show compassion, even to yourself.

Good night, Mama.

Good night, Oregon.

## 17. 1997

THERE'S SHAGGINESS TO being a student. Clothes pulled out of the dirty laundry. Ponytails sticking out of ball caps for quick, unwashed hairstyles. Beards on faces that haven't been shaved for weeks. With classes bearing down, self-care is a low priority.

So once a term, on the last day of Dead Week, the barbershop/salon in the Student Union gives free haircuts.

By the time I get there, unshorn heads fill the doorway and the line twists down the sidewalk. Students stand or sit. Some try to nap or study. Others chat. Our physics group brings chalk so we can work problems on the concrete as we wait.

Most of us look like castaways or prisoners.

The line moves quickly. Stylists wield clippers in three standard cuts: short, medium, long. Whichever we chose, we emerge from under the cape looking different—almost newborn. Foreheads and ears exposed, necks untanned, our heads lighter and easier to rub. We'll tug what's left of our hair during finals.

## 18. Prom and Other Stupid Ideas

### ON AIR

IF ANYONE IS listening, good morning. I'm The Navigator and we're taking a break from this riveting music to talk about a painful time in growing up. A time when the situation isn't over, but the book has been closed. This is a story of my first heartbreak.

In 1987 my mama stood at the door, holding the car keys, jangling them like they were carrots and I were a horse. "What *is* the matter with you, Stiks? Get a move on. We'll be late."

At sixteen, I was sullen and hated everything. "You drive," I mumbled, walking past the keys. Her eyes latched onto my back; her silent questions pricked like darts.

We got into the Chevette. "What's the matter?" she asked.

"Nothin'." Heading down the dirt driveway, I stared at the two cows in the pasture. Their jaws worked sideways. Their calves chased each other. The first calf ran with his tail straight up. The second hopped like a rabbit, kicking his heels behind him.

My easy life of wandering pastures and hanging out with friends had stopped several months ago. Mama had arranged a job for me at the grocery store where she worked. My shifts at D-Sacks were on weekends and two afternoons a week. Mama ran a register. I sacked, answered stupid questions, and spent ridiculous amounts of time shoving cans to the front of shelves, turning them so their labels faced out. A worthless gesture. If people couldn't recognize a Campbell soup can, no matter which way it faced, they were too dumb to open it and eat. I also did cleanup—usually in produce where kids grabbed the bottom apple in a pile. I was starting to hate little kids.

"Hon, treat this as a real job. You won't be doing it forever, but it's embarrassing for me when Duane has to constantly reprimand you." Mama pulled out of the driveway onto the gravel road.

I stared at the countryside. "Cows are lucky. All they have to do is graze all day."

"And then they're slaughtered for hamburger," she said. "Your life would be easier if you'd follow instructions without the attitude."

"Ugh. Attitude is the only way I can get through that job."

Duane, the manager, didn't have a sense of humor. He'd made me rip off the *Assembly required* stickers I'd put on boxes of fried chicken. He also told me, "Stop using the donut sacks as puppets to talk to the customers!"

Each time I worked, he ragged me about some nonsense. Earlier this week he'd told me, "When someone asks for vanilla extract, direct them to the baking aisle, not the Safeway in Eugene."

Mama interrupted my silent rant with, "And you need to tell Duane you want next Saturday off to go to the prom. Don't expect me to make all your arrangements for you."

I braced myself, finally saying, "I'm not going to prom."

"What?" Her voice pitched up. "Why?"

"Because Samuel backed out."

"Why?"

I shrugged.

"Well, he had to give you some reason. What'd he say?"

I let out a long put-upon breath. I'd never noticed how many cows stood around, twenty-three so far, eating and doing nothing. "He stuck a note in my locker."

"A NOTE! Flames alive! What'd it say?"

This was why I never wanted to get into a car with Mama. I was trapped. The only exit was jumping out at thirty miles an hour or waiting until she stopped, but then I'd be stranded in the middle of nowhere. I didn't want to talk, but maybe Mama could provide some clues about being dumped. She understood the gobbledy-gook logic of a male brain.

But Samuel wasn't an airhead, which was why I liked him so much. He was my lab partner in biology. And he could discuss Benford's Law or the Purkinjie effect or Fraunhofer wavelets. "I don't know what happened." I held out my fist, calculating the new moon's angle from the horizon. "His note said he didn't know his family was going out of town when he asked me. So he was sorry, but he couldn't go now."

"Oh, well, that's too bad."

"It's a lie. He's actually going with Melinda Kucher. He dumped me to go with her and her cute little nose."

"Aren't you two friends? Didn't you do a science project with her?"

That was another thing Melinda had ruined for me—the best moment I'd ever had in high school. Unfortunately, I'd asked her if her uncle, who was a welder, could get the chemicals I needed for my project: Determination of Planet Composition by Light.

"I don't have a project yet," she'd said. "So, if I can join your experiment, I'll see if he can get the stuff." I agreed, knowing she wouldn't be much help, but her Uncle George gave us $100 worth of supplies that I never could've afforded.

Leading up to the big day, she created lots of "buzz," dropping hints around school. "It's so dangerous, we have to do it outside. There may be explosions." There wouldn't be, but for a few days I was a celebrity, quizzed about "playing with fire."

I spent several nights drawing posters explaining electrons, photons and how gaps in atomic energy levels created different colors, thus allowing astronomers to determine the composition of stars. They were great. On Science Day, the principal allowed four classes outside to see our project.

Melinda and I looked cool in our safety glasses. She'd quiet the group and, like a circus ringmaster, announce the chemicals. "Strontium chloride!" Then I'd put a match to the little pile of powder, telling people to write down the color of the flames. Only a few people took notes. Mostly they *oohed* and *aahed.* After burning twelve chemicals, I brought out the posters.

Several times the principal had to tell the group to quiet down and listen, but overall it was the best experiment I'd ever seen at that school—or so I thought until P.E. class.

I was changing clothes and overheard Melinda in next row of lockers. "What a drag to work with such a nerd. And those awful posters. Tiny little print. Trying to cram so much on them. I told her nobody cared. People only wanted to see fireworks." Melinda and her followers left the locker room, agreeing I'd proven I was a goober to a third of the student body—more people would know about it by tomorrow.

I should've confronted her. I should've never let her be my partner. I should've gone into the gym and beaned her with a volleyball. Instead I sat there. Staring. Grieving. How could such a wonderful moment become so tainted? I skipped gym class. Nobody missed me.

"Are you sure?" Mama's voice jounced me out of the memory. "Maybe it's just a rumor Samuel's going with Melinda. Did you ask him—or her?"

I gave Mama a dark glance. "Oh yeah, like I'm going to confront either of them and be embarrassed face to face."

"So what? You're a couple classes ahead of her." She gripped the steering wheel harder.

"You forget Melinda and I are the same age. Samuel wants to go with someone who's pretty."

"Well, good riddance to that hobknocker. You can ask someone else."

"Samuel's different. He doesn't fart or make rude jokes. He talks about the new Apple Macintosh computer and why a Walkman works. He's smart."

We drove, listening to the gravel ping the undercarriage. Finally Mama spoke, her voice barely carrying above the noise. "Sounds like you really like him."

I bit my lip. It sounded worse when she put it into words.

"Well, that's just despicable," she said.

I looked at her. I hated her saying crappy things about Samuel. "No. I get it. He's big-time and good-looking. I'm dweeby, poor, and grody-looking."

The car braked so hard, the back end slid sideways a little as we stopped. Dust flumed forward around us. "You stop it, right now!" Mama ordered. "There is absolutely no excuse for anyone, not even this David Hasselhoff wanna-be, to accept a date then cancel it because he wants to go with someone else. I know you think I'm not with-it, but here's the truth. I watched him when he came into D-Sacks to pick up detergent for his mama and kinda flirt with you. I didn't like him much. I could see he had a self-centered side.

"And his dad always carries that big phone the size of a brick when he comes through the checkouts. He makes a show that he has the latest gadgets, calling his wife to see if she needs anything from the store before he leaves."

I didn't say a thing. I couldn't. A single tear escaped and I looked away. Her hand caressed my hair, barely stroking it. I didn't like to be messed with, so Mama didn't touch me a lot, but her fingers delicately tucked strands of my hair behind my ear as though she were working with threads of silk. "This will pass. Trust me," she whispered.

I don't know how long we sat like that. Finally I wiped my eyes. "Aren't we gonna be late?" I hoped to end this conversation. I didn't want to talk about it again—ever—especially after hearing Samuel had come in to get laundry soap. I thought he'd come to see me.

Mama crammed the shifter into drive and took off. "I'm telling you there's nothing wrong with you. Not your age. Not your looks. Not your brain. You're the smartest kid in that whole school. He's the one who messed up. Be true to yourself. Keep being you."

We didn't say anything more, and I would've never admitted it at the time, but I felt better. At least someone thought I was worthy, even if it was only my mother.

Mama pulled into the back of D-Sacks and parked. "I know you're having a bad day, but please try not to rile Duane."

We got out of the car and trudged through the steel delivery door. All the nametags were stuck in a corkboard by the timeclock. Usually I wore someone else's so if there were complaints, they'd report the wrong person, but today I didn't have the energy to be clever. I bagged groceries like a zombie, ignoring shopping life around me.

"What the hell kind of place is this?" A customer yelled, startling me from a review of every nerdy thing I'd ever done in front of Samuel. Mr. James, a bent-shouldered geezer, lived down the street and sauntered in twice a day, squeezing fruit, reshuffling cereal boxes, and reading the paper for free.

D-Sacks was a tight-fisted store, and one of my jobs was to go through the egg cartons, replacing slightly cracked eggs. I was supposed to batch six defective eggs in a sack labeled. "Fragile Half-dozen 75% off." It probably broke several health codes, but Duane squeezed every cent out of his stock, and it was a poor town. People bought cracked eggs.

Sometimes I added more eggs if the numbers didn't come out evenly. Often I penned comments like "Laid by cracked chickens" or "Quality-checked with a hammer." Duane would make me re-do the sacks if he saw them.

Old man James was a regular fixture in the aisle, counting eggs in each bag so he could get the most. His actions didn't go unnoticed by Duane, who'd make me re-bag the eggs with only six. Today the old coot pointed a crooked finger at my nose. "I've been comin' here fifty years. But you don't give a damn."

Actually, he was right. I didn't give a bugfart where he bought his daily donut, drank free coffee, and stole sugar packets. But he'd ambushed me with his comment. I wore the wide-eyed look of a spooked cow when a truck is honking at her. "Uhh ... can I help you find something?"

He shouted at the same decibel he'd used when he'd owned the tire shop, bossing his minions over the whine of pneumatic drills. "You don't say 'Hi' or 'How you doin?' I gotta yell to get some attention!" Duane Unsinn came running from produce.

"And you ..." the old fossil took a couple of steps back as the manger arrived, then his bony hands clawed an imaginary pile of coins together. "You're only interested in takin' my money. I'm movin' my business elsewhere."

Duane spent ten minutes calming the old crank. He spent another five minutes chewing me out in front of everyone about greeting folks because I'm usually closest to the door, bagging groceries.

I took his advice to heart and spent the next hours making nice signs, attaching them to baskets and putting them at the front of the checkouts. "Off-load whatever you don't want here." I thought it would be a great help since Duane informed us employees he'd narrowed the checkout lanes, making it harder for customers to ditch items as they unloaded their baskets onto the conveyor belts.

I also added a pretty sign to the deli samples, identifying them as "Mystery Meats—Free!" The pranks lifted my spirits for a few hours, until stoop-shouldered Mr. James came back that afternoon.

Grabbing the old galoot's hand, I pumped it in a handshake, greeting him like a rich uncle. "How ya doin? Lemme get a basket for you." He eyeballed me as though he couldn't decide if I were a monkey or a dog. Ignoring the red plastic basket I held out for him, he tottered off to see if the price of canned corn had changed since that morning.

When he returned and paid for one can, I bagged it, assuring him he'd made a wise choice and rolled the top of the sack so it'd be easier to carry. "You doing okay today, sir? How do you feel?"

"Why do you care? What's it to you? I can't even come in here without you jumping all over me, trying to sell me crap." He grabbed his bag and shuffled through the door.

I threw up my hands. On another day, it would've been funny, but today, it wasn't. From her register, Mama gave me a sympathetic look. The dark feeling returned, circling my head like crows looking for a place to roost and crap. No matter what I did, it didn't make a difference. Samuel didn't want to be with me. Not even an old geezer wanted to be around me. I went back to silently bagging groceries.

That night, after supper, Dad stood with the screen door half-open, calling back to the kitchen table where I sat, "C'mon. Help me fix fence."

I looked at Mama, but she was focused on scraping plates like she was doing surgery. "I've got homework."

"Help me. It'll go faster." I could see by the quirk of his eyebrow he was lying, too.

Huffing a put-upon sigh, I got up, followed him to the pickup, and got in, dreading the father-daughter talk Mama had surely orchestrated.

Without speaking, we drove through the pasture and pulled up to the fence next to the pond. Evening was coming on fast. Dad tossed me a pair of gloves. Using the wire stretchers and the fewest number of words, we spliced ends of barbwire where it had snapped when a tree limb fell on it.

When we finished, he stowed the tools in the truck bed and sat on the tailgate. "Your mama tells me you're having trouble getting along at work."

I shrugged, relieved the conversation was about bagging groceries. "I suppose."

"Well ..." There was a long pause as he watched a Jesus bug walk across the pond. "I couldn't do what you do. Old women standing in the middle of aisles, yakking as if they're at a high school reunion. People weighing boxes of fried chicken, trying to find the heaviest one. Old nutjobs gripin' if you've moved their butterscotch candies."

"The kids are the worst," I said. "They take bites out of apples and put them back. People let their children run like wild raccoons."

"Jackasses."

"Yep."

"But still ..." The Jesus bug had met another one and they were circling each other, leaving no trace as they skated on the water. “If you take a man’s money, then you gotta do the job. If you don’t wanna do it, then don’t take his money.”

“I do what I’m supposed to do. I just add a few jokes so it’s fun.”

“Sounds like you’re bored—like this isn’t the job for you. And that’s the tricky part of working. If you want money for a car or college or goin’ somewhere—you hafta to work. To work, you hafta ask for a job. And if you ask, more often than not, you’re gonna get rejected. That’s a fact of life. You’re gonna get turned down for all kinds of things you want. Jobs. Baseball teams. Dates.”

The last word hung in the air. I glanced at him. He was watching the waterbugs coupling.

“The past few years have been rough in the oil patch,” he said. “I got my hopes up about a job with GeoWiredlines. I really wanted it. Cleaner, safer work, better hours. They told me I had it, then hired someone else.”

“That stinks. What’d you do?”

“Drank for a while, but that didn’t pay the bills. That’s when I started working two jobs. Exhaustion will take your mind off depressing crap until the worst of it passes.”

“How long does that take?”

“A while. But here’s the thing, there’s other opportunities out there. Have you asked around? Seen what else is available?”

“Are we still talking about jobs?”

“Probably not. Why don’t you ask someone else to the prom?”

“It’d feel weird, and I don’t want to.”

He patted my shoulder. “You got hit hard, shug. I’m sorry. It may not seem like it right now, but I guar-ron-tee in the grand scheme of things, prom is pretty meaningless.”

"I know. It's just ... nobody ..." My words stalled. The two bugs had finished and were going their separate ways.

"You keep wondering what's wrong with you?" he said.

I nodded.

"Here's something you're gonna have to trust me on. If you keep hangin' onto the past, second-guessing yourself, thinking 'If only I'd said this or did that' ... well you're locking yourself into a life of misery. Look at ol' Olly Crawford. He's over there, misered up in his house because he's afraid to take a chance. He won't let go of the fact kids laughed at him when he was little, and people think he's a jailbird."

"Well, he is."

"That was forty years ago, and the sentence was overturned. And why should he sit over there alone when your grandma is next door and sweet on him? But that's another example of hangin' on to hurts. Her husband—your grandad—was as good-natured as they come. And as gullible as a blind sheep. Married life was hard for her, so she decided not to give it a go again. She just hangs around makin' my life miserable."

"So what are *you* doing about it?"

"There's nothin' I can do about *her*, but I'm tryin' to convince *you* to stop worrying you're not pretty or smart enough or some yahoo is better than you. I'm the first to admit I'm not good at this dad-stuff, but I know for sure that life is easier when you stop caring if your dreams are crazy or your family is embarrassing. Or if anybody really knew what you thought, they'd say you're weird. So what if you've failed once or a buncha times? You've got two close examples of what happens when you give up and hang onto criticism or rejection—two dried-up, lonely lives."

A breeze surfed ripples across the pond. Water bugs rode over the waves. Swallows dipped and darted through the evening sky. Dad twisted his head side to side, rubbing his neck and shoulder.

I remembered he'd gotten banged-up in the oilfield this week, then it dawned on me that after a twelve-hour drive home, he probably wanted to lie down. But here he was, sitting on a tailgate with me, watching the sun color the water orange and purple.

"There's one other thing you need to know," he said quietly. A couple of heartbeats passed before he continued, "I won't bullshit you. You never forget your first love."

"Really?"

He nodded. "If I think about it—which I rarely do—there's a pinprick wherever her memory is stored. Sure, you heal. You get over it, but you always carry that person with you."

"Who was she?"

"Nah, it worked out better. There's nobody like your mama. She's a tiger about keepin' me in line." He tapped my knee twice with the side of his fist as though driving his point home. "And she's worried about you."

"I'll be okay." I let out a long breath. "Growing up sucks."

"I think it's as hard on a mother as it is the kid."

The sinking sun had striped the sky with fire. The last rosy layer spattered into darkness. "This acreage will be yours someday," he said, looking around him. "My dad gave it to me. I'll pass it onto you."

"You ever sit at this pond and talk with him like this?"

He nodded. "As a matter of fact, we talked about a girl. Someday, you'll sit here with your kid and talk about their disastrous foray into love."

He pointed at the first star of the evening. "And you can tell your kid the world will keep turning, the stars will keep shining, and ... for sure ... it's all going to work out. I gar-ron-tee it."

I don't remember how long we sat there, the light fading, the stars showing themselves one by one, even though they'd been ever-present above us.

And that's the story of my first heartbreak. There would be others, but that night, I learned hope always lives on. It's ever-present, though hard to find in the darkness. I'd have to lift my head and look for the light.

Take a risk. Show compassion. Every day.

Good night, Mama.

Good night, Oregon.

## 19. 1997

"WHAT WERE YOU doin'?" a student in the hallway asks as I come out of the radio rooms after my broadcast.

It's 2:30 a.m. and he's leaning slightly forward as though he can't decide whether to run away or push past me into the room.

"Checking equipment. Why?" I say it in an edgy voice, looking around for others.

"Was that you on the radio?"

"No. A recording. Why?"

He doesn't move. Just looks at me. My voice becomes harsher. "The lower frequency range has been cutting out of the SM70. Why's this concern you? Are you the idiot who spilled coffee on a mic? Because we don't have money to replace everything students break. This station is a graveyard for old, junk equipment. The electronics can't take it."

"No. No." He shakes his head. "Are you always broadcasting this time of night? I thought it was only recorded music."

"A voice-over is more accurate for bandwidth and modulation tests." I use my bear-scare tactic, putting my hands on my hips and scowling, as though it will make me bigger and meaner. "Why? How do you propose I calibrate?"

"I ... uh ... don't know. I do the afternoon show, Let's Go To Town."

"Never heard it. What's it about?"

"I mostly read from a *USA Today*."

"Well, a dose of news never hurt anyone." I nod. "Why're you here at this time of night?"

"Looking for my notebook. I'll come back another time." He turns and cuts into the stairwell.

"Hey, how'd you get in this late?" I shout after him, my words echoing off the walls.

"Somebody let me in with the pizza guy." His voice bounces among his footsteps galloping downward. The exit door bangs opens, then hushes shut.

I stand for a minute, wondering if he's a spy checking on me. This calls for an interrogation of the students who ordered pizza. I follow the scent of pepperoni.

# 20. Commencement Exercises

## ON AIR

GOOD MORNING. I'M The Navigator, and this is a story of how I learned who my friends were.

There's a reason we remember misfortunes. Negative events wake up the emotional processing center of our brains. Then, to protect us, those feelings are stored in the amygdala in case we need them. To help handle future situations, they're stored with a lot of facts.

For instance, I remember in great detail the gut-plunging shock of January 28, 1986. The Challenger orbiter broke apart. Two minutes and forty-five seconds later, the crew-chamber hit the ocean with an acceleration of 200 Gs.

I heard about it at lunch break. We were pinning on *Just Say No to Drugs* buttons. A couple of us math nerds rushed to the library to see the news.

In '87 Baby Jessica fell into a well. Each classroom with a TV was tuned to the rescue attempt. I have memories of our class drama queen, Jana Beth Flesing, crying the entire two and a half days it took to dig the child out of the twenty-two foot well. Both of them survived.

Memories of catastrophes stick with us, which explains why I remember May 9, 1988 clearly.

I was graduating from high school in a few days, and had a scholarship at Valley State University in the fall. Dottie, Billy, and I planned to celebrate. I didn't know them well, but being younger than all the seniors, I didn't have many friends in my classes. I sat next to them in assemblies. They were funny, and sometimes I told Dottie my secrets.

That evening Billy drove us to the cemetery. Dottie brought wine. I contributed two six-packs from Dad's stockpile. Billy had some weed. It rained, but it didn't ruin the party. Dottie took pictures of us being wet, stoned, and drunk among the tombstones. She even got one of me mooning the moon when the skies began to clear.

"Gimme that! You can't take a picture of my butt." I grabbed for the camera, knocking it from her hand, cracking the lens on a granite marker. She was outraged. I gave her the rest of the beer, and it seemed to calm her down. Then we drove around the countryside, looking for something to do.

After a while, Billy braked to a stop. "Look what that creepy ol' fart has done!" The headlights shone on furry coyote heads on top of fence posts, their eyes reflecting the light and glowing like the undead. I stared. Usually Olly put them on the back of his property and blackberries covered them. What had he been thinking?

Billy goosed the car and pulled up to the gate.

"Whatta ya doin'?" I called from the back seat.

"We're gonna check out the place. Get the gate, Dottie."

"He's a ol' man," I slurred. "Leave 'im 'lone."

"An ol' Satan worshiper with hellhounds is whut I heard." Billy drained his Budweiser and tossed the can out the window. "Get th' gate, Dot."

"No killer dogs, there." Dottie grinned at me. She pointed, gooning me with a ha-ha face, then popped open the door and stumbled out.

"Shut up!" I pawed for the door release. "You swore not to tell whut I tol' you 'bout him." Finally, the door cooperated and opened. I rolled out, blundering into Dottie, putting an armlock around her body, dragging her backward. "Get back in th' car."

"Don't touch me!" Dottie beat my arms.

"GET IN TH' CAR!" I roared. "You're jus' tryin' to impress Billy. Stop doing what he wants."

"Screw you. You're always tellin' me what to do. Like you're so smart, graduating early." Dottie rammed her shoulder into my chest, using her twenty extra pounds to slam me against the metal bars of the gate.

Billy beat on the horn and pumped his fist like we were in a knockdown behind the school. "Whoo! Chick fight! Go girls!"

I swung, slapping Dottie across the face—hard. In the headlights I saw her head jerk back and her eyes stare upward for a couple of seconds. Blood began to trickle from her nose. "Oh no! I'm sorry! Sorry!"

I'd walloped the only senior friend I had in high school. The one who knew my secrets—or at least the few I was willing to tell her. Neither of us were "cool kids," but we were okay. Good-enough company. Why would I mess her up to protect an old man? "I'm sorry. I—"

Dottie popped me hard in the nose. Inside my head, the cartilage sounded like crunching popcorn. Then a jab to my gut had me caving forward. She grabbed a handful of my hair, yanking me down to my knees. "You always think yer better, don'tcha?"

"Wherz this comin' from? Stop it. Stop!" I gasped, my hands holding onto my scalp.

The car horn honked, Billy yelling, "Go. Go!"

"Go hit *that* asshole." I pointed at Billy hanging out the window. Dottie banged the back of my head with her fist.

As I toppled over, I swung and missed, thudding into the ground with a groan.

Twenty feet away, a shotgun blast exploded the air; the flash lit the night for a second. Pellets whizzed overhead. I stayed curled on the wet ground.

A door banged. Headlights backed away. The car fishtailed down the road, gravel flying behind it. My friends left me.

I rolled onto my back, listening to the sound of the engine fade over the miles. What shitty friends. Maybe it was the alcohol that made them crazy. Maybe the weed? I had no idea they could be so mean.

On the opposite side of the fence, footsteps and paws crunched the gravel. A dog stuck his snout through the gate. A *grrrr* hummed in its throat. The grinning dog. I didn't even look. Just stared at the Milky Way. Billions of stars. Each one a solar system. Some with planets. Maybe somewhere up there, on one of those worlds, there was another poor girl like me getting the crap beaten out of her by a friend.

"Who's there?" Olly's scratchy voice came through the darkness.

All I could manage was a whisper to whoever was running this Universe, "I ...hate ... this place."

I'm not sure how Olly got me up his long driveway to his house. I threw up twice. He helped me clean up. He said purple bruises were blossoming under my eyes, so my nose was probably broken.

"Don't worry. I've seen worse." Olly popped ice cubes from a tray, put them in an empty bread bag and handed it to me.

"I can't believe this." I groaned, gently touching the ice to my face. "How did you ever survive jail?"

"I found the biggest guy in there and tried to beat him up. After that, nobody messed with me."

"Didn't he come after you—get revenge?"

"Yuh, yuh. I was in pretty bad shape. This hand still hurts when it gets cold." Olly flexed his right fist as he sat across the table. "We ended up being friends by the time I got released."

"I thought Billy and Dottie were friends. I don't get it. Why'd they do this?"

"Booze and anger."

"I didn't mean to break her camera. I thought she was over it."

"Hell, as a young pup I didn't know what I was feeling half the time. That's how young men are—confused. I don't know about women. But men ... especially when we're scared ... we wanna hit somethin'."

"Dottie musta been wanting to smack me for some time. Was it like that for you? Did you wanna whomp the guy who beat your sister?" I kept the ice pack over my nose and eyes, not looking at him.

"He was a weak pissant. He took his shortcomings out on Della."

"I didn't even know Dottie was mad at me."

"She probably didn't either. The hootch helped. Took me years to figure out I was mad at the world."

"Are you still?"

He didn't answer. Through pieces of ice, I stared at the ceiling, counting the ways I'd screwed up the last of high school, burning friendships, getting drunk, puking, and having a broken nose I couldn't hide.

Headlights flashed across Olly's windows. I shot to my feet, grabbing the table to keep my balance. "They're back!" I looked around for a stick, a broom handle, or a bat.

"Sit down, Joe Louis. It's your grandma. The last time you were outside, upchucking, I called her. She's got a key to the gate."

I dropped into the chair like he'd stunned me with 100 volts. My voice coughed up my throat. "I forgot you lock the gate." I stared at him. "The fight wasn't even necessary. They couldn't have driven in."

"Drugs, booze, and youth. Shit-for-brains," he mumbled as he left to escort Gramoo through the dog pack. It took a while for them to come inside. That was fine by me. I was preparing my excuses starting with, "It was Billy. He's a pot-smoking jerk ..." By the time they finally stepped through the door, I'd gone through every rendition my foggy brain could think of and blurted out, "I'm sorry, Gramoo. I screwed up."

When she saw me, her hand went to her mouth, fingertips pressed against her lips.

"Is it that bad?" I gently pinched the edge of my nose and winced. "You got a mirror, Olly?"

But that wasn't the worst part. Dottie was busy the three days before graduation. She got the film in the camera developed. There were pictures of me relieving myself on the Jackson family's tombstones. Another photo showed me bare-butted and howling at the moon. The snapshots circulated through school.

Principal Jackson called me into his office. I wasn't sure if I should dread it or be relieved this would be his final lecture because I was graduating.

He was more agitated than usual, making me stand while he paced in front of me. "Your grades make you valedictorian of the senior class, but your actions are far from the leadership we expect. Unfortunately, I cannot strip you of the academic title you've earned, but you won't be giving the valedictorian's address. Sean Greil, the salutatorian will speak instead."

I nodded, silently comforted that I wouldn't have to stand in front of an audience looking like hammered dog crap.

He continued, "The rumor floating around school is that as soon as you take the stage, some of your classmates are going to hold up moons. Rather than ruining the event for everyone, I'm removing you from the spotlight. The programs are already printed, so you'll remain Valedictorian in title only, but you won't speak, nor will you walk the stage to receive your diploma. Look for it in the mail."

"Wait a minute! I earned the privilege to cross the stage."

"You lost it when you urinated on my mother's grave."

We argued, but I didn't have much zest for it. My face hurt. I felt embarrassed about my stupidity and wished there were do-overs for first-time drunks. I was silent while he gave me another long lecture—the kind adults use to assure themselves of their own convictions. For my part, I tuned him out, thinking how I didn't fit into this school or this community. I didn't even fit into my own family. I wished for someplace I could belong. When I noticed the room was quiet and he'd stopped talking, I told him, "I never felt like I was part of this class."

"That's what happens when you skip two grades. I tried to warn your mother."

I told Mama what the principal had said, and then declared, "I'm not going to the ceremony."

"Your father is driving in for it. I think he'll have something to say about that."

Gramoo scowled. "He doesn't have a right to say anything. He's pulled plenty of bone-headed stunts."

"Ha! You look like a sick raccoon," Root sneered, circling her eyes with her fingers.

"Shut up." I swatted her.

"You've already got your cap and gown. You can sit at the back of the group. We'll put foundation over those bruises."

Mama chewed on her thumbnail, studying my face. “Or maybe sunglasses. We’ll act like it never happened.”

My voice came out low and desperate. “But it did.”

She sighed, rubbing her eyes. “Pretending makes it easier to handle. I’ve pretended most of my life hasn’t happened.”

“Oh, Mama, that’s illogical and sad.”

She shrugged. “I’m going to pretend you didn’t say that.”

When Dad arrived we were dressed and ready to go. He listened to the story, shaking his head. “You may have the highest grade point—but obviously you’re not the brightest bulb in the Class of ’88. That award goes to the little wiseass who got you on camera. We’ll go down to the ceremony, and I’ll have a word with the principal.”

I stared at him, imagining how *that* would turn out. This fiasco just wouldn’t stop.

Mama picked up her purse. “Actually, I’ve been thinking about it.” She turned and fussed with my dress, smoothing the collar. “Honey, did you know you’re the luckiest kid in school?” I brushed her hand away. “Listen to me, you don’t have to give any dratted speech. That’s a relief right there. And nobody can take away what you’ve accomplished, whether you walk a stage or not. I think you should stay true to yourself, and we should celebrate your graduation elsewhere. That way none of us have to sit, watching people who aren’t your friends.”

Dad looked at me. “I’ll make sure you get on that stage if it’s what you want, shug.”

I shook my head. “I don’t want to see any of them or high school—ever again.”

As we walked to the car, Dad slipped his arm around my shoulder. “Pissed on the principal’s family plot? That’s better than the time I put a ’possum in my English teacher’s car.”

Mama shot me a sly smile, the kind which rarely passed between us. She understood I didn’t want Dad making a scene.

And I sure didn't need to hear any more comments about my face or those photos.

We went to a cafe in Eugene, celebrating with hamburgers and milkshakes. Mostly we laughed, talking of other graduations I'd have—but back then, I didn't understand the future rarely went according to plan.

That's the way I remember this catastrophe. Perhaps it's not quite right. Researchers say each time we examine a memory, we corrupt it. Our minds edit and reconstruct it, always attempting to make ourselves heroes of our own myths. Maybe it's part of survival, or maybe it's the psyche trying to heal itself.

But I'm pretty sure I remember it correctly because the hero wasn't me. On this rare occasion it was my mama, quietly showing me that learning who we are, and who our friends are, is simply part of the journey. The lesson doesn't need to be on display for others.

Take it. Learn from it. Go forward.

That's tonight's story. Take a risk. Show compassion. Every day.

Good night, Mama.

Good night, Oregon.

## 21. 1997

IT'S TWO IN the afternoon. Sleeping in the janitor's closet is like living under a car. It's hot, smelly, and too tight to get comfortable. But it's free. I get up, grab a cup of ramen noodles, and peek out the door. Something is different. There's an energy in the air, more people in the halls, and a low bass thud vibrates the walls. I slip out, plodding to the faculty lounge to microwave my breakfast.

"Where have you been?" Mina calls down the hallway.

I squint at her. I'm not saying anything until I know why she's asking.

"I've been trying to call you, but keep getting a recording saying your number is disconnected."

"Yeah. I'm saving on my phone bill."

"We've got a crisis. C'mon."

"Another one? Can I eat first?" I look longingly at the remaining cinnamon twists on the table in the lounge, but she's already hurrying down the stairwell. As we near the front of the building, heavy metal music thumps louder. In the lobby, it blares through the speakers. Outside, three campus security cars are parked in front of the building, their lights blinking in seizure-inducing flashes.

"What's going on?" I shout over the music.

"Do you know how to cut the radio feed? Some student took over the campus radio station."

"You're kidding!" I'm sure my face is sparking an array of emotions. After a moment, I yell at a kid on a step ladder, unscrewing a speaker from the ceiling. "Hey! What do you think you're doing?"

"She told me to disconnect this," the kid hollers, pointing at Mina.

"The noise is interfering with classes," she yells. "That's Jason, the student who's always taking the copier apart, so I thought he could—"

"Good grief! Next thing I know you two will be rewiring the proton accelerators. Is the copier working, Jason?" He nods. "Good. Pack up your ladder. Why are you in physics? You seem more of a mechanical-engineering guy to me. C'mon."

The three of us make our way back upstairs and Jason tells me, "The speakers were already disconnected in the labs and computer rooms. Don't blame me. I didn't do it."

"Yeah, physics and engineering students don't want to hear announcements or the radio. They neutered those speakers a long time ago." We exit onto the third floor. It's quieter up here, but the banging bass of drums and guitars travels up the stairwell. Doors along the hallway are closed. Three young men are trying to stick a reticulating saw blade between the double doors of the radio room. "Hey! Quit it! What in the name of Newton are you doing?" I ask.

"Dr. Klein recruited these engineering students to open the door," Mina says. "So, do you know how to cut the radio feed?"

"I said, 'Stop it!'" I yell at the engineering students. "You're ruining the sound-deadening seal on the doors. Figure out something else." I skewer Mina with a glare. "Where is Dr. Slompka? What does our department head say about this?"

"He's in Portland at a meeting. He hasn't gotten back to me. Dr. Klein is acting in his place. And the head of the Communications Department is here too. Dr. Whisher."

"Radio talent is his domain. What's he say?"

"The hijacker's name is Kurt. He used to be a student, but recently left the program."

"I've heard of Kurt. His name used to be all over the bulletin boards. Why can't you use your keys to get in?"

"There's a metal broom through the door handles," says an engineering student, and his focus returns to diagrams of breaching equipment the students are drawing.

I shake my head. "All this technology, and a stick provides security just like it has since humans began walking upright."

Mina nudges me. "Come on. Go talk to the professors."

"Uggh." I rub my impatient stomach as we walk toward them. Giving Dr. Klein a nod, I introduce myself to Dr. Whisher and ask, "Have you talked to this Kurt fella?"

Dr. Klein wears a testy scowl. "We've got this handled, Sophia."

Dr. Whisher gives his colleague a perturbed look, adding, "Kurt won't come to the outer door. He's staying in the broadcast room."

"Let me check something." I leave, wishing I'd had my soup-breakfast. It'd make it easier to deal with so many brilliant minds preoccupied with being in charge. "*Vlileg in een olifant.*" I grumble the old Dutch for "making a fly into an elephant" and trudge the stairs to the next floor.

In Mina's office, I grab the phone and dial the radio station.

A young male answers, yelling like he's at a football game, "Welcome to Dead Week's psychedelic-acid rock! It's DISTORTED. EXTENDED. AND REALLY LOUD!"

"Yeah, yeah. You go, Kurt!" I yell back. "Listen, flip the three white switches on the top row. If you don't, you're going to blow out the board. Then you'll be sitting in a dead room, listening to silence."

"This is what college students wanna hear. Not the lobotomized music-therapy BS they make us play. Those switches broadcast everywhere!"

"Nope. Well, they used to, but they were never used, so I rewired them to cooling fans. Now flip those white switches, or the board will overheat. This station is a graveyard for old, junk equipment. It can't take it."

"Hey, you said that the other night!" The background music behind him lowers to a less-deafening decibel.

"You were the late-night visitor?" I said. "*You're* the guy they call asshat-Kurt on the bulletin boards?"

"In the flesh."

"You realize you're proving their point about being a jerk? Well, whatever. Listen, can you flip the white switches, and please make a public service announcement about tomorrow morning's traditional Dead Week breakfast in the Union, from eight to ten. Free. All students and staff are invited. Eat. Keep up your strength for finals. Tomorrow. Eight to ten. Free. Will you do that?"

"Sure thing, LateNightWoman." He hangs up.

Mina looks at me. "Why not let it overheat, then all this will stop?"

The music cuts off in the lobby and hallway.

I smile at her. "Nothing will overheat. The switches still control the feed within the building. Well, my work here is done. Radio talent is the Communication Department's problem. Physics only takes care of the equipment. Don't let them ruin the doors." I move past her to leave.

"There you are." Dr. Klein steps in front of me with Dr. Whisher behind him. "Can you cut power and phones to the radio room?"

I take a breath. These guys have been watching too many *Die Hard* movies. "Holy Rackenfratz!" I run my fingers through my hair, staring at the ceiling. "That's a lot of cables to sort through. And would you really want to? How can you talk to Kurt if the phones are cut?"

There's silence as they consider this. "Why not let him broadcast?" I say. "How's this different from regular programming? If he weren't there, you'd have somebody else talking about cheap pizza or playing different versions of Pink Floyd's 'Pigs.'"

Dr. Whisher readjusts his glasses. "This programming hasn't been approved. And only one of those Pig-songs is the clean version."

"We cannot have students taking over the station." Dr. Klein's hand slices the air. "We cut the feed. I'll take responsibility. Just show me which cable to sever."

Dr. Whisher is still fiddling with his glasses, mumbling, "What if he gets out of control and starts cussing? Profanity is a thirty-two-thousand dollar federal fine—per word."

"You've got to be kidding! That much?" I try to keep the shock off my face. "But someone has to report the offense, right? And the radio signal isn't strong. It's a squeaker. Believe me, he's lucky if four people are listening. I'm guessing if nobody makes a big deal out of this, he won't become a 'pirate of the air waves.' And if anybody asks, you can say you decided to change the format for Dead Week."

I catch Mina's face. She's standing behind the two professors, giving me a shut-up scowl and shaking her head in micro fractions. I ignore her, continuing, "You trained and trusted him enough at one time to let him broadcast, right? He knows what to do. He only wants better music. He just did a public service announcement for me. Why not give him a PSA to do each hour? Make him work for you."

Mina's stare becomes fiercer. Her eyes dart to Dr. Klein and back to me. It takes several slow seconds to interpret her eye code. Once again I wish the caveman who'd developed silent social cues had been eaten by tigers, saving the rest of humanity from error-prone communication. Finally I add, "Dr. Klein, what do you think?"

"I think the radio station shouldn't be in the Physics Building, and the young man should be forcibly removed from campus." He gives Dr. Whisher a so-there nod.

"Really, Dr. Klein?" I blink. "I'm surprised because creative thinking is your strong suit. If anyone can figure out a way to end this without ruining a young man's future and jeopardizing the broadcasting program, I'm sure it's you and Dr. Whisher."

There. I've sucked up enough. I don't have any more to add, except they're both nincompoops looking for merit badges. I stare at the young men by the door. "What are they drawing? Excuse me."

I quickly extricate myself from the professors and join the engineering students, telling them we won't be using saws, explosives, acid, or any sort of force on the doors. They should go back to their studies. They amble off, still discussing plans, which look like a laser robot. I follow them, then take a quick exit to another floor.

Outside the faculty lounge, Mina catches me again. "Are you crazy? You stepped in front of Dr. Klein's spotlight."

I keep walking, determined to make it to the microwave. Damn! All the cinnamon twists are gone. Mina follows me, whispering, "You should hear the discussions Dr. Klein has with Dr. Slompka, telling him how he should run the department—but I can't say anything because I'm not supposed to be listening. Isn't Klein on your committee? This was his one chance to stand out in a crisis, and you took over."

"No I didn't. I acted as a consultant. I gave them an experienced opinion and left them to make a decision." I fill the ramen cup I'd been holding all this time with water and stick it in the microwave.

"Well, Dr. Klein still wants you to figure out how to kill the feed and cut the phone."

"*Ufff.* "Forget that. But if he asks, say I'm sorting through a metric shit-ton of cables. That's a scientific term, by the way."

Through the rest of the afternoon, Mina gives me Kurt-updates. "Now he's saying things like, 'Never miss a chance to stick it to the establishment.' He's asking listeners to tie shoes together and throw them on a telephone line to protest against 'the man.'"

I don't even look up from my text. "All the phone lines on campus are buried. And how did you find me? There're five floors in this library."

She doesn't reveal her methods, but her last report is, "Rather than shut off the phones or electricity or break down the doors, they're leaving Kurt alone as long as he keeps his words civil."

I look at my watch. "It took three hours to make that decision?"

"And Kurt is urging everyone to meet at the stadium at midnight and howl at the moon. Blow off some steam. Scream our frustrations out loud."

"Maybe I'll start now."

"Three people have called the station, saying they like the music. Dr. Whisher says it's more involvement than he's heard all year. Of course, they're probably Kurt's friends."

I stay clear of the building until eight p.m. then begin my cleaning rounds. Hallway by hallway, I turn off the lights. I tune into Kurt's broadcast of heavy metal, jokes, and announcements. Around 9:30, he begins a game: The one food he'd trade for sex. His raunchy description sets the tone for a couple of callers to copy him. They get worse. I go to the roof and cut the feed.

The sun has dropped beyond the earth's curvature, leaving the June sky black in the east and crimson in the west. A cool breeze turns the anemometer. Someone has set up a hummingbird feeder next to it along with a tripod, a camera, and some electronics. An experiment, but I have no idea what's being tested. I suppose Kurt is conducting an experiment, too. Some kind of accidental-coming-of-age try-on.

Back inside, ten minutes tick by before the phone to the radio room rings. I silently listen in as the caller reports he can't hear the station. A half-hour passes before Kurt slips from the radio rooms and pads down the dark hallway. When he reaches the stairs, it sounds as though he's taking them two at a time. At the bottom, the side door opens and closes with a *click*. I don't look outside to see if he's spotted by the lone Campus Security cruiser sitting in front with its lights off.

Instead, I muse over the fuss today. It seems so overblown. What would the professors do if they knew I pirated the airways several times a week? I even boost the signal when I broadcast.

Surely interrupting late-night cowboy music with stories isn't as irritating as Kurt's head-banger music. But I guess that depends on the listener. Anyway, I'll keep taking the risk.

I suppose we're both doing experiments without a conclusion or hypothesis in sight. We simply want to change our world. We have something to say. To share.

I have no cause to throw stones.

# 22. You Just Thought It Was Over

## ON AIR

HELLO, THIS IS the Navigator. This is the story of how it takes years to figure out what you're actually talking about.

Before you reach the age of twenty, most things that have happened to you weren't experiences you planned. Someone else was busy organizing your life: parents, teachers, babysitters, adults. You were on the receiving end—the participant.

Around the age of sixteen you began taking control ... or so you believed. You were told you're in charge of your fate, but actually it's about a fifty-percent probability. And the sooner you accept that you control only part of your world—then the less moaning you'll do when events don't turn out like you expect.

In 1989, I was eighteen and almost finished with my bachelor's degree. I didn't go home often. I stayed at the university because my hometown was full of morons. Our farmhouse was rundown and needed repairs. My sister had discovered boys; her brain was saturated with giggles and mood swings. Mama and I constantly argued. Dad was in the California oilfields and rarely around—except for one weekend when we were both home at the same time. It's stayed in my brain since it happened, and began like all uh-oh situations.

"Hey." Dad tapped my shoulder, "Let's walk to the pond."

"Dad, I've really gotta ..." I looked up from my paper on Spatial and Temporal Damping of Fluid Perturbation. His face said he hadn't been drinking, and we weren't going to fish for perch.

I followed him along the narrow rut the cows had hoofed through the pasture. It used to be hard to keep up because the weeds hit me in the face, now they slapped my waist. His body bobbed each time his right leg swung forward. "You hurt yourself?" I asked.

"Winch hit me the other day. Getting too old to jump outta the way."

"You're only ..." I searched my brain. "Oh crap! I'm sorry! Happy birthday. With classes, I lost track. I wondered why Mama was so insistent I come home this weekend."

"Yeah, she was with me, too." He climbed the bank and cut between two willows, startling a frog into the pond.

My eyes followed the concentric waves emanating from the splash point. "Well, I wish Mama would've reminded me so I could've gotten you a present. I'm sorry. Did the well come in?"

"Nope." He gazed ahead, not looking at anything. "I gotta go back and finish 'er up."

"You drove for two days just to get here for your birthday?"

"Flew."

"Wow!" Nobody in our family had ever flown before. Either this was one of those times he was flush with money or ... I studied his face, but he walked away. "Everything okay?" I asked.

He didn't answer, but stopped near the water's edge, staring at ripples. A spark of worry began in my gut.

"Your mama says there's no physics in the middle of a pasture. You'll move to Switzerland near that atom-smasher gizmo or go to New Mexico and build a bomb. You won't want this place—this land."

I breathed a long-suffering sigh. "I've told you, that's not the kind of physics I do. I study gravity. We have to leave the solar system. People are destroying the planet."

"Oh hell, don't tell your mama. It'll be one more reason to sell out for sure. She'll wanna move to town before the earth explodes."

"It won't happen like that." I sigh again.

"Root doesn't want this place. You're always gripin' 'bout being here."

"Because I had a terrible time in school. I felt like a chick trapped in an egg, waiting to break out. Go somewhere I could actually learn all I wanted. Do you know how many people in my senior class read a book cover to cover?" I held up two fingers. "The kids were proud they hadn't wasted their time. If they had to do a book report, they watched the movie version. And the weird thing was they even complained about that. I griped because there's no future in this place. You and Mama barely had enough to survive here, and yet you decided to add kids to the situation."

"Well, not everybody plans everything like you do."

It took a second, but my eyes widened. "Are you saying I was an accident?" My voice was loud enough to flush a duck from the reeds.

Dad watched the drake flap to the other bank. "Shug, for a smart girl, you've got a ways to go in field experience. Lemme tell ya ... most of life is an unplanned event. You deal with it, and then it's part of you, like me getting Gramoo for a mother-in-law or you getting a broken nose."

"If we were rich, I'd get my nose fixed." I rubbed the bump on it, and added, "You could send Gramoo somewhere. She's always wanted to see Florida."

"Oh no, she'd bring back an alligator to chew on me. She never forgave me for getting your mama pregnant. Sometimes I think your mama hasn't either."

"It takes two." I plunked down in the grass. "I can't believe I was a mistake. This is what you wanted to tell me for your birthday?"

"No! But it hasn't turned out so bad, has it? You almost got your degree in two years. I've bragged to ever'body. Pretty good for a poor family, huh?" He groaned a little as he lowered himself to sit beside me.

"I had a lot of advanced credits in high school, but I couldn't have done it without your support."

"Listen, shug, you helped, getting scholarships and grants. Until you came along, nobody, especially not Gramoo, ever accused our family of bein' smart. I want you to get the biggest damn degree they got. Prove 'em all wrong. Thumb your nose at everybody. I'll help out when I can. Truth is, I don't mind working. I like moving 'round job to job. Keeps it exciting. Unfortunately, it makes your mama unhappy."

My ember of concern flared brighter. I was pretty sure we weren't talking about birthdays or schooling.

"And you gotta travel," he added. "There's lotsa places to see. That's somethin' nobody can take from you."

"Uh ... haven't you heard me talk about getting away from this burg since I was little? I'm going to do big things. Save the human race. Travel to the stars." He didn't reply, so I waited for him to say why we were really here.

After five minutes of watching swallows swoop above the pond, he finally spoke. "I need you to make me a promise."

Aaaaah. Here it came. "Depends on what it is."

"Sometimes the logical part of your head wears me out. Just promise me you'll go as far in college as you can before you get tied down with a fella or kids or debt. And if you find yourself in a job or situation that becomes a rut—leave it."

"Well, that's easy to agree to."

"No, dammit. It's not. Life jumps on you fast as a mad dog. It bites before you know it. It's like falling down stairs. One misstep happens, then another. And you won't be happy—then *nobody* around you will be happy."

"Are we talking about you or me?"

"Dammit," he grumbled. "Just don't make *my* mistakes. Promise!"

"Okay, okay, I promise." Of course I wouldn't make his blunders. Any intelligent person wouldn't have chosen the life my parents had. "And I'm ahead of you about traveling. I already have my passport and I'm studying German." I gave him a Cheshire-cat grin.

"Good." He nodded. "That's all I wanted to say." Dad pushed to his feet with another groan. As he tugged me up, he pulled me into a hug. "Remember, after you change the world, me and this land will be waitin' here for you."

For a long time I thought of this conversation as the Birthday Talk. The type people make when they're getting older. Each Christmas and Easter Gramoo gave a similar speech, always adding she didn't expect to be around next year because life sucked, she was feeling rickety, and the government was bankrupt.

But life went on, one day after another. I finished my Bachelors and studied for two years on my Masters.

Over the years I've reflected on that father-daughter conversation. At first I thought it was about my dad's unfulfilled dreams. Probably because I was shocked to discover I wasn't lovingly planned, but only an accident of passion with all the ensnarement that followed.

It would be handy to have a video of our lives, so we could replay past conversations. We'd see maybe we actually did act like jerks in high school. Or when our siblings argued, "I never said that!" We could push a button and show them exactly when they told us, "I promise, I won't tell anyone!"

Maybe mankind would be better off if I invented a life-recorder instead of trying to navigate the stars.

Three years and a lot of experiences would pass before I realized our talk wasn't about me—or Dad.

It was about Mama.

So anytime you find yourself wondering, "What was that all about?" You'd better write it down so you can look at it later. I've discovered it sometimes takes years to decode human language.

Actually, the best advice I can give you is never assume a conversation is over. Even if you're just talking to yourself.

Compassion and risk each day, my friends.

Good night, Mama.

Good night, Oregon.

## 23. 1997

"SOPHIA! IS THAT you?"

I arrange my face into a smile and turn around in the hallway. "Dr. Klein, how are you?"

"I have corrections and suggestions for your dissertation, if you'll follow me to my office."

I trail behind him up two flights, neither of us speaking, but that's not strange for scientific folk. Both of us are ensconced in our own thoughts rather than make small talk. "Wait here," he says. "I'll grab your file." He unlocks his office, and I'm feeling relieved this will be a short exchange. I wasn't ready for a long sit-down critique today.

Reappearing, he hands me the thick file. "Sorry it took a while to get back to you. I feel there are a number of gaps that must be addressed, particularly in the area of resources." He relocks the door.

"Oh?" I frown. *Now* I'm interested in a longer discussion.

"It's all in there." He taps the folder and begins walking quickly. "I disagree about some points in your gravity model."

I follow him. "But I modeled it using Dr. Slompka's work—"

"Perhaps that should be revisited." He waves at the file as we hurry down the hallway. "I was precise in my notations. Excuse my rush. I'm late for an appointment. Don't worry. It's all in there. We can talk, perhaps next week—no, it'll have to be the week after—if anything is unclear."

I stop walking. He doesn't seem to notice. His back is diminishing down the hall. Maybe Mina was right about his ego and he's punishing me. I flip open the folder. Red ink scrawls on each page: corrections, suggestions, diagrams, and notes. Some with exclamation points.

I am screwed.

"Oh," he calls back to me, "good job cutting off that radio interloper. It took a while, but you finally figured it out. Way to stick with it."

"What?" I look up from his notes. He waves, turns, and continues walking.

"*Mierennueker,*" I grumble. What a nitpicker. When I started the doctoral program, there weren't any available teaching assistantships. I paid my own way and figured I could tell people to go to hell if they tried to make me kiss their ring or butt or whatever. But then I had to accept the custodian job and then the technician job to stretch my savings. I can't take another delay; I'm at the bottom dregs of money. Maybe Kurt, the radio pirate, was right. "Never miss a chance to stick it to the establishment."

Unfortunately, working for the department makes it hard to be an open rebel. And like kings and queens, the faculty have thumbs-up and thumbs-down power over my life right now.

I close the file and stare down the empty hallway.

Or do they?

# 24. Take Your Daughter to Work Day

## ON AIR

GREETINGS FROM THE Navigator. This early morning, I'm going to tell you the story of how I became sure of what I wanted to do with my life.

You probably know people who've settled in the wrong job, and they stay there no matter how bitter it makes them. And why's that, you wonder?

Because there's safety in having a job, even a miserable one. The wolves may be circling the house, but having a steady income feels like you have a stick to knock a few of them back into the woods.

Some of you may remember 1985, when the price of a barrel of crude oil dropped to $8. The oil boom had crashed. U.S. producers took ninety rigs offline every week. The number of wells drilled fell to its lowest in forty years. Investors abandoned their fantasies of riches. Banks sold those oil-rig dreams for scrap metal.

"That's the way it is in the oil patch," Dad said. "Sometimes you feast on pheasant, sometimes all you get is the feathers." Those were bad years for our family. Dad knocked about doing odd jobs. He traveled to the few drilling sites across the U.S. and even went overseas to Brazil to work. Mama took on more hours at D-Sacks grocery. I was at college and had a part-time job at a grocery near campus.

I pitched my money into the family pot instead of the car I wanted. I thought it was a huge sacrifice.

After several years, the economy climbed out of the hole and by 1991, drilling was picking up. Dad got hired in California and wanted the whole family to move there for the summer. Usually I found a way to stay year-round at the university. But I'd be turning twenty in a month—and now had a chance to get out of Oregon with Dad paying for it. You bet. I was in!

I was the only one who wanted to go. Mama said she couldn't leave the grocery store. My little sis and Gramoo wouldn't leave the adventuresome life in podunkville. So it was just Dad and me in sunny Bakersfield for three months.

I did three things that summer: work, work, and more work. Most of my labor was spent tweaking the final sections of my Master's thesis. But to nest-pile money for my next degree, I also stacked oranges at the local fruit market. The rest of the time, I helped Dad. He'd rented a farmhouse, and—no surprise—he'd wangled a deal, promising we'd farm the acres for reduced rent. That's how I came to be driving his truck one late afternoon while he bucked hay bales into the back.

We were taking a break, sitting in the shade of the vehicle, eating bologna-pickle sandwiches, when he wished for a decent tree.

"It's illogical to put a tree in a hayfield," I said. "The baler has to loop around it. Messes up the rows. When I inherit our land in Oregon, I'm cutting down that lone cedar in our hayfield. The cows have rubbed it to pieces. It's ugly and in the way."

"Leave it alone. Still gives shade. That's why me and the cows like it. Poor old tree. Maybe I'll get buried there and really mess up your rows." He looked at the pager on his belt. "Hell."

"What?"

He stood, crammed the rest of his sandwich in his mouth. I knew what that meant.

"What about this hay? It looks like it might rain." I pushed to my feet.

"Gotta go," he mumbled around the food. "And we got one truck between us."

"I hate the oilfield." I opened the door of his Chevy S10.

He drained his beer and pitched the can in the bed as he got in. "Yeah, me too."

But it wasn't true. He loved the clank, bang, roar, and hard-hat danger of it all. As soon as we arrived at the site I could tell by the way he walked he felt he was accomplishing something more important than hauling hay.

We stopped in the graveled lot they'd made in the pasture, and it was obvious something was wrong. There was only one truck there. The white and red tower stood tall over the countryside, but no roughnecks were on the rig floor. No one stood at the cat walk or racks of drill pipes. Most telling was the missing grind of the kelly and the growl of motors pumping mud into the casing.

A man in a polo shirt stood in front of the logger's hut. "Tonk!" he yelled and beckoned with his three-fingered hand. Dad left. I got out to explore. Even the shade provided by the platform where the blowout preventers were installed was empty.

I walked the surrounding weeds, looking for beer and soda cans, dumping what I found in the back of the truck. California grocery stores paid two-and-a-half cents for each one of those. I came across the Geronimo line. The long escape cable draping from the top of the derrick was attached to a loose stake. Using a rock, I was pounding it farther into the dirt when Dad came out of the hut like a man on a mission. "Stop messin' around!" he called. "C'mon!" I hurried to the truck.

"Hit a vug," he said as he got in and slammed the door. He was pulling out while I still had one foot on the ground.

"Wait!" I yelled, hopping along until I could jump in and yank the door shut. "What's happened?"

"They drilled into a cavity, lost all circulation."

"Does that mean it's a dry hole? You're out of work?"

"Not yet. They pumped more mud in, trying to fill the hole so they could drill past it, but it keeps flowing off to Tanganyika."

"And the pump's pressure keeps the mud flowing so the bit stays cool, right? Why not put something else down the hole, like ice to cool the bit?" I said.

"Won't work, Einstein. The mud carries out the stone it's grinding up. So we're going to the store."

"Why?"

"You'll see." He began one of his oil drilling stories, and forty minutes later he was still talking as we parked in the loading zone behind a small-town grocery. "Nab something to haul stock," he said, popping open his door.

As we hurried through the backroom, I grabbed a platform dolly and wheeled behind him. "Where do they keep the lady stuff?" he asked.

"How would I know? I don't work at *this* store."

On aisle six he stopped in front of purple and pastel-pink feminine products. "Excuse me, ma'am." Dad reached past a skinny woman with tightly-permed hair. "Stiks, get all this stuff you can." He grabbed packages of Kotex, two at a time, stacking them on the dolly.

I died a thousand deaths, forcing myself to ask, "Do you want tampons, too, Dad?"

"My heavens!" The woman's narrow-set eyes drilled my father.

"Better make your selection now, ma'am." He piled packages higher, shifting his attention to me. "We won't use those. Check the stockroom for more stuff."

When he was sure we'd cleaned out the store, he counted product, then ordered me to load the truck while he went to the register to pay.

I tossed products in the back with the cans and hay, but before I could push the cart back into the store, he was walking toward me, thumping the fender. "Leave it. Let's go!"

We drove back to the rig and I huffed, "Tell me what we're doing."

"You'll see. It's physics."

I made a doubtful eye roll. "What'd they say at the checkout?"

"Had to cut in front of that poodle-dog lookin' woman. I told her it was an emergency." He chuckled. "The ol' gal squeaked, 'What kind of emergency?'

"I told her it was a crisis at Saint Mary's convent up north." One side of his mouth turned into a half-grin. "That shut her up long enough I could pay and get a receipt."

I rubbed my face, deciding that was another town I'd never visit again.

He shot me a look. "Don't turn into a Barbie doll, here. This is science-shit we're doin'."

"With sanitary napkins?"

"With any damn thing that works. If the job of handling intimate stuff like rubbers, hemorrhoid cream, or feminine hygiene products disappoints you, or if having people look at you funny swills you down an emotional toilet, I got bad news about what the rest of life is gonna be like."

"That's not the problem. I work at markets. Remember?"

"You're turnin' into a chicken-wuss. We gotta get you outta that line of work. Put you into one where you learn to take a risk. The only peril at a grocery store is when an old fella drops a jar of jam on the floor."

"I don't like to start conflict. I'm not like you."

"Nobody likes conflict, but are you gonna spend your life stuffing what bothers you down your gut instead of dealing with it? You worry too much what others think. This is what happens when everybody gets a blue ribbon. Giving everybody a certificate churns out kids who expect the world to be nice to them. They think nobody's gonna have more toys than the next guy. They're shocked when the economy tanks, jobs roll up, and it all turns out to be chin music. Tell me this, hotshot, do you think all the other kids shoulda skipped a coupla grades like you?"

"That's different. They couldn't do the work. And I've paid for it. Skipping grades still gets me picked on, even in college."

"Damn right. You have to work harder. Take risks. It may not get you more money, but you'll make your own opportunities. You're livin' instead of hidin' where it's comfortable and being bored outta your mind. You have to find what you love to do."

"I've heard all this."

"Like hell you have, or you wouldn't be ruffled about handling a few women's products in a backwater grocery."

"That's not why I'm bothered!" My voice filled the cab. "It's easier not to stand out. Sometimes you're embarrassing to be around. Maybe you don't care, but you leave everyone else to deal with the consequences. Mama's always doing cleanup after you."

He didn't respond. Both of us stared out the windows. Dusk was settling on the pastures and half-shadowing our faces, giving us relief from seeing each other clearly.

I had clawed open a raw spot. Neither of us had talked about Mama's breakdown two years before. She'd fixed a big party because I was the first in the family to graduate from college. She'd invited everybody—friends, neighbors, and anyone who came through her grocery line. Dad had celebrated on the drive home. When he stumbled out of his truck, he had a crazy applejack gait.

We expected Mom to cuss him, but she simply took off crying and walking across the pasture. We let her go, figuring she needed some time to collect herself. The party didn't happen. That evening, instead of crossing the stage, wearing a mortarboard, I was out searching for Mama with the rest of my family. We found her sitting in a cattle shed three miles away. She was rocking back and forth, her knees drawn to her chest, sobbing into her hands. Mama went to the hospital for two weeks until they could get her to eat again.

The truck jounced over the rough roads. Finally Dad said quietly, "I've done some jackass stunts. I can stir up a tornado pretty damn quick. But I don't drink like that anymore. And one of the unintended effects of livin' with me is it's made your mama stronger.

"When I first met her, she wouldn't walk down the road in the dark. But last time I was home, I saw her mouthwhip Dell Jenkins for dinging her car. I bet he'll cross the street every time he sees her comin' from now on. And if something bad happens—like me losing my job—she pretends I never had a job in the first place. That doesn't make any of it right, and I know I'm still a jackwagon, but the consequence is your little five-foot mama's learning to take care of herself." The tone of his voice was urging me to laugh just a little.

I stared at the rig lights that had blinked on, visible a mile away. Mama had once told me Dad's swashbuckling spirit was what had drawn her to him. "Like a moth to a flame." I guessed the quality she admired most was also the one she hated most.

"Look," he said as we turned onto the newly-made road into the pasture, "work anywhere you want. I don't care about that. It's simply a stepping stone to what you wanna do. What I'm trying to get through your skull is you *do not* let anyone or any situation define you. If somebody gives you crap about handling Kotex, ignore 'em. You know who you are—the woman who gets the job done." He pulled next to several other trucks and cut the engine. "Got it?"

I nodded. We got out and carried our purchases to the mud pit, passing men traveling back and forth, joking as they toted packages from their trucks. The entire crew had been sent to surrounding towns to buy sanitary napkins. I felt a pang of concern that local women would have to drive two counties away if they were in need.

"Do you do this all the time?" I asked Dad as he slapped a hard hat on my head.

Nearby, a guy grinned at the others, mumbling, "Every thirty days."

"Okay, cut the shit." Dad shot the men a bull-elephant glare. "Try not to act like barbarians. My daughter, Stiks, is visitin' this summer. She'll finish up her Master's degree in physics soon. We were bucking hay when the call came, so she's with me to see what oilfield work is like."

"It's pretty damn mind-consuming," said a pudgy fellow they called Wisp. "Ya gotta grab this by the right end." He picked up a package. "Give it a rip." It took him two tries, and then someone pointed out the perforated lines. Several pads fell out when the package ruptured. He picked them up, stripping off the wrappers. "Throw 'em in the mud so the pumps pick 'em up, and fill the vug." He stared at me a moment, then looked away as though he just realized he'd explained sanitary napkins to a woman.

"Aren't they going to plug the pump?" I asked.

"Shee-it!" a guy named Gap declared. "You're already actin' like an engineer."

Roughnecks stood in a circle, tearing open packages and tossing handfuls of pads. Cases and cases of them. Silence, silly grins, and mumbled comments circled the group.

A twenty-plus-year-old cleared his throat. "Well, I had some luck. My purchase was so big, I was approved for a discount and an executive credit card."

Dad threw a pad, hitting him in the face. I knew what he was doing. He was the king of easing tension. "I bet it was a gal who talked you into that credit card, wasn't it, Lott? You young worms think every woman's attracted to you and likes you."

Lott shook his head. He was splattered from hard hat to boot with gray mud, even across his face. "Tonk, whadda you know about being attractive—or liked?"

"That gal's not your friend or giving you anything. The store will make money every time you use that card," Dad said. "They're hoping you'll stay cash-poor and credit-bound."

That started a round of money-stories. Dad glanced at me and winked. He was in his element. Exhausted as he had to have been, his eyes gleamed. Here in the oilfield, he was a respected, hard-working, experienced statesman. But out in the world, most folks saw him as a rough, uneducated smart ass. It amazed me he didn't let others define him.

Eventually the foreman yelled, "Deep 'nuff!"

"Huh?" I whispered. "Why's everybody stopping? What's that mean?"

"Enough stuff went downhole to plug the void. No sense putting more money and time in just for the sake of prettying something up. The pressure readings say we're good. We'll start drilling and casing again. Move back, shug."

We stood, watching the pumps work. Wisp yelled, "Well, that was a first. They'll be telling this pad-story at every drill site from here to Saudi. Even though no one's supposed to talk about it, and it never happened."

"Now you're part of the myth." Belott slapped my back, knocking me off balance. I teetered on the plastic edge of the pit.

Belott's face registered horror as he grabbed for me, but I was already stumbling forward. I stayed on my feet, tripping down the embankment and expected to end up calf deep, but the gray drilling sludge was as slippery as a butcher's apron. I fell on my knees and hands, my face and chest dunking under the muck.

"Move, dumb shit." Dad elbowed Lott aside. "Reach my hand, Stiks!" He held it out.

In a flash, I was on my feet, stepping on the black plastic embankment. And just as quickly, I smacked into the sludge again. Every attempt to stand slid out from under me. I bit my lip, getting madder and madder.

"You're okay. Spit it out. It won't kill you," Dad said.

"Leave me alone! I'll figure it out!" Slowly, in jerks and with flailing arms, I rose upright. My teeth clenched, my glare red-hot, and my hands full of mud and rocks, I looked for that idiot Belott.

Then I saw Dad's face. He stared at me with his don't-turn-into-a jerk look.

I blinked, weighing all the wisdom he'd ever given me. He was an embarrassment, but he'd never steered me wrong. "Okay." I shook the muck and rock cuttings from my fingers. "*Now* I'm ready. Throw me a rope."

Laughter broke out. Soon, someone tossed me a line, and as I was climbing to the lip, men slapped Dad on the back. "Chip off the old block, Tonk."

I wasn't sure how my handling the situation had become his accomplishment, but understood somehow we'd both racked up points on the tough-enough scale.

To clean up, Dad suggested, "There's a crew shower." But I refused, quietly telling him, "I'm not taking anything off. I don't even like to use public restrooms."

He shrugged and hosed me down, fully clothed. My eyes squinched closed, mouth blubbering and spitting as he sprayed me.

I was still dripping when we got in the truck. "See. Didn't I tell ya we'd have a great summer?" he said. "You're taking chances. Learnin' things not in books. Your mama's not gonna be pleased, so don't tell her. I won't always be 'round to help you. So don't be stubborn. That was smart, asking for the sandline."

I shrugged. "Thanks." By the light of the dashboard, I could see exhaustion lining his eyes. He sat slump-shouldered but wore a contented smile. I didn't mention we still had hay in the field or needed to unload the bales in the truck. By the time we got to the farmhouse, I'd dozed off.

He shook me awake and handed me a box of chicken tenders and jo-jos he'd bought at a gas station. As I went to bed, I thought about Dad. He made sure we had food in our stomach and a roof that didn't leak. It was a job that had to be done, and he wore the role of husband and father like an ox wears a yoke.

On the oilfield, he shined among the vibrations and pounding noise. Someday he'd be too old to climb the derrick. I wondered what he'd do then. Would he be content to work a desk job like the three-fingered man in the trailer office?

That night I decided no matter what, I'd work at what I loved. I wasn't sure what I'd be doing, but it'd be in physics. I'd learn to take chances. I'd figure out how to be at the top of my field, collecting big checks from big companies. And when the market went belly up, as it always does, I'd have a list of other jobs I could fall back on. I'd never work in a grocery store again.

Of course, I was younger then, but I had a dream. And lots of dreams have been born in oilfields.

Comfort and security, on the other hand, are actually built somewhere else.

We all need dreams. They keep us going forward, even if we can only move a little at a time. Tonight and always, let go and find something you love to do. Take a risk and do it. Then show compassion every day, because we're all on the same journey.

Good night, Mama.

Good night, Oregon.

## 25. 1997

IT'S TWILIGHT WHEN Mina and I leave the Legless Pub where a few staff and grad students have met for drinks. As we cross a dorm parking lot, returning to the Science Complex, she points to a dark mound behind a car. "What's that?"

"Somebody lost their coat." I keep walking, but Mina veers off to investigate.

"It's a student," she calls. Sure enough, a young woman, stinking of beer, lies on the asphalt, her head under the back of a car.

We try to get her up, but she's loose and limp. I check her pulse. Feel her head for bumps. "She's okay. Just drunk. Celebrating the end of school by the looks and smell." I slap her cheeks, first one then the other. "This is what I used to do to my dad."

"Is this why you don't drink more than a glass?"

"You're counting?"

"When a pitcher is being passed around, you don't refill."

"I don't drink much. Alcohol screwed up the big events in my life." I flick the end of our sot's nose. No response. "Hey! Wake up!" I lift her arm and let go. It flops to the pavement. "Well, let her sleep it off." I stand, wiping her beer sweat off my hands.

"We can't leave her here."

"We used to let my Dad lie in the yard when he couldn't walk from the truck. It'll be handy when she pukes, and she *will* puke." Mina's shocked expression tells me she hasn't dealt with drunks. I look around. "I suppose we should move her behind those bushes."

"You. Are. Kidding. Me."

"She'll be safe there. Nobody can see her. And she'll have a doozy of a story tomorrow when she sobers up. Maybe waking up in the bushes will be the alcohol deterrent she needs."

"Did it cure your Dad?"

"Okay—no. Mama's nervous breakdown put the skids on his drinking."

"Richard, in campus security, likes me," Mina says. "I'll call. He'll know how to handle this. Hey! What're you doing?"

"Instead of calling your wanna-be beau, I'm riffling through our boozer's pockets, looking for I.D. We'll phone somebody to come get her. Well, no luck. Her pockets are empty. Not even a dime or a key. Okay, call Ricky."

"Richard," she says, pulling her cell phone from her purse.

While we wait for Security to show up, we sit on a car bumper. Every few minutes I nudge our guzzler with my foot to see if she'll wake up. Mina says, "I heard your last broadcast. It was good."

"Couldn't sleep?"

"Yeah. Aren't you worried someone will figure out who you are? You talk about physics and your family."

"Low probability. Evidence shows few people listen to the station. It's a logical risk."

"Why are you science types so ... unemotional? The whole department is that way. The fire alarm went off the other day, and everyone ignored it."

"Would you rather we run around screaming and wetting ourselves?"

"No, but—" A cruiser pulls up and a good-looking guy in a brown uniform gets out. He puts on his hat and saunters toward us.

“I don’t like him already,” I mumble.

“You haven’t even met him,” Mina hisses. “Richard! Thanks for coming!” she gushes like he’s rescuing us from crocodiles. “I’m sure you deal with this all the time.”

Mina has turned into a simpering belle. She presents our carouser. “We found her like this. We’ve already checked for ID. There is none.”

Richard squats and looks at her. He scans the area. Finally, he concludes, “Well, the only thing we can do is call the city police.” He stands, placing his hands on his hips. “Campus security doesn’t accommodate drunks, and the infirmary is for colds and allergies. They don’t have beds for the inebriated. The city has a drunk tank. They can take care of her.”

“Wait. Wait.” I step in front of him. “If you do that, she’ll have a record. It could affect her chance for a scholarship or a job down the line. She’s only a kid, celebrating the end of the year. She must have crappy friends or no friends at all to leave her here like this.”

“Part of a college education is growing up. Some students learn the hard way,” he says.

“Okay.” I wave him away. “Thanks for coming, Ricky. We’ve got this. Mina’s taking her home. She’s the one who’s most worried about her.”

“Well, *you* should be. ‘Compassion every day,’ remember?”

“I’ve already done my kind deed for today. I helped a kid study for finals.”

Mina’s voice becomes more forceful. “I can’t take her. I live with my folks. I can’t bring home a drunken stranger. You take her. You live alone.”

“I don’t have room. My place is the size of a closet.” We stare at our boozer for a moment. I nudge her with my foot again. She groans something.

Richard's voice sounds disgusted. "I think she said she's going to be sick."

"You know a good bathroom to be sick in?" Mina says. "The one on the sixth floor of the Physics Building."

"I admit that bathroom looks like something the Russians built for a community housing project. You couldn't pull a sink off the wall even if you used a car. Ricky can haul her in the cruiser." Mina and I heft our drunk by the armpits. "C'mon, Ricky, grab her feet."

He stares at us. "I can't haul an incapacitated student to another building and dump her there."

"Oh, good grief," I growl. "If you ever want a date with Mina, get your butt over here and pick up our party-girl's feet."

"Maybe *I* don't want to date him," Mina says, struggling to keep her side of the body lifted.

"Well, I wouldn't blame you. He won't even give two women with a sick friend a ride to safety."

"Okay. Okay." He grabs the feet.

We make it to the Science Complex, stopping once, opening the cruiser door, and letting our drunk vomit onto the pavement. Before carrying her into the building, we pause near the shrubs and encourage her to hurl once more. Ricky spends his time glancing over his shoulder for witnesses.

In the lobby, the elevator dings as soon as I hit the button. The doors open; Mina and I pull our gal inside.

"Sorry, but anytime I'm called out, I have to make an incident report." Richard gives an apologetic shrug.

"Then it's a good thing it was a normal Thursday night disturbance in the dorm parking lot. Rabble-rousers dispersed." I push the button for the sixth floor. "Thanks. We'll drag her from here." As the doors begin to shut, I add, "If you call for that date, remember there's no kissing. No sex. I'll chaperone."

The doors close. For several seconds Mina and I don't say a thing, staring at our reflection in the polished steel, then she bursts out laughing.

Our sot belches and both of us jump back. "DO NOT throw up in here. You hear me?" I yell. "I mean it!"

We drag her to the toilets in time for her to make another deposit. She lies on the cool tile floor and passes out again.

"What a night, girlfriend. I can't believe how you talked to Richard."

"What a *gek*. He may be nice to look at, but he's about as smart as bait. Don't go out with him."

"I'll give him a chance." We both look at the girl on the floor. "How old do you think she is?"

"Not much younger than us. It could've turned out badly for her." We're silent, letting our imaginations run. I interrupt our thoughts with, "Go home. It's easy for me to stay. I live close by."

She stares as though trying to see through me. "Your employee card says your address is on the outskirts of town."

"I moved."

"Is that why your mail is coming here?" She keeps staring. "*I'm* a little smarter than bait. I know you had the lock changed on the custodian's closet. The paperwork was buried with your request to rekey the radio room door, but I caught it. I'm the one who signs off on these things for Dr. Slompka. What's really going on? Are you storing something illegal in the closet?"

"What could I stockpile in there? Black market Clorox? Counterfeit toilet paper?"

"Equipment that's gone missing. You keep telling me money is tight. I can find out. I have a new key, too. You don't think they only supplied one key and I gave it to you?"

"Then why didn't you go look for yourself?"

"Because of the way you dealt with Radio-Kurt. Directly. Voice to voice. You seem like that kind of person, so I'm treating you that way."

I let out a long sigh. "Let's find a place to sit."

We talk until midnight. I tell her where I'm living and why. "Sorry. I thought the less you knew, the easier you could claim ignorance if the whole situation went south. Besides ... it's embarrassing to be living in a closet."

"Well, if you can stand the smell of floor wax, then I applaud your determination. I'll make a postal box so you can have your mail and messages sent to the department. Your secret is safe with me." She adds, "As long as you don't put our sot in the bushes tonight."

"It was a better idea than your dreamboat's drunk tank."

After she leaves, I do my work, check on our drunk, and sleep for a while. At six, I get up to see how she's doing. The bathroom is empty except for vomit. I check the building, but she's gone.

I wonder how frightening it is to wake up, not knowing where you are. To stumble around until you find something familiar to mark your way home.

The hummingbird, which visits the feeder on the roof, has no idea who supplies its food. Our drunk has no idea who's taken care of her. Perhaps empathy is wired into us. Maybe in the infinite, black space of our Universe, kindness helps us feel secure. We create a place where we belong and can welcome others.

Last night, I helped a young drunk. I'll never know what happened to her or to other strangers I've shared odd moments with, but at times, I think about them. I hope they're safe—and living with people who care about them.

And maybe, sometimes, they think about me.

# 26. Choices

## ON AIR

GOOD MORNING. THIS is The Navigator. Today, I'll tell you a story about moving forward. This is how I made either the stupidest or the best decision of my life. I'll let you decide.

Do you ever wonder why people make the choices they do? Researchers say our brain weighs risk and importance against the urge to get the job done.

I once explained this to Gramoo and she told me, "Oh, sugar pea, with all your schooling, you use words that don't mean squat. Making a choice is simply walking into a grocery store, seeing chocolate donuts, and thinking oooooh, those look good. Then the overseer in your head says, 'Get your butt over to the carrots, that's what you came here for.'"

I believe each of us has a taskmaster in our head, but sometimes his or her voice goes strangely silent.

In 1992, I listened to that taskmaster and visited my home two week before the graduation ceremonies for my Master's degree. I didn't want to return there, but Gordon the bison had died. He was the closest thing our hermit neighbor had for a child. So I made the hour and a half trip home to support Olly.

He'd hired a tractor-guy to dig a hole and push Gordon in, but Olly wanted to use only shovels to fill the grave. Out of respect.

"Whoa. Wait a minute." I eyeballed the pit. Using a stick, I scratched calculations in the dirt. "Approximating the bison as a cylinder filling half the volume of this hole ... it's going to take at least 360 shovelfuls of dirt. We're going to have heart attacks and be in that pit with Gordon."

Olly reluctantly agreed to let the tractor do some of the fill-in. By nightfall, he and I finished topping off the mound. Exhausted, we sat in his kitchen, enjoying lemonade. Gramoo walked in, carrying the peach pie she'd baked yesterday.

"Ah ... funeral food has arrived," I said.

"What's th' matter, Winnie?" Olly asked. That's when I looked at her.

"Sugar pea ..." She set the pie down, slid her hands across the red and white checkered oilcloth, and gripped my fingers. Her appearance was congested. The corners of her mouth twisted. She swallowed. "There's been an accident. Your dad—"

I yanked away. The lines in her face were too deep. Too pinched with a kicked-in look.

"There was a flash fire—a gas surge." Her voice dropped to a whisper. "Your dad's gone."

"What? No!"

She nodded, but it was her eyes wincing into slits and mouth quivering that confirmed it.

I bolted to my feet, knocking my chair over. "He can't be."

"The drilling company called. They said it was quick. Not even time to get to the escape line. Another man died, too. Your mama's going to fly down there. We should—"

"No!" I rushed to the door. Everything seemed tangled and slow. My feet, my hands, my thoughts. The throw rug slipped, scuttling Olly's boots across the floor. The old black knob jiggled and twisted without opening. I yanked. Was that me screaming? If I could get outside. I could outrun this.

I yelled, pushing their hands away. Olly fussed me back and opened the door. I darted out, stumbling, tripping, falling off the porch. Lying in the gravel and dirt, I cried.

Olly picked me up, guiding me to the bottom step. Gramoo sat next to me. She tried to pat my leg, but I grabbed her hand in a death grip. Olly sat on my other side, pushing dogs away as they tried to lick my gravel-scraped knees.

No one spoke. Overhead, Hercules and Lyra glittered, but darkness was swallowing me, anchoring me in its black belly. My choked sobs barely carried up into the night. Dad and the stars above would never hear them.

One second, I'd been a young woman who'd buried a bison, conquered life, and was about to graduate, the next instant I'd lost my dad. The future seemed like an empty void. It wasn't right that the world could change in an afternoon.

We expected Mama to fall apart. She didn't—not then anyway. For an unplanned event like accidental death, she put a lot of planning into the funeral. Dad would've hated it. Gramoo helped, of course, and Mama took me along, saying it was time I waded into this part of life. All I learned was logic went out the window when it came to funerals.

Dad had been badly burned, so cremation made sense to Gramoo and me, but Mama wouldn't hear of it. "We're not going to incinerate him again. And he'd go crazy cooped up in an itty-bitty soot box."

"He won't know. He's not really in the box, Mama."

"Well, he'd find out somehow. I don't want him haunting me." She turned to the funeral director. "What do you have that won't break the bank?"

She picked an oak model with a little ivory satin pillow. Why Dad would need a pillow was beyond me.

Gramoo had a fit about the bill. "A hunnerd-seventy-five dollars for a viewing room?" She looked at the undertaker. "Haven't you got that room paid for by now?"

Mr. Daly gave her the same tired smile Sister Minnie handed out to sinners. "If you wish, the viewing could be at your house. Of course, there will be transportation fees to your home and back."

Mama hurried through the rest of the choices because Gramoo wanted to load the coffin in the back of the truck and haul Dad around ourselves.

It was my turn to have a fit when we chose the burial plot. "Dad wanted to be buried under the scrubby tree in the hayfield. He told me so."

"Well, that's not gonna happen," Mama said. "We're not turning the pasture into a graveyard. I think he'd like this tree." She pointed to a large evergreen in the town cemetery.

"Spruce?" I yelled. "He liked the smell of cedars!" We argued the rest of the afternoon.

Mama's boss called each night to see if there was anything he could do for the family. Duane Unsinn had been an annoying jackwipe when I worked at the store, but now I didn't have to put up with his smarmy concern. "No!" I yelled into the receiver. "Go away!" He continued to call. Gramoo was more polite when she answered, saying, "Thanks, but we've got it figured out. Don't concern yourself."

Lots of people came to the service and said nice things. But it started downhill when Zig Bunton spoke. The guy was stick-skinny with sucked-in cheeks, three days of beard, and a voice full of cigarette coughs. He began innocently with, "Tonk made me a loan. All of you know about me goin' on disability. And Twin Stars, hell, they wasn't good at payin' loggers. Anyways ... I always meant to pay Tonk back. But now it's too late. I used to cross the street if I saw him comin'. He wasn't shy about usin' his fist to remind you of your debts."

One person in the audience laughed. Zig took that as a sign to continue. "Most of you can testify Tonk could be a SOB, but he'd help you if you was desperate. If I saw Tonk today, I wouldn't cross the street. I'd grab his hand and shake it."

The next person reported, "Tonk and I once stole a car to go see some gals." He looked sheepishly at Mama. "I think that was before y'all were married."

Another guy blabbered for ten minutes, mostly about being out of work and bills piling up, mentioning Dad only once saying, "Tonk had a weird sense of humor."

I left while he was speaking, walking down the center aisle, feeling everyone's eyes on me. I slipped through the doors and sat outside on the steps, waiting for the debacle to be over. Why would anyone use a funeral to flap their personal woes?

Five minutes later, Mama's boss came out of the church and stood behind me. "You okay?"

"Yep." College had been useful; I'd learned never to give too much information.

"I think your mom would appreciate it if you came back in," Duane said.

"If that were so, she'd be out here telling me herself."

"She sent me."

I propped my elbows on my knees, resting my head in my hands, staring straight ahead. "Okay, got it. Thanks." I didn't move. Neither did he. "Message delivered. You can leave now," I added.

He sat down beside me. "Listen, your mom's been through a lot, even before your dad died. She's had to take time off at the grocery store. You're aware RuthAna has started working for me, propping your mom up, bringing home an additional paycheck."

"I've been sending money home, too. I work, you know."

"But it's not enough. RuthAna wants to go to community college and become a nurse."

"I doubt that. Root faints at the smell of blood. She doesn't know what she wants to do."

"Nevertheless, it's her time now. You're twenty-one. You've been at college four years. You need to come home or get a real job. Help your mama."

"Now? You want to do this *now*?"

"You've been gone. You have no idea how it is around here. It's time you shouldered responsibility." He cocked his head to study my face. "What? I'm only talking to you like an adult and a friend. Are you gonna be one of those forever students and burden your mom her whole life?"

"Leave me alone." I looked away.

His words turned sharp, running together. "You need to know the well has gone dry. There'll be no more handouts for your education."

"You don't know a thing about our lives. And it's none of your business."

"I know your mom and I are going to be married."

I shot him a look, my eyes trying to laser a hole through his head. "Bullshit!" But my mind whispered doubts. I'd heard Mama talk about the *brilliant* things Duane did like putting lip gloss at the register instead of the lotion department. She'd say, "He's such a clever retailer. He's going to own that store one day."

This couldn't be happening. I hopped to my feet, but Duane grabbed my wrist, jerking me back, gripping me as I stumbled into him.

"It's time you grow up. Help your mother. We're going back inside now." He stood up.

He wasn't expecting the fist I put into his gut, which made him let go. And he certainly didn't expect me to follow with a roundhouse, putting my full body weight behind it.

He stumbled backward, holding both hands over his nose. "You little bitch!"

"That's how Dad taught me to deal with bullies."

Blood streamed through Duane's fingers onto his white cuffs, into the sleeves of his suit. "Figures. The apple didn't fall far from the tree."

"You can be sure on the day of *your* funeral, I'll tell everyone how Tonk Bolton's daughter busted the nose off your face for disrespecting her mama. Oh, wait. I guess I *am* a bitch. Screw you!"

I turned and stumbled to a stop. Mama stood there. Right outside the doors of the church, watching. We locked eyes for a long moment.

"Oh, hon," she said and went right for Duane.

I left the funeral, catching a ride to Olly's house. At first I couldn't find our hermit-neighbor. I followed chopping sounds coming from the far corner of his property. Years ago, I'd stumbled onto his small fenced-in garden surrounded by shrubs. But by 1992 I'd become wiser and more worldly. "Is that marijuana?"

"What!" He startled. "You scared me!" He daggered a glare at the hounds stretched out on their bellies. "You worthless curs." He shifted his gaze to me. "Go on up to the house. I'll be along shortly. I thought ever'body was at the funeral."

"You grow pot?" I pulled a leaf off. "Holy moley! For eight years you told me you grew bamboo and rabbit ferns in here. I never bothered to look. How long have you been doing this?"

"It's mostly hemp. There's a difference. Now get outta here. I don't want you havin' any part of this."

"Why're you cutting it down? Is it time to harvest?"

"Because I choose to. Now leave." Olly hacked at another stalk, adding, "Without Gordon to chase trespassers, people can get in here. The dogs are growin' lazy." He spit at one of them. "I'm getting too old to do this." He picked up the plant and arranged it on a PVC pipe like he was hanging clothes on a rack.

I didn't say anything, my brain scratching to take this in. His surliness and the way he guarded his privacy. It made sense now. When my voice finally came back, I whispered more to myself than him, "You've got a fortune here."

"Nope. Only enough to pay bills for a year or so."

"I thought you lived on Social Security."

He shot me a narrow look. "I don't deal with the gover'ment. I don't take their money."

"Olly, you can't destroy this. What're you going to live on?"

He hung another stalk on the PVC pipe. "I've put some cash by. A truck will take this away tonight. This is the last load."

"I've never seen any trucks."

"Nope. It never goes local." He said it with such certainty I understood that not even the stars were aware of what had been happening beneath them.

"Those blue envelopes—are they payments?"

"This is the end of it! I'm not goin' back to jail because these damn dogs have turned into tail-waggers. And I'm too tired to train new mutts. I don't wanna worry about it no more."

"Could I have—"

"No!" He slapped a branch out of my hand, shaking his head. "Young people! Shit for brains. You shouldn't be here. Anything ever happened, you coulda said you didn't know squat about any of this. Isn't there a funeral you should be at?"

"People were telling pointless stories, so I left."

He scowled at me. "My dad died while I was in jail. I'd have given my left eyeball to go to his funeral. But you choose to sit here." He shook his head. "Shit for brains."

"None of the ceremony was what Dad would've wanted."

"He's dead. He doesn't give a rat's tail whether there's ukulele music or snake-dancing at his send-off. The whole show is for the living. It's your mom who needs help."

"Cheez," I sat down on a log, rubbing my face. "Everything is changing. That jerk, Duane Unsinn, is sitting with us like he's part of the family."

"Well, you aren't there with her, are you?"

"Why are you so angry?"

He gave me a severe look. "Maybe if you'da come home more often, you coulda helped."

"Helped what? You're saying this is my fault?"

"No ... no ... never mind," he mumbled and went back to cutting plants. "I guess we all got our burdens. You'll hafta figure out your own road. Where you movin' to?"

"What? I'm not going anywhere. I don't graduate until next Saturday."

"You're not livin' with your mama when you get outta school, are ya? Because your grandma won't. She's movin' in here with me. Your mother got preachy about us living together, but she's been diddling Duane, so she's not entitled to get righteous. Where're you gonna go?"

I stared, watching him work, but not seeing anything. Finally I mumbled, "Mama and Duane? How long's this been going on? I'm gonna be sick." He didn't reply, but kept working. My mind raced, piecing together clues I should've seen, but ignored. "So Mama's moving to town? Living with him?" It was like talking to air. "I guess I'll stay at the farm until I figure out what to do."

Olly stopped working and slowly closed his eyes. "Your grandma didn't tell ya, did she?"

"No one talks in this family. We ignore problems."

He hacked his machete into a log and left it there. Sighing, he sat down beside me, wearing the scrutinizing look professors use when they drop a question far beyond your knowledge, then watch your face for mental connections and computations. "Your mama sold the farm."

"She couldn't! Dad's only been gone a week."

"Your grandma says the deed isn't recorded, but there's a handshake, and a down payment with Dale Welks. Your mama and Duane are usin' the money to buy the grocery store."

"She can't. Dad promised the land to me," I whisper.

"Her name's on the property." Olly was still watching me. "Your dad didn't leave a will."

It was a pivotal day in my life. But really ... most bad days are pivotal, like hinged doors, swinging between choices and change. After I could breathe again, my world turned blood-red with anger. Legally, I knew I didn't have a chance of getting the land.

I stormed next door to our farm. I didn't take the cash in the lard can—that was for family emergencies. But Mama kept a stash hidden in her undie drawer. She didn't think Root and I knew, but kids snoop through every drawer in a house.

I took the $3,000 stuffed in a sock. I packed a few childhood mementos, and hitched a ride back to college. There was no guilt about my thievery. I'd sent her more money than that while I was working and going to school.

The next day, I expected her to call, telling me she was sending the sheriff after me, and she wouldn't be at my Master's graduation. So what? My family had never attended a graduation because I hadn't walked the stage for any of my degrees so far.

But I heard nothing from Mama. Not about money, nor my behavior, nor even an explanation about Duane. The sheriff didn't come.

A few days later I should've been walking across a stage. Dad should have been watching and waving at me. Instead, I was looking out the window of a train. My first. The *clack-clack* of wheels slowed as we pulled into the depot.

I'd settled my bills and left the university. Dad and I were the only ones who had cared about my graduation. He wasn't around, so why stay? It was time to follow his wise, unschooled advice: most of life is unplanned.

The doors on the coach opened. I wrestled my duffle onto the cobblestone street.

I breathed deeply, looking around. Romans had once walked here in Koln, Germany.

The taskmaster in my head had gone strangely silent. Not my Dad nor Mama nor conscience spoke. I couldn't hear anything except the sounds of a new strange adventure. I had a feeling I'd just enrolled in a different kind of school.

Go ahead. Take a risk. Show compassion. Every day.

Good night, Mama.

Good night, Oregon.

## 27. 1997

"GET OUT OF here!" Mina hisses. Her fingers freeze on her keyboard, eyes goggling like a bank robbery is in progress.

I'd only stopped by her office to say *hi* on my way to nuke a cup of breakfast noodles. She's out of her chair, glancing over her shoulder toward Dr. Slompka's office, then pushing me close to the doorframe. "Get out of the building! Now! I'll meet you in the library. Fiction. Romance section. Nobody in physics will find you there." She shoves me into the hallway. "Take the back stairwell. Don't stop to talk to anybody!"

I stare at her, but she fans me away like she's beating bees. "Run, idiot!"

Logical thought goes *poof*. Adrenaline takes over. In four minutes, I'm bumbling through the library with a cup of dehydrated noodles in my hand.

My radio hijackings must've been discovered. But how? I'd been careful, always tidying up. I'd even timed my broadcasts, then advanced the pre-recorded music so there weren't too many minutes left on the overnight program.

If I'm going on the run, I need my research files. Mina can get those. And my passport. Some clothes. And ... .

Staring at gray metal shelves stuffed with novels, I sigh, slumming down to the floor between the stacks. Across from me, a shirtless man moodily gazes from a book cover, beads of sweat clinging to his chiseled abs.

I pick him up; the paperback's spine is creased white with usage, the cover slightly curled. Probably a hundred people have read about ol' Hot-abs here. Two hundred pages of secrets and dark-eyed stares. It's almost the same length as my dissertation, which has taken three years to write. Probably only five people will read my words.

"Flaming monkey crap." I toss the book back at the shelf. It bounces onto the floor.

Mina's voice comes from the end of the shelves. "Be nice to the books."

"Listen"—I stand up—"I'm proud of my radio stories. It's satisfying to tell late-night anecdotes that may actually help people more than this romance crap. Why does the university buy this trash?" I kick Hot-abs, watching him slide across the tiles. "Let them come after me. I'm not going to run."

"Did they discover you?"

"I thought ..." We stare at each other, my brain clutching air like an arcade claw, trying to grab a conclusion. "They're not after me?"

"Not for that."

I close my eyes and let out a long breath. "Exactly *why* am I hiding here?"

"To keep from ticking anybody off. Jason, the copier-fixing kid tried to pick the lock on the computer lab. And—"

"Why? I left it open. There were a couple of students in there last night." I squint, fingering the keys in my pocket.

"Let me finish. I'm doing you a favor." She stares me into silence. "Early this morning Jason was waiting for his simulation to finish. For some reason—don't ask me why, I don't understand how you brainy-people think—he figured learning to pick a lock would be a good way to pass the time. Ben Frazer, a third-year student, was there and bragged that the Army had taught him how to do it. Problem was, he didn't have his service tools, so he borrowed a bobby pin from a girl passing by. They locked themselves out, and then surprise, surprise, the bobby pin didn't work. Now nobody can get in. Students are piled up in the hallway, ready to stab Jason with pencils."

"You've got to be kidding." I roll my eyes. "Are you waiting to use your key? Teach them a lesson?"

"Keys won't work. The plastic head came off the bobby pin and is jammed in the tumblers. Ben took off, leaving Jason to take the blame, and then Dr. Klein joined the fray."

"Well, it was stupid, but that poor kid. Somebody's got to help him."

"Nope." Mina grabs my arm. "They were looking for you, but trust me, there's nothing you can do. All the teaching assistants are involved and taking heavy flak. That room was designed to be secure because it houses the computers. The door hinges are on the inside. There's no window. They even tried sucking the key slot with a vacuum.

"Stress is running high with finals coming up. Dr. Klein is sniping at everyone. It amazes me that when someone is getting chewed-out, others just duck and watch. Dr. Slompka is the only one who has intervened, but he's really ticked, too. It's a minefield. Trust me. I'm saving you. Anyway, I handled the problem."

"How?"

"I called campus maintenance. They're over there now, taking the lock off the door. I told Dr. Slompka I couldn't handle the drama and was going on a long break. So whaddya wanna do while we hide from the department?"

I let her news sink in. "You're sure no one's coming after me for my radio broadcast?"

"Not that I know of. Are you still doing those?"

"Doesn't anyone listen?"

She shrugged. "I'm guessing anyone tuning in probably thinks the stories are a new part of the late-night format. I can't stay up that long. I've gotta work."

"Maybe that's why I've gotten away with it so far." I nod. "Well, thanks for saving me. How about killing some time by scavenging? It's the season for it." She narrows her eyes, but I'm already walking.

When we arrive at Delaney Residence Hall, we get someone to let us in, then work our way to the basement. Usually it's a lounge, but now clothes lie in heaps everywhere. Mounds of bedding nest in a corner. Pyramids of electronics rise from each couch and chair. "Behold!" I fan my hand. "My favorite fishing hole, but you can't tell anyone."

"What is this?" She picks up a string of skulls which light up in fluorescent colors.

"Excess consumerism." I set aside a rice cooker and dig in the pile, looking for the lid. "At the end of a school year, ten floors of residents move at the same time. It's like the biblical Exodus. They want out, and this is what they're leaving behind. This basement will be so full in a few days, you can't get in. Castoffs. If you find something you need, take it."

"How do you know if anything works?" She holds up an alarm clock.

"Try it, throw it away, or bring it back."

She picks through a box of sweaters. Both of us fall silent, sorting the piles.

Four years ago, I'd abandoned most of my belongings here after getting my masters and taking off for Europe. Since then, I'd discovered I didn't need much. I can't find the lid to the rice cooker—which is probably why they junked it.

Mina holds up a teal-blue sweater embroidered with flowers around the neckline and cuffs. "My sister would love this. It's missing a button, but I could change those out."

"Look for moth holes." I fling a cracked Frisbee across the room. "I didn't know you had a sister."

"She's older." Mina scans the back of the sweater. She's always cold since her accident."

"What happened?"

"A guy ran a stop sign. When I got to the hospital, a nurse told my family they'd stabilized Blair enough to operate. Of course, I wanted to see her."

"Mom tried to stop me, but the nurse said Blair had been asking for me, so I got to go into Pre-Op. No one prepared me. I hadn't thought how bad it'd be."

Mina stares at the sweater as though a video is playing across its bodice. "Blair's face was messed up. Split and raggedy ... like a tomato peeled back by the sun. Blood matted her hair. Dried along her nose. I just stared. Finally, a nurse patted me and whispered that I should let my sister know I was there. So I leaned close and said into Blair's ear, 'Were you wearing clean underwear?'

"One of her eyes opened in a slit. The other one was swollen shut. Her mouth was lop-sided, but she sort of smiled. A giggle tried to come out, but she began choking. Alarms and buzzers went off. They ran me out. I was sure I'd killed her.

"That was three years ago. She's stitched together now. She says she remembers getting into her car at work and then she woke up days later in the hospital. She doesn't know what happened. It's all blackness, except for a moment of light, laughing in the darkness."

Mina is holding the sweater against her heart, rubbing its softness. Finally she puts it down and carefully folds it. When she's finished, it looks like it came from Macy's. "This is second-hand, but I think it's all right. It's still pretty. I think she deserves to feel pretty, don't you?"

I can't answer. And when I do, all I can choke out is, "I'm a crappy sister."

## 28. Uh-Oh Moments

### ON AIR

GOOD MORNING. THIS is The Navigator. It's been raining since yesterday. I always feel gray days are depressing, so I'll tell you the story of how I found my way in the dark.

In 1992, when I was twenty-one, I angrily took off for Germany. It seemed like a good idea at the time. I'd just finished a degree. My Dad had died a week earlier. My life felt unraveled, and I was furious with my family, particularly my mama. I deserted everyone and everything.

On the airplane, it seemed each passenger was a seasoned traveler. They settled into their seats and introverted into their private worlds. I didn't want to stand out like a pregnant pole-vaulter, but it was hard not to contain my wonder.

How could people close their window shades when there was so much to see from 36,000 feet in the air? When land stopped appearing and the plane was over the ocean, there was still the changing hues of the water below and rag-tail clouds next to the window to marvel about.

We passed through a gentle rain shower. It was a little bumpy, but seven colors refracted into a perfect circle beside the plane, not the half-bows seen from the earth's surface.

Finally, it became so dark all I could see were the blinking lights on the wings, and I was awed, imagining seventy-five tons of metal coursing through the night, my face at a porthole.

The physics of flight was logical, but it was still amazing. I'd never traveled 534 miles an hour. How could people sleep through this?

But they did. Many were well prepared, putting on long socks and snugging under blankets when the cabin became dark. An older couple drank a nightcap. Several rows behind me a baby cried. Pools of light dotted individuals here and there, reading with tiny lamps clamped onto their books. We were a small community in a ship, sailing among the clouds.

Near dawn I kept my window shade cracked a couple of inches, peeking out, hoping to see the sunrise. "First trip?" my seatmate asked.

I was surprised he was awake. I looked at him and nodded. Soon a flight attendant came down the aisle handing out hot, moist towelettes. My seatmate rubbed his over his face, then his hands, then the tray table, so I copied him, feeling refreshed.

"You'll never forget this trip," he said, digging into the tiny containers of scrambled eggs and triangles of cheese they'd given us. But he was wrong. There was too much happening to remember every detail: imposing customs officials, long conveyor belts of luggage, walkways that moved people, arched ceilings of glass and metal. This was what the world had been hiding. All these wonders.

*Ausfahrt*. Exit. *Bahnhof*. Train station. Which *Bahnsteig*? Platform? *The uhr*? Time. *Ist dieser* seat *frei*? Like a sparkplug misfiring, my mind began to fritz into English, searching for too many translations. By the time the airport train arrived in the city and I stepped onto the cobblestones, my brain was foggy.

I stared at my feet for a long moment. Partly to memorize what it looked like to walk on history and partly to avoid seeing more stimuli. It didn't help. Sounds and smells poured in around me. Locomotives leaving. Four different languages passing by. Was that the aroma of hotdogs—here? Deep-throated bells pealed. I closed my eyes and counted eight gongs, trying to sense the pressure waves reverberating off the glass storefronts around me.

When I lifted my head, the Gothic spires of the *Kohler Dom* soared before me. It was mind-blowing to take in the size of the cathedral. Gap-mouthed, I walked toward it until a car honked, alerting me I was in the middle of the street.

It didn't cost to go inside, which was hard to believe, because even the toilets at the train station had a fee. Ten *pfennigs*. Cold water. No soap. Toilet paper—iffy.

I stayed near a tour group, pretending to study the floor mosaics of noblemen's crests. Actually, I was listening to their guide explain how it took six hundred years to build the *Dom*.

Men in red skullcaps and long robes began herding people out, unless they wanted to stay for mass. I'm not religious, but stayed.

The dark beauty of the chambers, the colorful leaded windows, the chant of the liturgy echoing up to the buttresses, the isolated serenity of the pews. It was impossible not to feel the presence of something greater than myself. Perhaps God? For the first time since Dad died, I cried. No one bothered me. No one comforted me, either—which was okay. I preferred to be alone with my emotions.

I found a hostel, made a few acquaintances, and toured the city and outlying areas for several days. It was thirty-two degrees Celsius—a joy to be in a country using the sensible and logical metric system, but it was still eighty-nine-degrees hot, and only retailers had air conditioning. People crammed into *Eis Cafes* for gelato and sundaes. I bought a cone at the counter and sat down like I'd always done in Oregon, but the manager asked me to leave. It cost an extra twenty *pfennigs* to eat inside. I quickly learned *zum Mitnehmen*. Takeaway.

Each day I returned to the cathedral. I'm not sure why. It was quiet amid the tourists and traffic. Perhaps it was simply because I didn't have to think, make decisions, or worry about what I would do next.

My German improved, but each evening, I was exhausted from translating and absorbing the scenes around me. The *schnitzel*, *brats*, *lebkuchen*, and *bier* grew heavy in my gut. I thought I'd have more stamina as a world traveler, but told myself I'd done well for my first foray.

Sitting on my bunk in the hostel, I dumped my backpack. I kept my money to get home in an envelope in the bottom. It wasn't there.

In a frenzied panic, I clawed through the pack again, then through several nearby duffles. Their owners shouted at me until a staff person intervened demanding, "*Denken Sie!* Think! Has your backpack been out of your possession?"

"Museums. Art galleries. I had to check it. There's no choice."

"No. Those are safe places. Nothing was taken there."

"But it's always with me." My voice was high-pitched like a child's. "*Immer mit mir*!" I slapped my chest. "Always!"

"Vhat about vhen you sleep?" a thin blonde asked, her English heavy with Eastern European consonants. "Do you use eet as a pillow? Lock eet to the bed if you stuff eet under?"

My lips trembled. My eyes stared. Someone in the room gave a heavy sigh, and the other guests' faces changed into sympathy.

"We will see who checked out recently," said the host, "but there is no way to be certain they took it."

My fellow travelers bought me brats and beer that night. The next morning as I left for the American Embassy in

Dusseldorf, the host handed me thirty *marks* and an old combination lock. "We took up a collection. No one travels alone, even if you're a party of one. We rely on others to get where we need to go."

Tears came to my eyes. Before Germany, I hadn't cried in years, and now I was weeping almost every day. There had to be something in the sauerkraut.

At the embassy, the State Department official listened to my story and read my intake documents. "You have no one in the States who will send you funds?"

I shook my head. Maybe Gramoo and Olly would, but they were old and needed their money. Besides, they'd be angry I'd left without telling them. I'd have to get out of this on my own.

"There is a limited fund for qualifying, destitute situations." He looked at me as though measuring my resources. "You have a Masters in Physics?" I nodded.

"The Kingdom of the Netherlands is particularly interested in people with science degrees. We don't find jobs, but we help our citizens be aware of international opportunities. Have you considered working abroad?"

I gave him my most professional, "Uh ..." and blinked several times, my mind warping at such a wild undertaking. In my pre-trip anger, I'd only thought about leaving, not staying out of the whole country. My long-planned agenda was to apply for grants and go to school in the States. I calmed myself, estimating the length of the pencils in his cup holder and adding the numbers together. 1.3 meters of graphite.

"May I give you a piece of advice?"

I nodded, thinking his question illogical because I was in no position to say no.

"You must be bold and ask questions or people won't know what you want. We cannot help if you don't ask. Speak your mind."

I mutely nodded again. His frown deepened.

I stuttered, "I don't know enough about being abroad ... to understand what to ask."

He stared at me, clasping his hands in front of him on the desk, and waited.

It took a minute to catch one of the thoughts torpedoing through my head. "Professor Slompka, my Department Head back in Oregon, told me there were no available assistantships for my doctorate ... I'd have to save my money before I could go back to school." I licked my lips. "So ... to work here and save money, do I need some kind of permit?"

He smiled. "That is a good, bold question. Let us begin ..."

That evening I boarded another train with a temporary visa and a small stipend in my pocket. By dawn I was toting my duffle across the cobblestones of Amsterdam in the Kingdom of the Netherlands.

It seemed most efficient to stay in the heart of the city near businesses, even though I wasn't allowed to look for employment until I received my residence work permit. I found a room in a thick-walled inn. It had been a warehouse in the 1700s. Upon checking in, Einar, the owner of *Brouwer Huis*, proudly pointed at the narrow, pie-shaped pieces of wood spiraling upward in a tight column. "We still use the original stairs." His great-great-grandfather, a sea captain, had the place built when the canals were young and Scandinavian wood, copper, and rye were global commodities.

A low-ceilinged passageway on the third floor ended at my slope-walled room. Heavy beams ran through the ceiling. It had a bed, desk, lamp, and wardrobe to hang my eleven pieces of clothing. It took all of three minutes to settle in.

The floors creaked, the plumbing rumbled, and the windows didn't quite fit the frames. Living in our old farmhouse in Oregon had prepared me well for this.

I swung the casement window open and leaned out. The morning sunshine looked the same. People looked the same, and I'd discovered most everyone, young and old, spoke a little English. But the landscape was very different.

Narrow, flat-faced buildings with fancy facades leaned forward, jammed against each other, their living spaces running deep behind them. I assumed it was a zoning rule, but later learned property taxes were based on street-front width. Some homes were only ten feet wide.

The brown-green water of *Singel Kaanal* lay where the street should've been. On each side, slim one-way lanes allowed passage for an occasional motorcycle or small delivery truck. Hundreds of bicycles sat on the sidewalks, chained to anything vertical, leaving a narrow obstacle course—if any at all—for pedestrians.

I navigated back down the death-spiral staircase. Its treads were six inches wide at the outer edge and an inch wide at the pole in the center. (Later, I discovered the inn had a one-person lift in the back of the building.)

"I'm going out to explore," I told the proprietor, who was placing cups and saucers on tables in the dining area. The patterns were mismatched and sections of gold had worn off the rims, but it was real china.

"No, no. Help with breakfast, please?" Einar said.

"O-kay?" I squinted.

He hand-waved my confusion away. "We will call it allowance on your room. I have no helper today. Guests are catching the tour bus to *Kinderdijk* to see the windmills. Breakfast will be crazy. You said you need to save money."

I spent the rest of the morning stepping over Einar's two miniature poodles, Mata and Hari. One of them had only one eye. They wandered between tables as I served soft-boiled eggs in the shell, warmed bread, some sort of hard cheese, and tiny pots of coffee or tea. Surprisingly, most of the guests were Americans or Brits. They asked me about working and living so far from home, and I answered like my Dad would have, lying like I was an experienced expat.

When I finally got to explore, I quickly discovered the danger in the city was bicycles. They traveled fast, made no sound, and there were thousands of them—multi-storied parking garages full of them. "*Domme doos!*" Stupid box! A man shouted when I paused on the course way, checking my map. It was a mild insult for a female; most riders rang bells when I unwittingly got in their path.

I settled into a daily routine, helping at the hotel, exploring the city, waiting for my documents, and worrying about my dwindling cash supply. Each day I asked about the post. "The government"— Einar would shrug—"who knows?"

One morning at breakfast, two pinch-faced old women, Virginia and Millie, said they'd pay me if I'd show them around the city.

Hospitality wasn't my strong suit, but I needed the money. At least I was honest, adopting the Dutch tradition of not mincing words, telling them, "I'm not much of a talker, not good company, and not from here." But the women insisted, saying they couldn't understand the accent of the Dutch tour guides. I wondered why they'd even bothered to leave the States.

I didn't have much gumption to visit the touristy spots, so I showed them things I thought were strange when I'd first arrived. I had them buy Amsterdam's favorite snack, *frites*. The fat french fries came in paper cones with a variety of sauces gooped on top. The women's favorite was the *oorlog*, a spicy combo of peanut sauce, mayo, and raw onions. When I told them *oorlog* meant war "indicating the chaos it takes to eat this mess," they were thrilled.

"See," Millie told her friend, "we wouldn't have gotten this on one of those Get-Around bus tours."

Inspired by their delight for the offbeat, we walked cobblestones until I found a street urinal; the tiny partial barrier concealed only the genital area of the man using it. "As you can see, it wasn't designed for privacy, but to keep guys from peeing in the canals," I said. "I'm told about fifteen drunks a year fall in and drown. But that's nothing like the 15,000 bicycles a year they pull out of the water. Vandalism, accidents. I guess there're lots of reasons to drown a bike."

Virginia turned away, her eyes wide. "I think we need to collect ourselves after seeing that. How about there?" She pointed at a storefront emblazoned in English, "Coffee Shop." Millie took a photo of the man in the urinal.

We entered the store, parting the haze of smoke inside. "Coffee *shops* are places to smoke marijuana," I said. "You can get a cup here, but if you only want caffeine, we'll go to a coffee *house,* Or is this what you prefer?"

"Oh, my heavens!" Virginia looked around the cozy bar with people chatting and smoking.

"Can I get a photo?" Millie said.

I hooked my thumb toward register. "Check at the counter." Millie sucked up the courage to ask, and I ended up taking a picture of the ladies holding a bong the proprietor provided as a prop.

I guided them through *De Wallen*, the Red Light District, warning Millie to honor the signs and not take photos of the women. She was surprised the workers had privacy rights and were unionized. It was morning, only a couple of mature women were in the windows, their sagging skin and wrinkles apparent behind the glass.

"Oh, Virginia, they're our age," Millie whispered, hanging her head. "It seems rude to look." But she stole glances, moving only her eyes. "It could be you or me, but for the grace of God."

"Hardly." Virginia walked on. Millie followed, giving one of the workers a small smile and a nod. The woman nodded back.

Passing storefronts, they studied the sex toys in all sizes and colors, causing Virginia to mumble, "I never realized how insulated my life has been."

To soften the culture shock, I found a street cafe. We sat in the sun, sipping coffee and eating *appeltaarts* piled with whipped cream. The women argued about getting rid of the marijuana photo because their children might see it. They were charmed when the waitress brought them red lap blankets "because the morning is a little chilly." They wanted a picture of that, too.

Ending the tour, I left them by Tram Five. "You'll need to see the *Rijksmuseum* and the masterpieces on your own. It takes hours to soak it in, but it's worth it. Stay on this tram and get off with the crowds. They'll lead you right to the doors."

I had promised little, told them what I knew without embellishments, and took them to oddball places. They thought it was the best tour ever and gave me a fat tip. Such generosity was illogical, and confirmed I didn't understand people at all.

When I got back to the inn, Einar was waving a government-stamped envelope at me. I immediately headed for the university.

Two hours later, I sat in the tiny bricked-in storage area Einar called a courtyard. When he saw me staring at the ground, counting bricks, he didn't say a word, simply brought me ginger tea and squeezed onto the bench beside me. Mata and Hari flanked us.

"I shouldn't have come here," I said. "I should've gone home."

"They will not let you teach?"

"I knew I'd have to have a doctorate before I could be an instructor, but I was sure I could do research on one of their projects. Unfortunately, not even their experimental department has anything in my specialty."

"What do you do?"

"Aerospace."

"Can you change? Maybe do a little of what they're looking for?"

I gave him a flat look. "Sure. I'll just whip out three years of materials science I don't have and change my specialty to something I'm not interested in."

"Sorry." He ducked his head. "Maybe if you knew Dutch, you could tutor first years."

"It shouldn't matter in science." I looked at the sky, imagining the constellations above. "Mathematics is the universal language to describe the physical world. It's as constant as the stars. All scientists use it. If I say Snell's Law, no matter your spoken language, you know the equation and can apply it."

"So why do they not use you? You know these things, right?"

"There's not a place in the university program. There's a corporate aerospace center in the city. I might be able to do contract work there, testing satellites or simulations. I'll have to make more inquiries, but it didn't sound hopeful." I ran my fingers through my hair as though that would settle the worries buzzing inside my skull. "At first this was an adventure, but now it's become tiring. Life turns on a single moment. A single decision. I'm nearly out of money. No prospects. An ocean away from home. I was stupid. I should've tried to talk sense into my mama. I should've never taken off 'horn mad' as she would've said."

"Aaah. Your *moeder* liked Shakespeare? *Much Ado About Nothing?*" Einar pushed the fur away from Hari's one good eye.

"If she quoted Shakespeare, it was an accident." I didn't mean to say more, but stories surged out. My redneck family, growing up poor, and how I'd always wanted to leave, but not the way I had. I'd wanted to hurt Mama like she'd hurt me. Instead, I'd jammed-up my own life. I'd botched things like my Dad usually had.

"*Dat is verleden tijd.*"

"Past time?" I frowned at him. "No it's not in the past. I'm paying for my mistake at this very minute."

He shook his head. "You should go to the Anne Frank House. She will remind you what to do about mistakes. She gives good Dutch advice. And you need to learn our beautiful language. Stop piecing-in German. Your life will change when you learn Dutch." He stood, taking the tea cup from my hand. "*In de benen*! *Nu*!"

"On your legs? Now?" I squinted at the translation as he walked away, the dogs following him.

He smiled, talking to Mata and Hari, "Look at the young American. We will have her speaking Dutch and ready for any job."

On my daily wanderings around Amsterdam, I had skipped the Anne Frank House. It required reservations months in advance, and I refused to wait two or more hours in the blocks-long line for the iffy chance to get a walk-up ticket late in the afternoon. Today wasn't any different. Hordes of people queued, hoping to see the hiding space for eight people.

I gave a miserable laugh. If my family had been hiding, one or two of us would've been ejected into the street for being a pain in the ass. But the Franks and their friends persevered for twenty-five months, until an informant tipped off the Nazis. All but the father died in concentration camps.

Einar probably wanted me to see the bond of family in the face of betrayal, but I didn't want to listen to a depressing story; instead I went to the nearby *Westerkerk,* the biggest church in town. A plaque on the cemetery wall noted Rembrandt had been buried there. Unfortunately, he'd been so poor he was put in a pauper's grave. After twenty years, they'd dug him up to make room for some other down-and-outer. The final resting place of his bones was unknown—as was Anne Frank's.

I sat on a bench in the graveyard. How could it be that two hundred years later the painter's masterpieces hung in museums all over the world, yet he died penniless? Anne Frank's words lived on, translated into seventy languages. Thousands lined up to see her bed, yet she knew little of life and died at fifteen.

Surely Rembrandt and Anne Frank had uh-oh moments? Desperate seconds of regret and panic where they'd done something stupid. They knew what they'd lost, but they didn't know what lay ahead. Nothing was turning out as they hoped. And yet they changed the world.

I frowned at the plaque on the wall next to me, unable to translate some of the words.

"*Vergeef me.*" A white-haired man stood several meters away. I'd seen him earlier, slowly strolling among tombstones, a green scarf around his neck, a cane in one hand, and a shopping bag in the other. He bent slightly to look at my face. "*Ben je verdwaald*?" Lost?

"In so many ways," I sighed.

"American?"

I nodded.

He nodded too, turning stiffly, looking at gravestones. "You are at the right place. These walls have words to guide you."

"Please," I pointed to the plaque, "what does *wereld verbeteren* mean? I mostly use German to translate."

" 'To improve the world.' Anne Frank said it." He smiled reading the words, "'You don't even have to wait a single moment *de wereld verbeteren.*'" He nodded, looking at the graves. "You should learn Dutch, then you can read all of these."

"A friend told me that, too."

The old man offered a tour around the cemetery. We ambled together as he commented on epitaphs on headstones and life. When he turned out of the churchyard onto the street, I stayed by his side. It seemed to me he wanted to chat. Or maybe it seemed to him I needed someone to talk to.

Evening was coming on. Soft lights glowed beneath arched passages along canals. "This is the way of life." He pointed at the water, now black and seemingly bottomless. "We cannot have the light without the dark."

At *Koningen Kaanal* he said goodbye. "Keep moving your life forward. A path will open." I watched until he disappeared into the evening, surprised at how much lighter I felt.

The streets were dark as I threaded through parked bicycles back to *Brouwer Huis*. How could it be Anne Frank had been gone over 70 years, Rembrandt over 350, and yet they were still changing lives? You never knew how your smallest work could affect others, even on your worst days.

Even if you're a lonely old man, strolling through the cemetery, stopping to talk to a sad young woman.

And that's why we need to take a risk. Show compassion. Hold onto hope. Every day. We'll find a way through the dark.

Good night, Mama.

Good night, Oregon.

# 29. 1997

TREVOR, A GRAD assistant, raps the lab's doorframe. His words are rushed and urgent. "Halsey Hall is having The Talk."

I look up from the circuit board I'm soldering. "When?"

"Fifteen minutes." He hurries away. Yanking the cord from the outlet, I drop the soldering iron on the steel table and follow him.

Trevor works one side of the hallway; I take the other. We Paul Revere the message throughout the Physics Building. Several students emerge from rooms in pursuit of us.

"C'mon, Jason." I slap the kid's shoulder as we pass through the lobby. "You need to attend this."

"I'm keeping a low profile. I'm not too popular since I locked the computer lab. Besides, I gotta study. Final tomorrow. Energy conversion equations."

"Two things you need to learn." I hold up one finger. "Don't let anyone else define you. Take the hit and get back out there. And two ... this will only take an hour. When it's over, I'll show you how to calculate potential-to-kinetic change so easily, you can get a job on Starship Enterprise."

Fifteen of us, including Jason, hurry across campus, grilling Trevor. "Are you absolutely sure it's now?" "Did you get double confirmation?" "Don't they always have this at the first of the semester?" "I hope there are graphics this time."

"Yes! I've got insider information!" he yells, throwing up his hands. "They forgot to do it earlier, so they have to make this presentation before the school year closes." We assemble in front of the doors to the dorm. "Okay. Everybody know the rules?"

Jason halfway holds up a hand. "I don't." Someone in the crowd snorts. Jason points at me. "She made me tag along."

"That's right." I give the group a don't-try-me stare. "In the past, I've made several of you attend. It's tradition, and your mothers will thank me. The newbies will carry on after us."

"Good thinking, Sophia. Okay, everybody, listen up." Trevor snaps his fingers, calling for silence. "No talking. No laughing. No heckling. Leave the chairs for the residents. Don't be first in line. We've got a reputation as silent geeks to uphold. Got it?" He turns and enters; the rest of us follow.

As we file into the dorm's lounge, a tall young woman with fuzzy red hair yells, "I can't believe this. It's the physics people! How do you guys find out about these things?"

"Some of us are girls." Patty, a junior, gives her an insincere smile.

"But we only announced this yesterday. Half of our dorm doesn't even know."

"We have curious minds." Patty shrugs and checks her watch. "Will you be starting on time? We've got finals tomorrow, you know."

Trevor shoots her a look, and she sits on the floor with the rest of us.

"Okay. How many students from Halsey Hall?" asks Red. Four hands shoot up. "Other dorms?" Two hands rise. "The physics department?" Jason starts to raise his hand, but I hold it down. The rest of us look around as though we don't speak English and are pleasantly waiting for a bus.

"Well, these are the science nerds." Red twirls her hand at our group. "They never say anything, but they're well behaved and increase our headcount. Thank you for helping keep our program funds." She gives us a little salute. "Now ... welcome to Sex Education Talks."

Jason slowly turns and looks at me.

At the end of the hour, each of us are given a bowl. "Why did everybody get so excited about this?" Jason asks as we get in line,

"Duh! Because there's ice cream!" Trevor says.

"Do they always pass around a basket of free condoms?"

"Yep. And free ice cream. As much as you want." I nod.

"I am *not* telling my mother about this." He looks worried as though she may find out anyway.

Trevor ladles strawberries into his dish. "The myth-buster section is my favorite. Some people actually believe a female won't get pregnant if she's on top."

Jason turns a deeper shade of pink. "How many of these have you been to?"

"Each dorm is asked to have one. Anyone can attend." I take the scoop and mound chocolate ice cream into my bowl.

"And physics students go to all of them?" He gives me a look. "Why?"

I stare at him as though he's forgotten which solar system we're in. "Because there's *free* ice cream."

The next afternoon, Mina finds me in the lab. "Jason told me you dragged him to The Talk. So ··· maybe you'd like to go to a church supper?" Her words rush together. "Tonight, Campus Ministry serves a meal for students. It's free. I'm going and you don't—"

"Sure. I'll go."

She's silent a minute. "Is it just because of the food?"

"Yep."

"I ... uh thought you might be offended because it's in a church."

"Why? I believe in God."

"You do?"

I smile. "I'm sure we'll disagree on theological details, but we'll leave it at that. This circuit board is due tomorrow. I'll see you tonight."

It's a surprising meal: home-cooked lasagna, three different salads, with fruit. Hot, fresh-baked bread and warm blackberry cobbler—with ice cream!

At the end, I brace myself for the proselytizing, but I only receive an invitation to return whenever I can on Tuesday nights for a home-cooked meal.

"Why do they do this if they're not using the opportunity to convert people?" I ask Mina.

She laughs. "Compassion. Every day, remember? This is Tuesday's kindness." She turns and calls to a rather nice-looking guy in a t-shirt. "Roy! C'mere."

"I've already met more people than I want to remember," I mumble, touching my crooked nose.

"Roy's in Engineering. You two speak similar languages." Both of us look at her, then shake our heads.

"Has anybody invited you on the July bike ride to the wildlife refuge?" he says. "We try to do something social once a month. I've got an extra bike if you need one."

I'm surprised the idea sounds good to me. "Sure. I'd enjoy that if I'm around. I'm on the tail-end of my doctorate. I don't know my schedule, but ..."

"Just let me know." Roy smiles as he's tugged into another conversation. I can't help but notice he has nice eyes.

I turn down car rides back to the campus and leave the church feeling guilty. I was so hungry I was willing to endure righteous arm-twisting to get food, but instead I received a meal and inclusion in a community.

What has happened to me? Since I've returned to school, my world has become smaller. I've focused only on myself and my own problems. Somewhere in my past, I was a bigger person.

I walk the two miles to the campus. By the time I reach my closet, I vow to grow again, reminding myself, "It's never too late to improve the world—along with myself."

## 30. Lonely Cobblestones

### ON AIR

THIS IS THE Navigator. Sunshine is promised tomorrow. This is the kind of weather that makes a person happy. It reminds me of the story of how I learned about happiness, avocados, hookers, and heavy hearts.

The year was 1994 and the hooker in Amsterdam spoke with a light Slovakian accent. She told me, "There is a difference between loneliness and homesickness."

It began earlier with her tiny dog sniffing my toes; his red leash dragged on the bricks between the hooker and me. Her toenails were polished in a deep-wine color and glistened from the ends of her sandals. Mine stuck out of flipflops—unpainted.

From my bench I squinted up at her, the sunlight coming through the trees, outlining her shape. She looked different on the street. Her hair was pulled into a ponytail. A loose bell-hemmed top swayed over her jeans which were destroyed at the thigh so her skin peeked through.

I shrugged. "If you say so."

"Oh, you care, or you would not keep coming here. You are looking for something. A distraction? A message? Maybe the answer to something, yes?"

"Maybe." Her dog sniffed the leg of my bench, then took a wide stance and lifted its leg. She gave the leash a shake and the little mutt scuttled a few feet away to sniff a receipt someone had tossed on the stone plaza.

"My name is AnnaLise." She stood without moving or saying another word until I looked up at her again. This close, it was hard to imagine she was the same woman I'd seen so many times from a distance. Usually her hair was poufed like a glam photo and her breasts bumped from the plunging neckline of her bathing suit. Her eyes were wide and brown and somehow communicated she could keep secrets. "You are?" She prompted me to be courteous.

I was tempted to say, "Nobody," but replied, "My family calls me Stiks." Her dog had meandered to the end of his leash and was having a stare-off with a bigger dog.

"Believe it or not, Stiks, I am a good listener."

"I'm sure you are, but I can't afford your time."

"How about a trade? I will listen, and you stop sitting near my window?"

I stood. "Sorry. I didn't mean to interfere with your business. Do your customers think I'm spying on them?" I glanced at the tall window where she usually posed or sat in her bathing suit, reading until a john stood in front of the glass. "I people-watch. There's some interesting—"

"I know the look on your face. I once wore that look. Come on." She gave a sideways nod, indicating we should move down the street. "We talk. There is not much I have not heard." She walked a few feet then paused, turning to give me the look a mother gives a dawdling child.

An alarm bell gonged in my head. "Uh ... no, thanks. I'll move somewhere else. Sorry I was bothering you."

She came back and sat down, patting the bench until I sat too. "I'm not working today. Look!" She opened her arms. "I'm dressed for the market."

Two guys eyed us—actually her—as they walked past, one turning to give her another once-over. The woman reeked of curves, softness, and sexuality. She must've had DNA from Marilyn Monroe *and* Sophia Loren.

"Listen ..." her voice was so soft I had to turn my head to hear it. "Lately, I look out my window and I see you on this bench. You look unhappy. It makes me unhappy. I know a thing or two about unhappy. Something has happened to make you sad? Tell me. I know many healthy cures for sad. Church, movies, a good talk." She handed me her dog. "You pet *Liecit* and tell me of sad. Everything is easier when holding little animals."

The mutt looked at me big-eyed, twisting his head to rub against my hand. I let out a long sigh and scratched between his ears. She waited for me to speak, finally giving me a nudge.

"About a year ago ..." I paused but she nodded as if she were really interested. "A dear old neighbor died of a heart attack. My grandmother lived with him in Oregon—in the States. I didn't go back for the funeral." I could hear the defensiveness in my voice and slumped.

"It is hard when we're so far away. I have missed several family funerals. I feel bad, but—"

"I was only thinking of me!" The dog pulled away from my loudness. I petted it. AnnaLise was right; it was calming to hold him. I continued more softly. "I figured if Olly was dead, it wouldn't matter if I went to the funeral. He wouldn't know." Her eyebrows rose slightly. "I mean, it would've been very expensive. If I'd left, I couldn't have flown back. I was trying to be independent and get my life started here. I was selfish."

A guy passed us, his hands jammed into the pockets of his tight, narrow-legged jeans. "Nice! Reeaal nice!" he called out, looking at the dog, but there was no mistaking who his remark was intended for.

She stood, pulling at my sleeve "Let's walk. I will listen. Not so much paparazzi that way." We strolled down the sidewalk, her pot-barreled pup in front of us, his stick legs quickly pegging the cobblestones.

"I should've done more for Olly when he was alive," I continued. "I wrote him and my grandmother. Even sent them small wheels of cheese for Christmas. The gouda probably clogged his heart. I might've helped kill him. I should've called more often. I should've gone back. He was a crotchety, grumpy old *slimmerik*, a codger who never left his farm, but he was the best friend I had growing up. He listened when nobody else would. The last time I saw him, we fought."

"Here." She stopped walking. "This is a good place."

There were hundreds of bars and backrooms tucked into the alleyways of the Red Light District, and even though I sometimes gave tours of the area, I'd never noticed the small signboard over the door, showing only a gilded skull and two crossed sabers beneath it. No words identified the place.

"What is this?" I asked as she pushed inside, revealing a tiny bar. I counted ten chairs clustered around five tables the size of chessboards. The walls were covered with old ship wheels, portholes, glass floats, and several anchors.

As soon as we entered, two round-shouldered men, hair graying at the temples, rose from their table, smiling shyly at AnnaLise. "Here. Here, take our seats."

She cocked her head, touched their arms, softly thanking them. "You are so nice. We appreciate it." She looked at the guy behind the bar and pointed to me then herself. Within a minute, he bent next to us, placing two iced lemonades and a dog treat wrapped in a napkin on our table. "Would you like anything else?"

Her full lips curved into a sincere smile, murmuring, "No thanks." He gave a nod which seemed more like a bow, and once again I wished I could figure out some way to bottle the grace and sensuality she exuded. Maybe I could attract a different boyfriend—one more to my liking. I concluded I was sitting with some type of royalty within the *De Wallen* district.

"Now we can talk without distraction," she said. But several people watched as she swayed the dog biscuit under her chair. Her tiny mutt grabbed it, curled up, and began gnawing. "So"—she turned her gaze on me—"you weren't there for this Olly, when he was there for you. Your guilt is chewing you up."

I blinked at her. Good grief! She went right to the core of a problem. No wonder guys were in and out of her room in ten minutes. "Um ..." I pulled my brain back to the topic. "At first I was guilty, yeah. But that was a year ago. I felt empty. Like my Dad had died again. I felt so alone. Mostly, I sat around feeling sorry for myself. My landlord got so tired of it, he made me join the *Fysica Club* at the University. I networked with professors and made contacts in my field. It helped. I got freelance work at an aerospace company. I'm dating a guy who's in the Ultimate Frisbee Club with me."

Her eyebrows rose again.

"I know." I looked down at my body. It wasn't gobby, but it wasn't model material like hers. "I'm not the athletic type, right? But I live and help out at *Brouwer Huis* and Einar, the owner, said I needed to exercise to shake off loneliness. So I joined the easiest sport I could find and now have a boyfriend he hates."

"If you're better now, why do you sit on the bench with such a long face? What are you looking for?"

"Answers." I shrugged. "I'm good with math and science, but not people. Crowds come to *De Wallen* to be happy. Tourists, customers. I want to see what they're happy about."

She rolled her eyes. Leaning close, she spoke so low I could barely hear her. "Many come for distraction. They think their lives are boring. They take pictures of us through the windows, even though they may get beat up for it. They gawk. The lady in the booth next to me is sixty-eight. You've seen her. She is tired. She is sad, and she feels bad when people laugh at her, but she works because she has to. We all do. She has her regulars. Some clients come back to us because they want connection. A few don't even want sex. Only a massage—or to massage me. That is why I'm a good listener."

"Does that take away their loneliness?"

She shook her head. "I was born in Czechoslovakia under Communist rule. My papa tells the story of my second birthday. I wanted a banana, but he could only get a banana on Tuesdays—just one for each family. He stood in grocery line for three hours, but when it was his turn, they were out of bananas. He paid more and got an avocado. None of us had ever seen an avocado. We didn't know what to do with it, but we each had a slice and celebrated as though it was a banana.

"He and mama once spent a whole week's salary so I could have a pair of Levi's. Can you imagine? And now look, I buy jeans with holes already in them. It's crazy. I miss my family. They don't know what I do here, but I'm lonely for them. Sex does not replace loneliness. It cannot fill the bond of a man who would stand in line for hours to get his daughter a piece of fruit. The good news for you is loneliness fades. It comes back, yes, but in smaller waves each time. Easier to handle."

I nodded. "I was doing well until my sister called last week."

The bartender set another lemonade in front of AnnaLise. I hadn't touched mine. I was a bit worried this whole place was a setup and if I drank it, I might wake up in the belly of a ship sailing to some forsaken country. I quickly continued, "I haven't heard from her in two years. She must've gotten my phone number from Grandma. She called, saying my grandmother was dying. I need to go home to help take care of her. I guess my mom is sick too. She's losing her memory." I tapped my head.

AnnaLise's hands flashed wide as though she were making a psychic revelation. "Then you must go home."

"But I was just offered a job. Full time work at the place I've been freelancing for. I tried almost two years to get this position. The salary was good, not great, but I'd be able to save enough to return to school in a couple of years."

"Tell the job-people to delay your start."

"I tried. They won't hold it. I'm sooooo frustrated!"

"Then ... I suppose you want to stay?"

"But if I stay, I'm abandoning my grandmother like I abandoned Olly."

"Then you must go."

"Why did this happen now? I just started feeling a part of this place. I look at community bulletin boards and I know what the signs are saying. When I go to the toilet and overhear a conversation, I understand what the women are gossiping about. I'm fitting in. The language and culture are no longer a barrier. And I can have a job in my field. It's a foot in the door." I took a sip of my lemonade, staring at the floor. "It's not fair I have to choose between my grandmother and my future."

A piece of orange rind landed on the table. AnnaLise swiped it away with the side of her hand. "There is a difference between loneliness and homesickness."

I let her statement hang in the air, not much interested in it. I took another sip, then remembered I wasn't going to drink it, and put the glass back on the table.

"Loneliness is feeling isolated, feeling left out. It happens when you leave your country. It happened to me. But it happens anywhere. In school, girls don't let you sit with them for lunch. As adults, women may not invite you to coffee or drinks after work. Who knows why they do it? But no matter what country you are in, there is always someone who is willing to make you feel left out. Loneliness is about connections.

"Being homesick is different. It is missing a familiar place or special person or tradition like my family celebrating my birthday avocado each year." She smiled and nodded. "You are not lonely. You fit here. You have a place now. I think you are afraid that if you leave, you will long for Amsterdam and be heartsick about the people you left behind."

"And the job I'm forfeiting." Another piece of orange rind fell onto the table.

She pushed it to the floor. "Listen to me. I tell you what my papa said, and it is true. He said, 'When that bell is rung, you can't unring it.' He was talking about my virginity, but it's the same here. If your grandmother needs you, and you don't take care of her before she dies, you will lug that around. It is like carrying the big bells of *Westerkirk*. You will be heart-heavy the rest of your life. You cannot unring it. And if you leave, yes, you will miss friends and this new job—but you might find a better job in America, or who knows, you may find a way to come back to us, yes?"

I took a drink of lemonade. She was quiet as I stared at the floor, trying on her words to see how they felt.

After a while, a peanut shell landed on the table. She picked it up and flicked it off her fingers. It somersaulted into a small cage over the bar where a tiny monkey grasped the bars, looking out. He threw another shell at her. "That is George. If you sit at a table too long, he throws things. Back in the 1700s this place was next to the docks. The owner traded rum for monkeys. The bar was full of them. Most were howling in cages downstairs. They say it stank, but sailors had been at sea for months, so they stank too. The same family owns the bar and they keep a monkey for luck. Even if he is an annoying little *stront*." She threw an orange peel at the cage as she stood up.

"I'm so sorry, but I must get to the market. No more long face, okay? Being homesick means you are blessed. When you are heart-heavy, it's because you have people or a place special to you. You are lucky. People care about you. I see many guys who have no one."

"I guess you're right. I've never thought of it that way."

"Trust me. There may come a time when you cannot go home—as I cannot—then you will curse yourself for not going when you had a chance."

"Why can't you—"

"That is a story for the next time we meet. And this is my treat." She pushed my hand away as I fumbled with my purse. "We are both strangers in a foreign land."

"But I want to thank you. What you say is logical. I'll have other chances at jobs and friends, but never with Gramoo again. I don't want to live with bells ringing in my head, reminding me of my failures."

"Good. You go home. When you come back, you sit where I can see you, so we can talk again." She smiled and held out her hand. "I do not say goodbye. Farewells are too difficult unless—you are a man, your thirty minutes are up, and you do not want to pay twenty-five marks more. Then I have no problem showing you the door. But for people I like, I only say, 'We will meet again. Somewhere. Someday.'"

"Until that day." I shook her hand, feeling sorry I hadn't met her before now. Sorry I hadn't trusted her lemonade. Full of doubt our paths would ever cross again.

As we left, an orange rind hit me in the head.

When I told Einar I was returning to Oregon, he was somber but finally said, "It is a wise thing you are doing."

My last day was spent in a rush because he insisted, "You cannot simply leave and avoid saying farewell to everyone. It's important to say goodbye well."

I broke up with my boyfriend—easier than I thought—then visited my favorite cafes and my almost-job-site. It was obvious some people cared more than others, but Einar was right. It was satisfying to tie up loose ends. Something I hadn't learned to do in my family.

"*Vaarwel.*" He hugged me in front of his inn, holding me and rocking back and forth. "The first morning you came so frightened and tired. Now you speak Dutch. I told you it would bring you a job, but now you leave. Who will help me? You must write. You call. Promise you won't lose me. I need to keep track of you. I send all the luck of Amsterdam with you."

"You'll never know how much you—" but that was all I could say before my throat closed. I knelt and petted the dogs, trying to hide my tears. When I'd wiped my face, I stood and gave him a Dutch goodbye, kissing first one cheek, then the other, then back to the first. He patted his face as though pressing my light pecks into his skin. "I promise," I said, "we'll meet again. Till then, *succes*."

He helped me don my backpack and handed me my duffle. With a final wave, I picked my way through bicycles, walking the same cobblestones I'd crossed two years ago, heading for the same train station, leaving a bit wiser.

Since then, bananas haven't been the same for me. They remind me how growing up works. Sometimes you have to accept something else like an avocado in order to understand what blessings you actually have.

Take a risk. Be compassionate. Every day.

Good night, Mama.

Good night, Oregon.

# 31. 1997

I CLOSE MY binder—I didn't take many notes. I'd been meeting Dr. Slompka regularly for the past year, discussing my hypothesis, techniques, comments from other committee members, and editing the phrasing of my paper. His mouth crooks into a smile as he looks at me. "I think this is ready."

I stare at him, waiting for a 'but.'

He clasps his hands behind his head and leans back in his chair, watching me.

I'd been exhausted when I came in, now my stomach has squeezed all of its juices into my intestines, and I can barely stay seated. "Now?"

He nods, leaning forward, scanning his calendar. "Three weeks or four weeks to schedule your defense?"

"Three weeks."

"Good, I think sooner is the best chance we'll have of catching the rest of your committee. Are you ready for this?"

My body goes limp as I lean back and stare at the ceiling. "I've been ready for the last year."

"So you've been telling me."

Suddenly I lurch forward. "Dr. Eaves seems satisfied, but what about Dr. Klein?"

A frown pulls a corner of his mouth into a *tsk* then disappears. "I understand Professor Klein has some concerns, but I believe you're ready. You will need to thoroughly know the body of work surrounding your subject to convince him. This is a private defense. Only your committee will be there. That should be helpful in providing some latitude to concentrate … and speak with authority."

"Are you saying I mince words?"

He looks at me as though he's revealing the formula for alchemy. "I'm saying prepare to prove you know what you're talking about. You'll need to substantiate you are correct—and then some."

My eyes widen as I sit perfectly still.

"Do you want more time?"

"No." I cough. "No," I say louder. "Let's do this."

## 32. That's Not The Way I Remember It.

**ON AIR**

GOOD MORNING, THIS is the Navigator. Do you have a brother or sister who's tiresome and vexing? This is the story of how my sister and I came to an unspoken truce.

In 1994, I'd just returned from the Netherlands. I didn't know my sister had married, nor that she and her husband had moved Gramoo into a hospital bed in their spare room. By the time I arrived, hospice had been called, machines hummed, and oxygen bottles stood in the corner.

"I can't ... believe you came," Gramoo whispered as I took her hand.

"I told Root I was leaving Amsterdam. Didn't she tell you?"

"No, sugar pea, she didn't."

I gave my sister a donkey-stare. I'd spent money on a phone call, hoping it would keep Gramoo from climbing the stairway to heaven before I got here.

Root began smoothing the sheets, tucking the corners. I recognized that fidget. She shot me a peeved look. "Well, who knows if you'd actually show up? We can't count on you. I didn't want to get her hopes up for nothing."

"I told you ..." I glared, noticing she was taller. Prettier. The ring on her finger was plain silver, no diamonds. At twenty she was three years younger than me, but she'd always seemed a kid no matter her age. No one called her Root anymore. She'd probably had a foot-stomping outburst and set everyone straight about that. I was glad I'd missed it. She could've at least sent me a postcard about her nuptials. My face softened. "I'm here now. What do you need me to do?"

"Talk to Gramma." Frustration lined her voice. She also didn't use the name "Gramoo." Okay. Obviously there were new traditions. I planned to ignore them because no one should change 'home' while another person is away.

"Don't you need a nap or something?" I used the tone we'd exchanged as kids when I wanted to get rid of her. She stormed from the room. I was surprised how easily I could ignore the anger she left behind. It was like stepping back into the dance we'd practiced as kids.

I'd adopted the Dutch trait of cutting to the core of a conversation, wasting little time with niceties. "Root says you're dying. Is she just being hysterical?"

"Lungs fill up ... stopped draining them. Why delay ... what's coming?"

"Are you ready?"

"Ready years ago." She adjusted the cannula in her nose. "I have no idea why ... He's kept me alive this long."

"Are you talking about God, or your doctor who checked under your skirt, even if you had a cold?"

Gramoo coughed. "Don't joke." She drew a labored breath. "Hurts to laugh."

"Is there anything you want to say?" I steeled myself.

"I love you. Olly loved you too."

The wall shielding me from scoldings and butt-chewings crumbled as I let out a long breath. Guilt pulled my heart to my feet. "I'm sorry I wasn't here for him."

"He surprised us all." She paused to collect air. "Just potting plants. Found him. Gone. Hands still in dirt."

"Was it his special plants?" I knew he still grew a few marijuana pots to make arthritis salve

She nodded. "Don't mention it to Root."

"You didn't tell me she'd married. Do you like her husband?"

Gramoo shrugged. "Don't matter. I'm not married to him." Her stare went out the window and through the years. "I liked your daddy."

"Oh, you did not." My eyes did a half-roll. "Now I know you really are sick. Is that oxygen turned on?"

"He was a darn sight better ... than your mama's last man."

"What happened? I've only been gone two years and Root says Mama's as goofy as a goose. Doesn't even know what day it is."

"The booger took her money ... from the sale of the farm ... bought the grocery store. Dumped your mama. Bought a bigger store in Eugene ... and a younger bride."

"You never told me this in your letters."

"What difference ... would it make? You had ... a new life."

"Duane Unsinn used to make me change the expiration date on bread tags when I worked at the store. I told Mama, a long time ago, he was a whopping jackass."

"Promise ... you'll be nice to your mama. She's always been fragile."

"No she hasn't. Daddy used to say she had a spine of iron."

"He brought that out in her ..." Gramoo looked out the window, adding, "Don't mention ... grocery store to Root. Sets her off."

"Good grief, is there anything we can talk about? Like the family farm? You know it was supposed to be mine."

"Olly left you his land." I squinted at her. She nodded. "In a little trust. You get it ...when you're thirty."

"Why would he leave me anything?"

"He cared for you. Thought you'd be more ... settled in a few years. Sister Minnie thought ... she was gonna get it for the convent." Gramoo closed her eyes. "Always stopping by ... bringing Olly pickles or bread."

"You're jealous of a nun? Remember, you're headed to heaven. When you reach the gates, I'd like to hear you justify your envy of one of the Lord's handmaidens."

"Don't have to ... Jesus died for my debts. Remember that."

"Well, good thing you've got that going for you. But now I'm worried about the debts Olly left me. I can't pay the property taxes."

"All ... in a trust." She shook her head, then adjusted the cannula again. "See J.J. Swank ... the attorney."

My eyes went damp as I leaned close, examining her face to see if she looked fuzzed-up in her head. Olly was a cautious old geezer. Nitpicky about the way I weeded or watered or pruned for him. "He actually left me his land?"

"He's buried there. Said to make sure ... no one ... puts horns on his grave."

"Ha!" A tear escaped with the memory of a humiliating day in high school. Olly had cheered me up by helping me cement goat horns and deer antlers on the family tombstones of my bully. "Olly said it was a long time coming and 'the whole buncha them were ditch slugs.'"

Gramoo gave me a knowing look. "Town council never figured out ... who did that."

My sister peeked around the door. "Did what?"

"Hey, Root." I grinned. "You'd enjoy living in the Netherlands. Your family can't disinherit you there."

"What's that supposed to mean?"

"But they can take their revenge after you're dead. Graves are limited. You can only rent a plot for ten to twenty years. If your family doesn't cough up more rent, you're dug up and put in a mass grave. You might end up next to Rembrandt."

She gave me a sarcastic look. "I'm almost sorry I asked you to come back. Let Gramma rest from your awful stories. Tom brought Mom from the care center. You can entertain her while I cook. And don't tell her any of your depressing crap." She left, her footsteps clacking down the hallway.

I made a fake-frightened face. Gramoo returned an equally aghast look. I took her hand. "I've really missed you."

Her chest worked to build up air. I counted twenty breaths in a minute. How much life could an E canister of oxygen labeled 625 liters provide?

"Glad you're back," she finally huffed.

"Me, too," I whispered as I stood. Around 4,992 life-giving breaths. Then it ran out. There was a termination point to most things. Maybe it was also true about home. It didn't feel like I was back. This wasn't home. Everything was ending again. People had changed.

Gramoo grabbed my wrist. "Promise you won't sell Olly's place."

I kissed her forehead. "Don't worry. I'll make sure you and Olly always have a spot to rest in peace."

"Don't sell out. Not the land. Not yourself." She leaned her head back and closed her eyes. "He wanted you to go ... as far as you could go."

I didn't know if she meant geographically or educationally, so I simply said, "I will. I'm just a little adrift at the moment."

"So's your mama."

I sighed. "I'll find my way—eventually."

"I know you will, sugar pea." Gramoo opened her eyes briefly. "And ... don't tell your sister ... about the land. She doesn't know."

***

Mama seemed smaller and thinner. Maybe it was the big recliner she was sitting in, but she reminded me of a bird hiding in the corner of its cage. She watched as I lowered myself onto the ottoman in front of her.

Root said, "Look, Mom, Stiks is home."

My mother stared like I was an insect with appendages and antennae in the wrong places. "You stole my sweater." She pointed at the pashmina wrapped around my shoulders.

"Uh ... are you talking about today or something I did when I was younger?"

Her forehead wrinkled into a scowl. "That's mine."

"You want it? I got it in Delft." I began unwrapping the long scarf, but Root stopped me.

"She thinks everybody steals her stuff. Her dishes, her pencils, her magazines, her clothes. As you can imagine, she's real popular at the nursing home." Root bent over, patting Mama's shoulder. "It's not yours. You've got your sweater on."

I held out the garment. "Here, Mama, you can have it."

She gave me a hard look. "I'm not your mama."

"Don't you recognize me? It's me, Stiks. Your daughter." I urged, pushing the shawl at her.

"My little girl is smart. You're not little. Your cheeks are wrong."

I looked at my sister who returned my gaze, her face expressionless. I turned back to Mama. "It's me. I'm older. My hair is a little shorter."

My mother shook her head. A rough voice came out of her I'd never heard, "You got any cigarettes?"

I leaned back. "You don't smoke!"

"She does now," Tom said as he came into the room. My sister had told me her husband was assistant administrator at the hospital twenty miles away. He looked older than her by about ten years, a small man with a soft voice and forgettable features. How he'd snagged a looker like Root must've had something to do with his steady job and his willingness to commute from Rain. After we'd exchanged introductions, he told me, "Charlie Owens, in the nursing home, gives your mother cigars." He turned to Mama. "C'mon, Grace, you can take a cancer break while I fire up the grill." Without hesitation, Mama trailed him to the backyard.

"She'll follow a man anywhere, " Root huffed. "Come make yourself useful."

I tagged along to the kitchen and took the onion and cutting board she set on the counter. "Does she know *you*?"

"Most of the time. But *I've* always been around."

I let her dig pass. "How long has she been like this?"

Root gave me a peeved look. "A year. I didn't know where you were, so I couldn't tell you. She had a car wreck. She'd been drinking because of Duane Unsinn."

"Gaaah! That man! Do you think he was after her money from the start?"

"Nope. Mom was so smitten with him, she even gave him Dad's death benefit, to help buy that stupid grocery store. Fortunately, she had enough smarts back then to put ownership into a contract. You know they were doing the pickle-tickle while Dad was alive, don't you?"

"I still can't believe it."

She gave me a needling look. "You were at college. And when you visited, you didn't notice much. After they were married, he continued his mattress dancing with others. Mom started drinking. After the wreck, he divorced her. The settlement covers her monthly expenses."

"Will she ever get better?"

"There was swelling on her brain. We thought she'd come out of it, but she floats between different periods of her life. She especially likes ten–fifteen years ago, when she was in control of us."

"Good grief, I wasn't gone that long. I can't believe you didn't tell me."

"You left. It was obvious you wanted nothing to do with family." She ripped the paper wrapper off the ground beef.

"Just because—" When I looked at her face, drawn and tired, I fell silent. This wasn't the time to fight. We worked quietly until I could think of something neutral to say. "Did you get a chance to go to nursing school?"

"Hated it. But nobody expected much outta me. Are you in line for a Nobel Prize? What've you done with the family's share of brains?"

I chopped the onion faster, not looking at her.

She stopped pressing ground beef into patties and stared at me. "You got all the talent. The adoration. The brilliance. And you're doing zilch?"

"I quit everything to come back here and help." I slapped the knife down. "Happy now? Each time a door opens, something jumps in front of it. It's like I wasn't meant to fulfill any objective, so I take off in another direction. I was going to get a doctorate, but dad died. He was the only one who cared if I went to school. I was out of money. Then Mama betrayed us with that jackass, so I left. I had a decent aerospace job in Amsterdam, but Gramoo is dying, so I came here to be with her. I can't afford to go back to school. And yes, I already checked into scholarships. They're gone for the year. I'm like a pinball, banging around."

"You and Mama both." Root shook her head, smacking a blob of meat, flattening it.

I began chopping celery and red peppers. Root started a salad. Tom came in, got the patties, and left.

She broke the silence with an accusing, "Did you know Olly grew weed?" She didn't wait for an answer. "Gramma called when she couldn't get him conscious. Tom and I hurried over and found marijuana plants. Ten of them. Giant ones. I thought Tom was going to have a heart attack, too. He was frantic, yanking them up and hiding them before the medical examiner got there."

"Why? They weren't his."

"Oh, for heaven's sake! How would that look in the local newspaper? 'Hospital Administrator's Family Growing Their Own Pharmacy.'"

"You and Mama..." I shook my head. "Always worried what people think."

"Gramma told us the ol' fart didn't even want a coffin. He wanted to be dumped in the ground with mushroom spores on top of him so he would compost faster."

"Where do you get mushroom spores?"

"I don't know!" she squeaked then lowered her voice to a whisper, stirring the salad so hard, celery jumped from the bowl. "How crazy is that? We didn't do it. Don't tell Gramma. Let her think it was perfect."

I shrugged and began unwrapping cheese slices for the burgers. "Was Mama mad about me taking her underwear-drawer money when I left?"

"If she ever figures out who you are, she might cuss you out, but I doubt it."

"I'm sorry."

"What're you apologizing to me for? You beat me to it. I didn't hang around either. Unsinn was making passes at me. Mama was crying and drinking. I couldn't stand it. I moved in with Tom. That made Mama drink even more. She was wailing about Gramma living with Olly. You'd ran off. Dad had died. We'd all abandoned her."

"I guess we sort of did."

We were silent, moving around the kitchen, our regrets shadowing us.

After five minutes a thought made me smile. "I hated working at that stupid grocery store so much, I'd go to the toy section, get plastic snakes, and hide them in the cabbages. You should've heard customer complaints. It was great."

"You ruined it for me working there. Unsinn didn't keep me around long. Thank you for that. Didn't you draw faces on eggs in the carton, using a black felt-tip pen?"

"Oh, yeah. I forgot about that."

"That's not the way I remember it." Mama's voice trailed from the living room.

I looked at my sister, my eyes large.

Root held a finger to her lips, waited a few seconds, then murmured, "Sometimes she'll recognize a voice, but when the face doesn't match the picture in her mind, she's confused. 'Course, all her mental images are from the time we were kids. Remember Cindy Heath from 4-H? She's Mama's caregiver. Mama will talk as long as she doesn't see her, but if Cindy steps into view, Mama zips her lips. Stay here and answer her. You'll see."

Frowning, I called out, "I thought you were outside, Mama. What do you remember about the eggs?"

"I remember you got your bottom tanned for messing with them, so you switched to drawing mustaches on the babies of diaper packages."

I raised my eyebrows at Root. She giggled and whispered, "My favorite was when you replaced Unsinn's photo with Hitler's on the employees' Wall of Fame. It took him a month to notice."

"What are you two snickering about?" Mama called. "Don't you be planning anything."

"I was just saying," Root called out, "once, when I had to hang around the store after school, Stiks gave me a bottle of clear nail polish and told me to paint a bar of Irish Spring."

I laughed out loud. "That thing stayed in the soap dish for years. I bet it's still there."

"You were always putting your little sister up to something so she'd get in trouble," Mama said. "If we didn't keep your mind occupied, you were into mischief. I don't know why you had to cause problems for me. I was always apologizing for you and your stunts."

"I was bored! You made me work for that numskull, doing mindless—" I walked toward the living room.

Root grabbed my shirt. "Don't! You can't convince her. You'll be arguing with the ghost of memories. She wouldn't let go of her problems, and now they won't let go of her. Trust me. It's never her fault. You can't change her version of things. It's her new comfort zone."

I yanked away and kept walking. Mama was sitting on the sofa rolling an unlit cigar between her fingers. She startled when I walked in, tucking it in the folds of her dress. Her voice came out like a child's. "I wasn't smoking in here."

"Do you recognize me now?"

She stared at me.

"Mama?"

She said nothing.

For the next few days I watched my sister run the world. She served coffee and cookies and chatted with neighbors and church ladies who came to say goodbye to Gramoo. She organized Mama's activities and cooked meals and cleaned house like a 1950s housewife. She was dressed, with her makeup on, before Tom left for work. Gracious. Happy. She'd achieved the life our mother had always wanted.

On the fourth afternoon after I'd arrived, Gramoo turned and looked out the window. It was a windy day. The tree boughs dipped and swayed as though moving to music. "Look," she whispered, "the angels are waiting. Their wings ... stirring the air." Gramoo didn't move again. Her eyes didn't close, but she was gone.

A short memorial was held a few days later at the Lutheran church. I'm not very religious, but I said a thankful prayer there was no open microphone for people to gabble their random thoughts. And it was nice that the church ladies made a community dinner for everyone.

It was calmer than Daddy's funeral. Mama spent the day in foggy bliss. She liked being dressed up and meeting new folks, even though all of them already knew her. When she was drowsy, she catnapped in a lounge chair. We were supposed to wake her so she'd be tired and sleep through the night, but we didn't. It was easier on us when she napped. We didn't have to monitor her unfiltered stories or make sure she didn't hike out of the building.

When it was over, Tom took Mama back to the care center. Root and I went to her house and drank beer.

"You were super today." I sat at her kitchen table, gnawing on chicken wings the church ladies had sent with us. "You went around talking and thanking everyone. I didn't inherit the hospitality gene. As a matter of fact, I don't like most people."

Root shrugged. "This is what I want to do—be part of a community and have a family."

"Pleeease," I groaned, "don't raise them here. There's so much more in the world. This is the black hole of creativity and progressive ideas."

"Oh, stop whining about this town. It's safe. People know each other, help each other. I like it. You know what's the matter with you?"

I gave her a withering look.

"You need to do what you set out to do. Go back to school. What happened to your dream of getting a doctorate? Was that your idea or was it what everybody expected you to do?"

"You wouldn't know about being pulled away from your goals or about being alone or life's roadblocks, prissyboots. It's frustrating and damn hard."

"It's supposed to be hard, blockhead. If it were easy, everyone would do it." Root retrieved two more beers from the fridge. "How many people are given the smarts to understand your Einstein gibberish? And if you're gonna hang around here, lemme tell you something ..." She twisted off the caps with more force than necessary and threw them at the sink. "All my life I've had to compete with you. When you were here, I was invisible. Even now, people at the funeral were saying, 'Oh, your sister, she gave up work and traveling so she could come back and be with her grandmother.'"

"I never said that! Well ... I may have mentioned being abroad."

"And once again, you're the hotshot. All the time you've been gone, I've been the big deal. Believe it or not, I make the decisions in this family. Mom's world operates around me. When you were here, it was all about you. You're the one Mom and Dad bragged about."

"I don't remember it that way. And when did you start calling her 'Mom?'"

"When I stopped being a little kid. Except I was always treated like one. I didn't even get to help with Dad's funeral. Nobody asked me what I thought, but Mom took *you* to plan the service."

"I don't know why. She ignored everything I said. If Dad had been here, he would've skipped his own ceremony and gotten drunk. It was an empty show, but it was what Mama wanted. She had to have it her way."

Root smacked her bottle down on the table, beer splashing out. "She *always* has to have it her way!"

"Until now. I really don't think she wanted to live an addle-brained life."

Both of us were quiet, lost in the pieces of life that weren't fair. Finally I said, "I should've been here with you. Maybe together, we could've helped her stay sane."

"I doubt it. Tom says it's guilt that keeps us enslaved to this family. You wanna know the truth? I was jealous you escaped the whole mess."

"And yet, here I am—back again."

"Crap. Why do we inherit the problems our parents create?" Root peered inside her bottle, as though the answer might be floating in there.

I picked at the label on my beer. "I don't know why you're bellyaching. You inherited all the charm and looks."

She beamed. "I did, didn't I?"

I threw a chicken bone at her. "And you're lucky with Tom. He puts up with a lot. Where is he? He's been gone too long."

"Mom sleeps the same as when we were little. Awake all hours of the night. He's probably telling her a story. It helps her drift off. If he's not there, she listens to the radio."

Maybe I'll try the radio. I don't sleep well either."

"That's because you've given up on your dream."

"I don't have the money, prissyboots."

"Then work, blockhead! Geez, you're supposed to be the smart one."

I tossed another chicken bone at her. "Not that it's any of your business, but I called an old college friend yesterday. He offered me a job. It's mindless, dangerous, and a lot of travel, but pays really well."

"Tom has accounting jobs at the hospital." She didn't look at me. "If you don't try to take over, I could learn to put up with you again if you want to stay closer to home."

"Accounting? *Uglaaak*. I feel like a stranger among everyone. I don't have a home anymore."

"Well, Gramoo once told me, 'Wherever you are—that's home.'"

The corner of my mouth turned into a slow smile. "You know ... she was a wise woman."

"That's the way I remember her."

We tapped our bottles in a toast.

Since then, my sis and I live with an unspoken agreement. It's a cranky-glad-to-chide-you understanding. We no longer have to compete to get attention from our family. We've buried most of them.

What we are left with is each other. We still disagree often, but we cannot deny there is an invisible chain of memories binding us together.

It took getting older to be happy about that.

Take a risk. Show compassion. Every day.

Good night, Mama.

Good night Oregon.

# 33. 1997

MINA KNOCKS ON my closet door at 8:10 a.m. whispering, "Your sister just called. She wants you to phone her right back."

Rousting myself from my lucky sleeping bag and two hours of rest, I crack the custodian-closet door and peek at Mina. "Is this a trick? A surprise party or some joke?" Mina shakes her head. I dress and traipse to her office because I can't afford a mobile phone and the department phone has become my personal number.

I dial and as soon as I say, "It's me. What's happened?" Root blurts, "I told you the wrong date for Mom's doctor appointment; it's today, not tomorrow. Can you still do it?"

I'm silent, filtering my reply. My knee-jerk response would be *You're on your own, prissyboots. I've got to study for my orals.*

Instead, I say, "Okay, but there are two things you need to understand."

"I knew you'd try to get out of it."

"No, you have to admit I've been helping more with Mom. I'm simply warning you my carburetor has become persnickety. It might take a little snooze at an intersection, and then Mama and I will have to sit about fifteen minutes before it starts again."

"So begin early. What's your other excuse?"

"I'm not shirking, only explaining possible problems." I huff out a breath. "Remember how Mama made a fuss when I took her to Wal-Mart a couple of weeks ago? She thought I was a hitchhiker stealing her car and heading south with her in it? Stop laughing. It wasn't funny."

"Okay. Okay." Root clears her throat. "I'll call the staff and tell them to prepare her, but who knows where her brain is today? Look, I'm sorry about mixing up the dates, so I'll tell you a trick." She pauses. "Promise Mom a treat and she'll go with you. And if she makes a fuss, then tell her she'll wake the baby."

"What baby?"

"Just say it, blockhead. You don't have to have one around. Works like a dream. She'll shut up if you scold her for disturbing a sleeping infant."

Moments pass. I try to control my breathing. "You're just now telling me this? The last few years I could've ... you've got a mean streak, you know that?"

Root laughs. It's high-pitched. Squeaky. Almost maniacal.

I hang up and tell Mina, who's been pretending not to eavesdrop, "I think my sister is losing it."

When I pick Mama up from Stoney Park Care Center, she's dressed to the nines. To get her to go, the staff has told her I'm taking her to a party. I groan. There will be hell to pay, unless the doctor's office is playing music and serving cocktail wieners. Mama happily gets in the car, asking, "Now what did you say your name was?" She repeats the question every ten minutes.

Her physician is a soft-spoken woman named Dr. Chu. Confused, Mama squints at her Asian features asking, "Are you saying 'Jew,' like the people who killed Christ?"

I rub my face, which I do a lot during this checkup. The nurse advises me, "It's easier if you pretend you're not related. That's how I handle my mother." I try her technique, but each time I look at Mama, memories leak out. Her younger self would be mortified at the social faux pas she's making.

Neither Mama nor I are good at discussing her health history. "This is a terrible party," Mama replies to most of the doctor's questions.

Finally, I simply ask, "Do you hurt anywhere, Mama?"

"I have headaches and I'm dry." She touches her mouth. "I use a lot of lip balm. It works well on my downstairs lips, too."

Now I begin to wonder if ol' Charlie, at the care center, is giving out more than cigars. "You'd better check her lady parts, too," I tell the doc.

Mama puts up a small fuss, but when the exam is over, Dr. Chu says there's no sign of sexual activity. Mama seems happy to be sitting around naked. I take away her magazine so the doctor can tell her, "We're going to schedule you for a MRI for those headaches. You seem in pretty good physical health, but you should stop smoking."

"And you should wear your hair out of your face," Mama snaps back. "You'd look more professional that way."

It takes a bit of coaxing and the promise of a treat to get Mama dressed. The nurse has given her samples of lubricant as "party favors." The whole ordeal makes me realize how much craziness Root has put up with.

As we drive away, Mama's mouth works like a door on a windy day, never fully closing. "Lookit that hippie. I hope he trips on those long pants." "My neighbor thinks she's interesting because she's old." "Look! That man is pregnant!"

"Mama, you can't say that just because someone is overweight."

"*Pffft*. Old people are deaf. He didn't hear me. Those young people are gonna get cancer of the butt for keeping phones in their back pocket."

While she jabbers, I pull into the Rainbow Drive In. I'd spent most of this week's food allowance on gas. I"ll blow my remaining cash here. "Give me two small chocolate Dr. Peppers," I say to the intercom. "And I need the senile citizen's discount on one of them."

Mama is still yapping when the carhop brings our drinks. I pay in quarters and dimes. But when my mother takes a sip, she falls silent. I relish the peace, closing my eyes and breathing in the quietness. How has Root dealt with this? I visit Mama several times a month, but Root is doing something for her every day. I'm surprised my sister isn't a howling nutter by now.

I glance at Mama. She's staring at me, watching my face like a cat about to lick her kitten, her pale blue eyes shiny.

I see her in there—the mother I grew up with.

"You know"—her mouth softens into a sad smile—"you taught me to drink these. You're the only one who would buy them for me."

"You know me?" My heart melts and spins. I paw at my seatbelt, trying to get it off. "You recognize me?" The catch pops and I reach for her. Tears blur my sight. I lean against her. "Mama, I'm sorry." Her hand barely brushes the top of my head. I whisper, "Sorry, I left angry. Sorry I wasn't here to help you ..."

Her shoulder is warm; her fingers are cool. Like she had so many years ago, she delicately tucks strands of hair behind my ear as though she were working with threads of silk.

"I'm sorry I took your money. Maybe you could've used it to get a better lawyer. Then all this would've turned out differently. Forgive me," I whisper.

"Oh Stiks, this will all pass. Trust me."

I lie still, sniffling, grabbing her words as a form of forgiveness. An untethering grows in my chest.

"I heard you on my radio one night."

"Which story?"

She doesn't answer. I don't push it.

We sit. Sunlight warms us through the windshield. A breeze rustles the trees. Comfort trails from Mama's touch.

"Those hotdogs I ate this morning—I think I've got diabetes now." I look up at her. The face is the same, but the window has closed.

I try to pry open her memory again with, "Do you remember my driver's test?" She does, but she answers yes to all my questions including meeting Elvis Presley and fighting in Normandy.

It takes me a while to dry my puffy face and collect myself. I start the car and we begin driving back to Stoney Park. Mama is gabbing about one of the residents who listens to a song her grandkids left on her answering machine. "She plays it over and over. It's special because she was lying in the shower with a broken hip as they sang 'Happy Birthday.'"

I smile. I understand completely.

I plan on pulling out this memory of the Rainbow Drive In and playing it repeatedly. Mama may have forgotten today is my birthday, but knowing me is the best gift she could've given.

# 34. Falling

## ON AIR

I'M THE NAVIGATOR. It's a quiet night. The kind of night that makes you ponder the past, and that makes it the perfect time to tell you about the worst feeling of all. This is the story of how I dealt with fear.

It's a feeling similar to walking past an unfamiliar dog. The animal doesn't look mean, but its tail isn't wagging. The nearer you get, the more details you take in, black nostrils flaring, analyzing what you're made of—cold sweat or brutality.

Its eyes watch the swing of your hand, the stride of each leg. You have to walk near it if you want to get where you're going. And then there's the moment of trust. The hope that you haven't misjudged the animal's attitude or the reach of its teeth.

Fears haunt us as we go about our daily business. We're all tested.

In 1994, my big fear was falling. I talked myself past it each day. Height didn't bother me. It was the thought of a misstep that ghosted my feet.

Eight months earlier, I'd called a friend who was preparing to take over his uncle Manny's company. During college, I'd let him sleep on my couch when vandals had torn up his home—a tent. Now he offered me a well-paying job. A year of work would almost be enough to finance my doctorate. The only problem was the probability I would slip. The numbers demanded it. According to the Department of Labor, fatal falls were increasing by nine percent each year. Four-fifths of fatal falls were from a height of thirty feet or less.

*Thirty feet or less. That's only a three-story house*, I told myself and tugged the lanyard at my waist, mumbling, "So why do this?"

The steel cable covered in crinkly yellow fabric pulled tight. The snap hook gave a *clank*, assuring me it was anchored to the tie-line. "Because I need money. And to prove to myself I'm courageous." I also told myself to quit thinking about the statistics.

One hundred and thirty feet below me, horizon to horizon, a few lights shone around Dillon, Kansas. Golden streaks bruised the sky to the east. The colors indicated the sun was still six to twelve degrees below the horizon. Nautical twilight. If we were old-time sailors, we'd now be using the horizon to navigate. But we were water-tower painters, and here in the Sunflower State, Manny used nautical twilight to start work. Ten hours of daylight left to finish this job.

I transferred my lanyard to another tie-in. With the securing *clank*, I paused. At this height, how many seconds would I see sunrise before Manny did as he barked orders from the ground? I stared to the north, my mind calculating earth spin and altitude.

Several miles away, the headlights of a tractor circled a field, plowing before the wind came up. Here, the dirt left for Canada on the slightest breeze. The growl of the engine carried across the open air to my ears.

"Hey!" Manny hollered from below. "Where's your head at?"

"Okay. Yeah." I grabbed a 4'X 8'sheet of polystyrene and shuffled along the narrow walkway that circled the water tank.

The templates of letters were my guide to paint the town's name on the tank. I almost finished yesterday, but a breeze rolled up while I was holding the last sheet. Like a sail, it lifted me several inches before I let go and watched it windmill into a backyard blocks away.

This morning the template was sitting next to our powerlift. Someone had brought it back. I carted it to the top. Small town. Nice people.

"Is it useable?" Manny shouted.

"Yeah. Can you see the sun yet?"

"What? No. Pay attention to what you're doin'!"

I pulled my flat pencil from my vest pocket and wrote on the tank, calculating at one hundred thirty feet, how many seconds I'd see the sun before Manny did.

I'd written other calculations on the tank, like how long it would take to hit the ground. If I fell, it would probably be the first thing in my mind: How long do I have? So I did the numbers ahead of time and can spend my last 4.8 seconds pondering something else.

Like?

How fast I'd be going. One hundred six miles an hour, but that was only a first-order approximation, not including air resistance and—

"What in God's green earth are you fiddling at up there?" Manny yelled.

"Making guidelines." I kept scribbling. "You want the town name tilting off the tank?"

"It doesn't have to be perfect. Slap it in line with the other letters." He picked up an empty paint bucket, mumbling about damn numbers-people.

"Just tell me when you first see the sun on the horizon," I called out.

He snorted and threw cable climbers into a crate.

In the flat country around me, trees stuck up like pins in a map. Most of the leaves had fallen, exposing the roofs and farmland beyond the city limits. Black branches were silhouetted in the pink dawn.

On the next street over, Bike-girl winged a rolled newspaper at a house decorated with Halloween spiders. She threw to three more houses before she disappeared down the block. She had a good arm, but it was 7:05. She was late.

In the house below me, Mr. Crott had taken up his post. Each morning the old codger brought his coffee to the front porch, settled into his padded rocking chair with his newspaper, and watched us work. He saw me looking at him, and we did our usual exchange. He lifted his cup, calling, "Hold on."

"Always." I gave him a nod.

Four weeks ago, on the first day we began painting Dillion's water tower, a representative of the *Chronicle* arrived, snapping photos and asking for details.

The lanky, young man held a recorder under Manny's nose, saying, "Can you tell us exactly how you'll be doing this and how long it'll take?"

Like a football coach, Manny preferred talking to his team rather than reporters. His scowl pivoted back and forth, watching two painters already on the other side of the tank and Dez, still on the ground, arranging tools on his platform. "What we're doin' is puttin' paint over every square inch of your elevated water tank. Stand back." He flipped ropes, keeping them untangled as the swinging stage lifted my former college roommate up the side of the tower.

The young reporter stepped a few feet away, avoiding the uncoiling cables snaking upward. "Sir, this was a controversial project. The town council fought over this expense for almost a year. Our readers want to know exactly what their money is being spent for."

Manny was silent, watching Dez tie in and then arrange welding equipment next to the squatty tank that looked like a big pill on steel girders.

"Sir?"

Manny's eyes stayed focused upward as Dez yanked on a steel ladder curving to the top. The stout black man wore the same frown he had last night when the waitress delivered our Dr. Peppers with her thumbs in the glasses. He looked down at Manny and shook his head.

Other neighbors and looky-loos gathered around the interview. Manny stared at the reporter for a long second. "You tell folks this tower has been neglected for so long, the tie-off points built into it are too eroded to access the top. So we're gonna hafta bring in a hundred-fifty-foot crane. And that fella up there's gotta check each curved seam and re-weld anything iffy.

"Then because you folks are tired of dingy laundry, itchy skin, and buildup in your pipes, we're gonna climb inside and sandblast the scale outta it. And since the only lick of paint this steel has seen in twenty years is graffiti on the legs, we're gonna prime and coat the whole shebang in a durable epoxy that's baby blue. Then people will have fresh water, a landmark you'll be proud of, and hopefully it won't be another twenty years before everybody decides to take care of their primary water reservoir."

He pointed at me to watch Dez, then walked away, leaving me with the reporter. Above us, my friend was putting on a show. His muscled arms gripped the swinging stage, as he leaned way over it rather than move the whole metalwork to check another area. Behind me, his audience whispered nobody could pay them to do that.

"Ma'am, what do you do?" the reporter asked me.

I took the Manny approach. It worked so well for him. "I paint water towers."

"Are you scared being up so high?"

"Good grief!" I kept my eyes on Dez. "Of course it's scary. Fear of heights is hard-wired into us. It's a survival trait. Without it, the whole human race would be falling off roofs or dancing across electric lines like squirrels. If you ever lose your fear, you need to quit. You have to focus on what you're doing. Always be aware of where you are."

Except that wasn't exactly true for me. When the wild dog of fear crept up on me, stiffening my body, I distracted myself with math. I'd become an expert at calculating water pressure, where each foot of height increased force by .43 pounds per square inch.

"Are you a thrill seeker?"

I pondered that for a moment. I'd always considered myself a rebel not an adrenalin junkie. I gave him a flat look. "I'll just say, it's an adventure." I glanced at Dez. He loved being high above the ground. The higher, the better.

"Have you ever fallen?"

Why would anyone emphasize such a thought? No wonder Manny tried to avoid interviews until the job was finished. He'd been in a controlled fall once. Messed up his back. "Look, have you ever fallen out of a tree, off a ladder, down the stairs?"

"Yeah, but not way up—"

"It's simple," I interrupted. "Don't let go. Hold on to anything. That's all you have to remember."

"But—"

"Hey!" yelled an old codger holding a coffee mug against his poochy gut. He was hump-shouldered and built like a fire hydrant. Crusty, brown spots showed through his thinning hair. He looked like a poster for hard life. "I live across the street. This thing leaks like a minnow bucket. Dripping all year long. It's a damn mess. Let 'em get on with their work."

I felt relieved, but doubted if the ol' man noticed because now he was complaining about cracked sidewalks, dogs running loose, and the "stupid law prohibiting cars from backing into parking spaces." That began my relationship with Mr. Crott.

Fewer and fewer people showed up each day to watch us, but each morning the old goat and I exchanged a few stories while I put on my full body harness. One afternoon he caught me tossing pebbles off the top of the tower. I was timing them to test my calculations. The next day he gave me coins, saying it'd be better to toss nickels. More fun for him to pick up. Each morning when I reached the top, he was on his porch, raising his cup, reminding me, "Hold on."

"Hey!" Manny yelled, "Quit writin' on the tower!"

I shouted down, "You'll be happy to know at this height, I'll see the sun 1.6 seconds before you do."

"Big whoop! You're burnin' daylight." Manny knew I needed to acclimate by doing math first thing in the morning. We all had rituals. Delph and Shey slurped down coffee and tossed their paper cups, checking which way the wind blew. Dez liked to spit and watch it fall. The *ker-splat* on the ground reminded him to stay alert. I needed complex calculations. It was soothing knowing my numbers yielded irrefutable answers.

I placed the template even with the other sheets and secured it. Bike-girl was pedaling up our street.

*Whap*. Pedal. *Whap*. Pedal. *Whap*. Her missiles hit targeted porches and front doors.

A *thud* sounded as she passed Mr. Crott's house. "Sorry!" her voice trailed behind her. She sped on. "I'm late."

Mr. Crott's newspaper lay on the sidewalk at the bottom of his steps. I checked my watch. 7:20 a.m. She wouldn't make her bus. Slowly, the old man stood, unkinking his vertebrae one at a time. My roller brush sopped up thick paint. I liked having the stick in my hand, it made me feel balanced. I ran it over the templates. Black, blocky letters appeared that would be visible for miles.

The sun had topped the horizon. Manny hadn't mentioned it. The long shadow of the water tank stretched westward over lawns. Dez was silhouetted on top, moving like a stick figure, untethered, rolling his brush in short sweeping pushes. You ready to come up here and finish this masterpiece?"

Manny would have a cow if he knew both of us left our initials on top of each tower we'd done. I got the idea when I read about building bombers during WWII. The women weren't supposed to sign and date their work, but no one would see their names in the floor plates unless the plane crashed.

"Help!" a voice croaked below.

Mr. Crott lay on the sidewalk. He was bug-eyed like a fish out of water, flapping an outstretched arm, gripping his newspaper, his hand shaking.

"Manny!" I yelled. "Get over here!"

The boss's squatty legs came at a run. It took a quick confused conversation to sort out I wasn't the one who needed emergency services. Shortly the squeal of a siren began in the east. From my perch, I spotted the red and blue lights flickering across town, working their way toward us.

My attention pivoted between Mr. Crott groaning and the ambulance wailing. Several blocks away, the emergency vehicle suddenly braked to a stop. A yellow bus blocked the road between cars parked on both sides of the street.

From the opposite direction, Bike-girl came pedaling, her legs pumping hard, her hair flying behind her.

The sirens gave a *whoop whoop* and brought a few people onto their porches. Slowly, the bus lumbered into a narrow driveway, the tires cutting ruts in the manicured lawn. The ambulance veered around the back of the bus and sped on.

Bike-girl swerved off the street, bounced across a lawn, and jumped off, letting the cycle's momentum crash into the porch of a blue house. She disappeared inside as the ambulance passed her door.

I stared at the bike lying in the yard, wheel still spinning.

Manny was kneeling beside Mr. Crott, speaking quietly, kindly. He was the right man for the job. He understood fear. Shortly, the ambulance pulled up next to our trucks.

Two blocks over, Bike-girl burst out the door, backpack over one shoulder. The bus lurched to a stop at her driveway. She wouldn't have made it if the bus hadn't pulled over for the ambulance. But the ambulance wouldn't be here if she hadn't missed Mr. Crott's porch with her newspaper.

I looked at the pivotal points in this drama: bike, bus, ambulance, Mr. Crott. All interrelated. It didn't seem fair that life insisted on connecting disparate people together.

I tried to live as carefully as I could, lower my risk probability. Maybe caution made me overreact, but it didn't seem right something unrelated may topple me.

What was the chance Bike-girl would be late this morning? And why the fluky throw at that moment? She usually hit the porch, sliding the newspaper next to Mr. Crott's feet. And what were the odds he'd fall down the stairs he'd been using all of his life? I'd need a computer to calculate the probabilities.

They were strapping the old fella onto a backboard. He'd stopped moaning. His eyes were wide like he was scared and figuring his chances of ever returning to his own porch. I'm sure he didn't want to recuperate at his daughter's house. One morning he'd told me, "She cooks so bad the crows won't even eat her grub." Then he flung a slice of her homemade coffee cake onto his lawn. A week later, it was still there.

Kitty Lane came from her bungalow, clutching her housecoat to her chest, walking a stiff-legged quickstep. Her hair was frizzed like Groucho's and her open mouth showed her twisted front teeth. "Wait ... wait!" she called, her arms reaching as she hurried.

The old man had once told me, "Poor soul. She's not much of a looker. But nice. Real nice. Name's Katherine, but I call her Kitty cuz her cats crap in everybody's flowerbeds. Never married. I don't think anybody ever asked her. Shame."

Each afternoon, from my tower perch, I saw her trek to Mr. Crott's, carrying a snack package of Oreos. They sat on the porch dipping them in coffee and solving international crises.

Below me, they were wheeling Mr. Crott to the ambulance. Kitty Lane followed, still reaching for him. The old man lifted a shaking arm and pointed up at me.

Grasping the railing, I leaned over to yell our usual, hold-on exchange, but the shadow of the water tower caught my eye.

The silhouette of Dez on top was jittering. He must have had his back to all the action, unaware of what was happening on the ground, because he was pumping his roller brush up and down, knee bent in the air, jumping on one leg then hopping to the other. He was doing his ritual I'm-Done dance. It always made him smile. "Because it's never been done on that spot and never will be again."

Mr. Crott was looking at my friend, not me. Dez—one-stepping, taking chances like a fool, the sort of risks young, immortal, untried people take.

Reality pinched Mr. Crott's face into mottled pink splotches. Or maybe it was pain. It was as if he realized life would never be the same for him. His routines and personal freedom were a thing of the past.

I looked around again. Many small unknowns had come together to create this very moment. Remove any one, and it would've happened differently. What was my role? Was there some secret lesson I was supposed to absorb so my brain could decrypt it later when needed?

The only thing I'd learned today was life was a crap shoot. A frustrating system of chaos. So I should stop planning because it rarely turned out like I expected.

People were messy and unpredictable. Maybe this incident was a message from the Universe telling me to chuck it all. Live large. We can't control meteors, falling trees, or misthrown newspapers. So take what comes and make it work. I figured it could work for Mr. Crott, too.

I leaned over the railing and yelled to the old man, "Let go!"

Dez hollered from the tower top, "I *am* letting go, baby!"

"What?" called the EMT, who stopped pushing the gurney, thinking I was shouting to him.

"No! I'm talking to your patient. Mr. Crott, let go. Move in with Kitty Lane instead of your daughter. Let go. Try a new routine. Maybe a better one. Instead of holding on, open your hand and accept what's falling into it. Take a chance. It'll be easier."

The old fella, still pointing at Dez, slowly turned his palm up, as though he was going to catch one of the nickels I'd tossed. The EMT shrugged and pulled the gurney toward the ambulance's open doors. I was left with the image of the old man, his hand up in supplication.

I stared at the emergency vehicle until it left for the hospital.

"Hey," Manny yelled at me. "Settle yourself, then finish up."

I pulled out my pencil, surprised I was so worried about these strangers. Mostly, I kept to myself, one of the benefits of working on a tower. Life was easier that way. I did a quick calculation. My math failed to calm me.

Late in the day Dez and I put our initials on top. We cleaned and packed our equipment, then headed to the next job. I took a detour, stopping by Dillon Hospital.

Mr. Crott was sedated. Kitty Lane was there. She reported he had two broken ribs, a broken hip and "bunged his head real good. But he's cussin', so he's okay."

Our crew moved on to Colorado. I called Ms. Lane the following week. I'm not sure she knew who I was, but she was full of information, telling me, "Oh, honey ... Edgar died."

"Whaaat!? Are you saying Mr. Crott is gone?"

"Yes ..." her voice broke a little. "It's hard to believe."

"How could that be? I thought he was doing okay!"

She heaved a rackety sigh. "I told him I'd help him. But he said he didn't wanna go on. He'd lived long enough."

"And he ... gave up?"

Silence reeled along the line for so long I thought she'd hung up, but finally she said, "I was with him Monday night. His daughter called me first thing Tuesday morning. He was gone. Simply gone. They tend to go in the middle of the night, you know. The hospital said it was his heart. It wasn't. He'd lost hope. No will to go on."

I sat in silence, ambushed by feelings. Could this be my fault? When I said, "Let go!" I didn't mean ... I never considered death an option.

But he must have.

Was that the role I was supposed to play? The reason I'd been factored into this drama? If so, I was ticked about it. And why was I concerned about people I barely knew?

It was that damn interconnected thing again. I'd lived among these folks for several weeks. I knew their routines, their attitudes, some of their hopes, and a lot of their fears. They'd rubbed off on me. I never intended that to happen. The more people get summed into your life, the harder it is to control.

It's the strange dog you encounter on the street. Go forward or go back. Connect with people and all of their messiness or avoid them. Even the tops of water towers weren't good hiding spots. Life would connect me, no matter what I did.

I told Dez and Manny, "I'm quitting. I'm not putting off my PhD any longer. I'm doing it before I become old, crotchety, and lose all of my hope in humanity."

"You think it'll make you happy?" Dez said.

"Who knows? But I think it's a good move not to think about falling every day."

"Did you run the numbers before you decided? Have you saved enough money yet to pay for it?" Manny asked.

I shook my head. "I'll make it work somehow."

"You can have my lucky sleeping bag," said Dez. "With it, you'll always find a place to sleep."

Manny stared at me. "If you didn't do calculations about this, the earth must be coming to an end."

"Naaah!" Dez pulled me into a bear hug. "My pal is learning to trust. Her world is just beginning."

That was three years ago. Since then I've discovered not all probability can be accurately charted ... not the dogs of fear running up my spine nor the faint breath of confidence whispering I made the right choice. I still second guess myself.

I assumed all of us gained different insights from Mr. Crott's fall. Perhaps I was included in that teachable moment to learn about fear and trying to outguess the future. Or maybe I needed prodding to get out of the tower-painting business and get back to school. Maybe it was all coincidence.

What I know for sure is that in Dillon, Kansas, the tower still stands tall on the flat horizon. Dez's and my initials are still on the top.

And here's something no one knows.

There is a calculation in the 'o' of the town's name.

My pencil scribblings show it will take 5.3 minutes to get Mr. Crott to the hospital. The rest is an ever-changing guess of how life will turn out after that.

Show compassion. Take a risk. Every day.

Good night, Mama.

Good night, Oregon.

## 35. 1997

THERE'S A CRYPTIC note in my mailbox. *Lay low.* I crumple it, wondering what's broken now.

Mina's in her office, putting folders in a cabinet when I stop by to ask about the note.

"Someone called the university wanting The Navigator from the radio program." One of her eyebrows cocks higher as she looks at me. "They were transferred to the Communications Department, and now Dr. Whisher is asking questions."

"I've got a fan?" I smile.

"This is serious! You've gotta stop doing those broadcasts."

"Maybe my stories are helping someone. I know I feel better after I tell one."

"Could it be it's more about you figuring out who you are than it's about—" Her eyes dart toward movement beyond my shoulder. "Hello, Dr. Slompka. Would you tell Sophia to stop fixing things and go study? She thinks these orals are going to be as easy as a dog licking its dish."

The department head pauses as he shortcuts through her office, heading to his own. "Mina's right. You need to be studying—everything you've learned since first grade."

"I skipped a couple of grades, so that may be a problem." I smile.

"See! She's always making jokes." Mina plops down in her chair. "You talk to her!"

I give her a wary look. Social cues have always confused me. I know we're shifting the topic from clandestine broadcasts, but double-speak subterfuge is far beyond my skill set. For some reason, I feel like a kid who's been passed off to the meaner, sterner parent. I'm not sure whether to act penitent or casually interested.

The professor locks me in a stare. "I'm telling you that staying calm and professional will be critical to your defense."

"As opposed to yelling and whacking dissenters with a stick, sir?" I frown and shrug. "What are you saying? Just tell me."

"I don't want to cause you additional anxiety, but I'm expecting your exam to be challenging. I'm saying *the manner* in which you speak and act will be as important as *what* you say. You *absolutely* must dialogue with authority without appearing supercilious. In other words, you should prepare for one or more of your committee members to grill you. When they do, resist becoming defensive. It's easier to be calm when you're confident of all your facts, even the ones you didn't think you'd be asked."

I glance back and forth between the two of them, but neither say more. I turn to leave; my voice has the enthusiasm of an undertaker. "Well, thanks. Now I *am* nervous."

"Wait." The professor looks at Mina. "Did you tell her Dr. Whisher wants to see the radio logs?" She shakes her head. He focuses on me again. "Are they current?"

"I need to enter last night's readings, otherwise, yes. Is there a problem?"

"Whisher is obsessed about pirating his airways. Don't worry about it. Right now your main concern is your orals. Prepare!" He turns and goes into his office. Mina grabs a sheaf of papers, gives me a hawk-eye look, and follows him.

Now I don't know which dilemma to be more nervous about.

Tonight, after cleaning the building, I enter Flippers' Corner with the one story I have left to tell. I pause in the anteroom to update the log. I'm supposed to take readings every two hours, but usually I take one per night and float the rest because they don't vary much unless the signal has increased, and I sure don't want that to show on the books.

Some entries I write in pencil and others in pen so it looks as though they were made at different times. A click sounds from the deadbolt of the outer door.

As the door bangs open, I slide the story I was going to read into the back of the logbook.

"Dr. Whisher. You scared me!" I lean back, letting out my breath as the tall, white-haired man walks past. I look at my watch. "What are you doing here?"

"I could ask you the same thing."

"I'm working."

He pauses to scan the room, then peeks through the windowed doors into the radio lab. All is dark except the yellow glow of a few buttons. "Are you alone?"

I pick up the phone and punch three numbers. "Security? I have a Code 300, third floor, Physics Department, please standby." I stare at Dr. Whisher. "Sir, I know who you are, but since someone pirated the airwaves, I call in anything that makes me nervous, and you're making me very uneasy. Why are you here at this hour?"

"I didn't know security had been improved since the incident. I'm impressed. That's good."

"Sir? You're still spooking me." Stone-faced, I waggle the phone. "Why the late night entry?"

"Oh! Sorry." He holds up his hands as though surrendering and yells to whoever is on the other end of the phone. "This is Dr. Whisher, head of the Communications Department. I mean no harm. This is a security check."

“Why?” I say.

“A caller asked for more stories about bullies on our late-night story program.”

“Okay, that sounds good. What’s the problem?”

“We don’t have a late-night story program. I suspect our radio pirate has found another way to hijack our broadcast.”

I let out a sigh, then speak into the receiver. “Security. All clear. Stand down. Sorry to bother you.” I hang up. Actually, I hadn’t called anyone, and Code 300 was the signal at D-Sacks grocery that a weirdo was at the register and the manager needed to come take care of the problem. But Dr. Whisher seems impressed.

I frown and point at the speakers barely emitting sound. “You can hear we’re broadcasting programmed music.”

“I wanted to look around. See for myself that everything was secure. Are you always here at this time?”

“I’m always somewhere in the building. Who was this caller? Where’s he or she from?”

The professor tugs on the broadcast room door, finding it locked. “Well ... it was a ten-year-old from Coos Bay. I called him back and interviewed him. This wasn’t the first time he’d heard The Navigator. He had details that made me think he could be telling the truth.”

“I’m sure he was telling what he remembered, but confused about the station. Our transmission range isn’t that far.”

“I know!” he says. “Perhaps someone is tapping our link to the antenna south of town.”

“That would take one heckuva technician.” I shake my head, open the log book to the entries I’d just made, and slide it toward him. “There haven’t been any spikes or dips in broadcasting amperage. There’s no evidence of what you’re saying. Have you driven out there to check the tower for extraneous wires?”

"I wouldn't know what to look for. Would you consider checking for connections?"

"Me?" I resist grabbing the logbook. "No. I'm not scaling that tower. I have a fear of falling. And I doubt anyone could climb over the razor wire platforms around each leg."

"Perhaps, you're right. I know I'm over-concerned, but airway infractions are serious offenses with hefty fines. We can't risk another breach." The professor stuffs his hands into his pockets, then takes them out again, rubbing his fingers as though they're itching. "We've brought trespassing charges against the young man who took over the station, but I doubt if they'll stick. He's out on bail and probably up to something. I'm glad Dr. Klein was able to cut the feed before the kid caused real problems."

"Dr. Klein did that? Interesting. I thought it was a group effort."

"Oh ..." he smooths his hair as though petting the words out of his head. "I'm sure others helped. If you were involved, thank you. I suppose I'm anxious about another takeover attempt."

"I think you heard from a confused little kid who really needs help dealing with bullies."

"Yes ... yes. It could be." He closes the log book and scoots it back toward me. He pulls the binder of announcements off the shelf, and studies the latest pages.

My heart is bouncing in my chest. I grab an amplifier out of the Fix-It box and begin metering it. He shelves the binder. "Have you noticed anything out of place? Anyone acting strange?"

"Besides the head of the Communications Department showing up in the middle of the night?" I give him a questioning look.

"Perhaps I *have* taken it personally." He scratches his fingers again. "Kurt was a very promising student, but he turned against me and endangered the program."

"I think he was just trying to foster a change. Trying to find his way—but aren't we all?"

"Right. Well, everything appears in order." He looks around the darkened room before moving to the door. "This is an off-the-record visit. I wanted to see if I needed to do anything official. No need to share this with Dr. Slompka. I wouldn't want him to think I don't have faith in his department."

"I understand." I give him a mechanical smile. "We're all simply trying to do our best."

"Right, right. Well, sorry for interrupting you." He heads out the door.

I let the silence of the room settle around me. My heartbeat slows to normal. I won't go on the radio tonight, but a smile crosses my face. Wow, Coos Bay. That's quite a distance. I only wanted to reach Rain, Oregon. Next time I'll dial it back a bit.

## 36. 1997

"I'M SORRY TO call so early," Root says. "I know you sleep in the mornings, but—"

"I was studying!" I interrupt her, glancing at the clock on the wall of Mina's office. 10 a.m. Twenty-six hours without sleep. I was in the lab when Mina tracked me down, saying my sister was on the line, waiting. "What do you want? My orals are tomorrow morning."

"Oh! Sorry. I lost track of when ..."

Of course she'd lost track. She's rarely paid attention to what I'm working on. To her I'm a satellite, circling, doing what I'm programmed to do. Forgotten until someone needs something.

"Well ... good luck tomorrow," she says. "You sound tired. Get some rest."

"Okay. Thanks. Bye."

"Bye."

But neither of us hang up. A message has traveled beneath our words. A tone, a pulse like when we were kids lying to protect one another. Both of us claiming we had no knowledge of why there was a hole in one of Mama's scarves or how the chickens ended up with no tail feathers. We listen to each other breathe for many heart beats.

Finally, Root whispers, "I hear typing. Are you alone?"

I glance at Mina's back, four feet away. "Why?"

"Never mind."

"Look," I growl, "you didn't call this early to say nothing. I'm too tired to play this game. If you don't tell me, it'll gnaw on me. I need a clear mind. Ask whatever you need me to do. I'm old enough to say no."

Mina has stopped typing. She touches the paper as though looking for where she'd lost her place. I pull the receiver from my ear. "Mina? Could you give me a moment with my sister? Thanks." With a nod, she leaves the room, closing the door behind her. "Now, what do you want?"

"Mama died," Root whispers. "I'm sorry to be telling you this now. I didn't know whether to say anything ... I don't want you to think I'm keeping things from you.

The world stops. Neither of us seem to be breathing. When sound finally returns, it comes as the *flap, flap* of a Valley View windsock twisting in the breeze outside Mina's office window.

"How? When?"

"In her bathroom. This morning. Aneurism. The nurse's aide found her. Tom said it would've been quick. Mama didn't suffer."

Mama, not Mom this time. A hundred thoughts crowd the silence coming through the phone.

*Flap. Flap.* My mind comes back to this room, this moment, this receiver in my hand. "Okay." I let out a long breath, rubbing my forehead. "I'll talk to my committee chair and be in Rain this afternoon."

"No. There's no reason to rush here. It won't bring her back. The only thing to arrange is the funeral. You know I'm good at that. Let me do it." Her voice is flat, without emotion. "I'll use the list I used for Gramma. We don't even have to have the funeral this week if she's cremated."

"I'm guessing Mama would want a big fuss and a beautiful corpse," I say.

"Heaven help us. She'd become so nutty, I don't think she knew what she wanted. Besides, you once told me every graduation in your life has been fouled up. I won't let that happen this time."

"Dissertation defense isn't graduation. It's more like the final test."

"Well, it's just you and me now. What do you want to do? I'll go along with whatever."

I stare at the floor, closing my eyes. I am so close. I'm so mentally ready for all of this to be over.

"I've been told ... when I get started on my subject, I talk about little else. So, yes, I'm pretty sure I can carry on. I'd like to do my orals as scheduled if it's all right with you."

"Good. I agree. I can drive up and be with you if that would help. Would it?"

"Oh, Root." My heart takes a dip and warps a little. "It's a closed session. There'll be nothing for you to do but sit in the library." My voice cracks a little, "But thanks ... that means a lot. How are *you* doing?"

We talk—she and I making plans for the future, being in charge.

When I leave the office I find Mina leaning against the wall next to her door, wearing a worried look. "Everything all right?"

"Yeah." I nod with a half-smile. "My sister was really supportive, wished me good luck tomorrow.

# 37. 1997

I'M WEARING THE best clothes I own, and wish I could take them off. I've been in this second-floor classroom without air-conditioning for an hour already, defending my dissertation.

I hadn't worn the business jacket since my interviews in Amsterdam. It's wrinkled from lying in my suitcase. I suppose I should've looked at it ahead of time and hung it up.

The day didn't start out hot, but sweat rings my arms. Perspiration trickles inside my shirt. I suppose I should've thought of that, too. If I take off my jacket now, my armpits would be too distracting. Strange little thoughts like this pop into my head, trying to get my attention. None about Mama—yet.

Earlier, a gust blew through the open window. It picked up my notecards, swirled them out of order, and junked them on the floor. Like my wrinkled jacket and underarm stains, I tell myself they don't matter. I leave them there, passionately presenting my findings and citing resources from memory.

Dr. Klein asks a question. I have no idea where he's going with this query. It isn't logical. I look at Dr. Slompka, my committee chair. He seems lost in my paper, silently tapping his finger as he reads. I swear he's tapping out S-O-S. I gather my notecards from the floor and pretend to look for a citation, attempting to calm myself. Dr. Klein tells me I should be more familiar with my sources.

Twice in the next fifteen minutes, I use the ol' let-me-look-up-that-citation to answer Dr. Klein's sidetrack questions. I finally deduce it's his way of asking for different explanations based on various publication sources.

Dr. Eaves asks many questions about the mechanical application of my conclusion. She seems genuinely interested in its possibilities.

My shirt sticks to my back. Brain cells fire that have awakened only for this ordeal and will surely die after this abuse.

I get a break when Dr. Slompka and Dr. Klein disagree about my usage of the term *natural width*. It's obvious they've had this argument before when discussing quantum mechanics and the indetermination of particle energy. I enjoy listening to them; it reminds me of my freelance work at the aerospace center when we were applying ideas and actually building something.

Soon enough, their attention turns back to me. Fifteen minutes of grilling continue, but it feels like an hour. Finally, Dr. Slompka excuses me. "You're free to stretch your legs while the committee discusses your findings. Be back in a half hour."

I trudge downstairs, wondering how long I've been ignoring the dull ache growing at my temples. I bang on the side of the soda machine, but it isn't rolling out any freebies today. I don't have any coins. Tweezing my shirt from my body, I step outdoors and circle around to the shady side of the building. It's a gorgeous day. Summer term has just begun, but the campus is mostly empty.

It's a coincidence that I sit directly under the second floor window where I'd just defended my findings. Voices travel down to my perch. Dr. Slompka says he's going to the beach for the rest of the month. He has a little condo and his grandkids will visit.

Dr. Eaves already has her train ticket through the Cotswolds. She and her husband will be hiking to several villages, then spend time in Oxford and Bath.

Dr. Klein is teaching a class and installing a new parquet floor in his house.

Their chatter continues. They discuss new departmental policies, the Cleveland Indians, and how to remove mold from basements. Time passes but I remain buckled to the sidewalk.

It becomes apparent they aren't going to discuss my work. Perhaps it's because they've already read and commented on it, so what more is there to say? Was this only a game? An exercise to ensure logical thinking and proper scientific method?

Now their topic has changed to President Clinton's speech on science and technology. I let out a long, low breath. All the money, the worry, and the time I'd spent. Of course, I'd grown in knowledge, but the entire process could've been done more efficiently. This was like an endurance test to join their club. Dorothy must've felt like this after seeing the man behind the curtain pulling levers.

What had it all been for? For letters behind my name. Perhaps it would get me better jobs—or at least an interview, but it was no guarantee. Strangely, at one time I thought I needed the degree to make my dad proud and to feel good about myself, but not anymore. As Mama once told me, "No one can take away your knowledge and skills, whether they give you a degree or not."

Images of her circled my mind. It felt strange to have her story end. There'd be no more opportunities to ask her questions. To hear her weird thoughts. I am now an orphan.

A stiff breeze rolls past, blowing the sounds of my committee down the street. My shock and disappointment follow it. With the next gust, I let out a long sigh. The curtains on both life and my dissertation have been pulled aside; now I know how surviving works. I've spent too much time worrying about dotting i's and crossing t's when I could've been discovering more useful things.

"Be true to yourself." Mama's words goad me as an idea grows. With three minutes to go, I hurry upstairs and wait.

When they call me inside, the committee members wear solemn faces as though they've been working on world population control.

"Sophia," Dr. Slompka says as Dr. Klein hands me a list of notes. "As you know, Dr. Klein and I have differing opinions about how to state your conclusions. You've provided us with revisions—"

"Twelve," I interrupt.

He looks at me, cocking his head. It takes him a moment to start again. "Ah ... well, yes, you've made several revisions, yet the committee isn't quite satisfied with the wording. So—"

"Excuse me, I need to clarify here." I ignore Dr. Slompka's stare. "Dr. Eaves, do you have a problem with the language in the conclusion?"

"I ... uh..." She is the outsider in the group, from the Engineering Department. She looks at my document in front of her.

"If I'm going to further amend, I must know where the confusion lies. I'm curious about your perception of the problem from an engineering perspective. Please?"

She again flips through my 220 pages formatted into a book then closes it. "I have no concerns about your methods or your writing."

"That may be," says Dr. Slompka a little too loudly, "but the committee is still asking for a revision. Obviously," he looks at Dr. Eaves, "we won't have to convene the entire group again. Sophia, if you could emphasize—"

"Wait." I hold up my hand. He stops talking. I don't speak, imagining how the future nitpicking changes will require more edits and delays because of summer vacations. Then fall classes will create more hold ups. It very likely could be next winter before this will be approved.

He lets the silence continue for a long moment before saying, "In the interest of present perspectives—"

Both my hands signal stop. His eyebrows rise as I say, "I need a moment. Please."

He leans back into his chair. Surely he understands. Sometimes while explaining a problem in class, he stops in mid-calculation, his mind circling in another direction until he can gather himself again.

Three sets of eyes study me. I want to be sure I've come to a calm decision, not a horn-mad impulse. Weighing logic against risk, I stare out the window, watching oak leaves twist in the breeze.

For some insane reason, Gramoo's voice pops into my head. "That's the angels waiting, their wings stirring the air and the leaves."

Good grief. What hokum. That isn't even remotely helpful. My synapses are short-circuiting. I'm losing it.

"Bifurcation!" I say loudly, jumpstarting my mind toward something mathematical. I search for cogent words as I turn and face the committee. "A split. I'm at the point at which something must divide.

"For most of my college life, I've worked toward this dissertation topic. It was in spurts and jumps—as money allowed. My papers, readings, and research have been in this area. It's my passion.

"But I've taken the modeling equation as far as I can today. As we would say, 'it's currently unsolvable.' My Dad would say, 'It's deep enough.' He was a rough man. Died in an oil field fire, but when he was around, he'd give my sister and me pithy advice such as, 'Be a hand, not a face.' He meant, get work done, don't stand around. Get your hands dirty so you know what's really going on.

"I'm telling you this because the timing for this oral defense couldn't be better. It's the beginning of summer. I'm sure everyone is eager to finish up and get on with their vacation plans. For instance, tomorrow, I have to drive to Rain to help my sister with my mother, then find work. You see, I'm out of money and time."

"What are you saying?" Dr. Klein's eyebrows squeeze together.

I give him a regretful smile, the kind which indicates politeness is covering a ditch full of problems. "I gave this doctorate my best shot within the allotted time and money I had. As you know, I actually thought I'd be done six months ago, but there were more revisions than I expected. I'm saying with all of your esteemed help, I wrote a paper that was as clear, logical, insightful, and as well researched as I could make it. I appreciate your suggestions, and I included them because it made the paper better.

"I understand not everyone agrees, but if it were a topic each person approached the same way, then I'd be contributing nothing to the body of research. It makes sense that Dr. Slompka would like more emphasis in his area of expertise, while Dr. Klein prefers more support of his field. I understand both perspectives. But here's the thing, I wrote not only what I found, but what I'm passionate in discovering. I can do no better at this time."

Dr. Klein stares at me. "By university policy, you have two more years to finish. You should—"

"For the last six weeks, I've been living off little packages of ramen and the donuts left in the faculty room. As I mentioned, I have family obligations. Besides, I don't know that any question about our world is ever finished. Wasn't it Einstein who said something like, 'Our attempt to understand reality is like a man trying to understand the mechanism of a closed watch'? I can't solve your split perspectives in this paper. Only you two can." I nod at the two men.

Dr. Slompka's forehead furrows. "Well now, I'm sure we can find some short-term position in the department to tide you over while you fix these things."

Dr. Klein scowls. "What about all the work you put in? All of us have put in?"

I hold out my hand to him. "I really appreciate the recommendations this committee has made, helping and guiding me. I hope very much the committee will conclude their differences and grant my degree. I've done the best science I can do. It's time for me to be a hand, not a face. I need to find full-time work."

I thank each one of them individually, and then slip out the door.

Outside, in the hallway, I cover my mouth, breathing heavily as I lean against the wall. I'm tempted to listen through the door, but I don't. I've played my hand. Taken the risk.

I feel different. Not angry or afraid. If I've made a mistake, I'll start over elsewhere; at least I have more skills this time.

A relieved sigh escapes. I straighten my spine and walk out of the building. As I stroll down the sidewalk the oaks sway in the breeze. For the briefest of moments I tell the scientist in me to shut up.

I imagine the clatter of leaves as the applause of angels.

# 38. 1997

"I CAN'T BELIEVE you didn't tell me your mother died." Mina scowls.

"I couldn't take the chance you'd tell Dr. Slompka."

"Of course I would've, because you're terrible at emotional stuff. Maybe alerting him would've kept you from screwing up your orals. Why are we celebrating?"

"I didn't mess up. I took charge. We're celebrating the end. The conclusion—one way or another." I signal the bartender for another Dr. Pepper, splurging and adding an order of chili cheese fries.

"I think you've set yourself up for more punishing rewrites," she says. "A doctoral committee doesn't allow uppity candidates. They have ways of humbling a person until they grovel."

"Well, they can't because I won't be around. And I wasn't uppity. I told them I was out of time and money—which is true. The funds I set aside for school ran out weeks ago. I'm done."

"You're done when they say you're done. That's how it works. Trevor Jaze has made ten revisions and lost twenty pounds since he started. Your committee is your overlord. If they want changes, you give it to them, or your future is stuck until you do."

"*Pfffft!* My dad was on top of a burning derrick. That's stuck. My mama thought it was always 1980. That's stuck. But being asked for another revision? That only means the choices get more difficult.

"I've learned the hard way you can count on something to go wrong. You either give up, or you try to solve the problem. Then go onto the next obstacle and the next one. I simply attempted to end the committee's nitpicking by telling them I was out of time and money."

"Why should they care?" Mina plucks a french fry as the waiter sets the basket on the table. "They've got their degrees, positions, and egos. Once they grant your degree, you become their competition."

"They care because of funding. Every department is expected to churn out a certain number of graduates in order to get grants and project monies. They're not worried about my research. It's solid. They didn't even discuss it." I hold up my hand stopping her question. "Because I eavesdropped."

"Let me get this straight. You listened in on a confidential faculty session? You told the committee you're finished? Not to mention you've used college facilities as your covert radio station, and you took over the custodian's closet as your personal residence? Any one of those could get you removed from the program. What's going on in your head?"

"I've done workarounds all my life. Haven't you listened to my stories?"

"So you're giving up on your doctorate?"

"I spent the afternoon making a few revisions."

"And if they don't accept it?"

"Mina, I've had a lot of practice in starting over. I'm good at it. I had a job at an aerospace center in Amsterdam. I'll get one again somewhere in the world. I'll do new research at another university. I'll find new people and new minds to work with. At some point while my committee was dillydallying about their vacation plans, I realized I wanted to create things, not kiss their rings.

"I know it's not normal, and grad students are expected to kowtow until signatures are on the dissertation, but that's not how I think it should be.

"I completed the research I believed in—not something promoting others' platforms. It needs to be judged on its own merits. And I didn't want to play the pity card. Either I earned the degree or I didn't. For me, it's as factual as that. In the meantime, please don't say anything about my mama."

"You're crazy."

"You're probably right." I wrap her in a hug and whisper, "And I'm saying goodbye tonight. I'm leaving in the morning."

"What?" Mina shouts, pulling away, staring at me.

"Funeral planning. I'm sure my sister has it all under control, but I'd like to be with her."

"I knew something was wrong when you came out of my office yesterday. I'll never understand you nerd-types. You'll let me know when the funeral is, won't you? I want to come."

I nod and pull her into another hug. "I need to say this quickly because the others are coming through the door. Thank you. You've kept my secrets. You listened to me rant. You covered for me. You dragged me to that church of yours so I wouldn't starve. You made a difference in who I am."

"Oh ... it was ... I wanted to. I'm sorry you're being pulled home again." She moves to break our hug.

But I hold onto her, blinking back tears. "It's different now. I'll be in Rain for a few days. Then I'm off, searching for a job—and a new home somewhere in the world. I trust I'll find people as kind as you."

Jason is hollering as he steps beside us. "I bet you're glad that's over, huh?" I let go of Mina and fall into his bear hug. "In your honor," he says, "I'm gonna disassemble the copier in the faculty lounge."

"No, don't do that."

"Screw 'em. They have PhDs. They should be able to put it back together."

"See what you've done!" Mina slaps my arm, giving me the quiet smile that passes between women who share a secret.

I grin. "My work here is finished."

Friends and students drift into the bar. Word has gotten around. No one is rich, but we're pooling money, buying pitchers of beer and soft drinks, ordering pub grub, and telling stories about each other. We're travelers on similar journeys, our paths intersecting, boosting each other along.

Never again will all of us be together in one room. As I look at each face, I remember some way that person has made my experience here more bearable. I've grown because of them. I suddenly feel unworthy. They've created a debt inside me. To repay it, I'll have to be a better person.

That seems more challenging than getting a PhD.

# 39. Last Story

**ON AIR**

GREETINGS FROM THE Navigator. It's the small hours of a long night. This is the end of a long quest. I have one final story, a modern fairy tale. This is the story of how to say goodbye.

There once was a girl. Not a princess or a cheerleader, just a plain girl with no super powers. Actually, she was sort of a dweeby tomboy. She liked to climb trees which was useful as a kid, but not that helpful as an adult—unless she wanted a job climbing towers.

She also liked numbers. She could sum, divide, and braid calculations into elegant solutions. And she loved looking at the stars at night. She dreamed one day she could use her numbers to travel between those bright specks of light.

Unfortunately, she was picked on for being different. Her dad told her "to pop those jerks in the nose"—unless they were littler than her. If they were smaller, then she should be nice, because a little-snot threatening a big-snot wasn't very smart, "but ya gotta admire the spunk." Her mother gave her the old sticks-and-stones advice—ignore the idiots and be true to yourself.

The girl figured bullying was the best she could expect from her tiny town populated with troll-minded jerks. So when she got older, she ran away to a new kingdom. The Kingdom of the Netherlands.

Regrettably, this place also had jerks. And even more shocking, she discovered *she* too acted like a jerk sometimes—okay, she was often a jerk—but she was stressed.

She would've starved and been forced to live under a canal bridge if it weren't for a kind wizard. He was actually an innkeeper, but for the purpose of this tale, we'll call him a wizard. He made her learn the crazy-vowel-language of the kingdom, and she watched and memorized his secret magic: Do at least one compassionate thing for others each day.

She practiced his sorcery and discovered there were more *not-jerks* than jerks around her. She made a lot of friends who were different. She grew and learned. And just when she was comfortable and in danger of settling into a rut—she had to leave the kingdom to continue her adventure. The wizard insisted she perform one final ritual.

All of these tales have rituals. Click the heels of the ruby-red slippers to get out of OZ. Melt a ring to get out or Mordor.

The girl had to learn to say goodbye well.

First, she had to find everyone who'd helped her and give them a hug. This worked well, unless they were British, or didn't like to be grabbed by an American, then a handshake was acceptable.

Second, she had to say what needed to be said. That was the hard part. Life had a wonky sense of humor, and if she were to tell someone they were a muttonhead or a gloomy pest, then it was likely their paths would cross again and that person would become her boss or mother-in-law.

So she decided what was truly necessary was letting folks know how they'd been significant in her life. Then she encouraged them to hang onto hope, and told them they'd make it, even if they didn't feel like it. She assured them life does indeed give second chances. Often not the way they expected.

Lastly, she had to wish the other person good luck in their journey. *Veel succes. Viel gluck. Bueña suerte. Bonn chance!*

Most importantly, she had to do each step as sincerely as she could.

The magic worked. In all this farewelling, she discovered the one person she'd never have to say goodbye to was herself. She'd met herself in each place she'd traveled, on every tower top and through dark streets and graveyards. And when it became hard to keep pushing forward, others had encouraged her. It was surprising how many non-jerks there were in the world. The memories of them were hers. She could carry them with her for miles and years.

She'd risked getting to know people—even those she didn't want to know. She took chances and looked stupid and felt insignificant. She made mistakes. She grew. In a quiet sort of way she was proud of herself. That's the best kind of adventure, surviving it and coming out wiser and satisfied at the end.

Tonight my radio journey is over. I'm moving on. As I look back, sometimes I've felt insignificant or stupid behind this microphone. I think only two people listened to this program—and I doubt my mama understood anything she heard. Mostly, I felt I was alone, talking in the dark. But if by chance, you heard one of my late night stories, then I hope it helped in some way.

There's a strange feeling about leaving a place. Like time running out or a door closing. It urges a person to speak the truth.

The truth is, telling these stories probably helped me more than anyone else. I see things differently now than I did at ages eight, sixteen, or even last year. Re-examining the past has helped me go forward. It got me unstuck. It reminded me to be plucky: Go after what I wanted. Trust that I could handle what came next.

That's the best kind of adventure—wiser and satisfied at the end.

So, if you're out there listening, thank you for helping me on my journey.

Now ... here's a hug for you.

Good luck on your own wanderings.

Somewhere, someday we may meet again. Until then, take a risk. Show compassion every day.

Good night Mmmm ...

Good night, Oregon.

Goodbye, Mama.

# 40. 1997

I FLICK OFF the microphone. The 'On Air' sign goes black. Another switch powers down the equipment. A couple of tiny LED lights glow from the console, interrupting the darkness. The quiet settles in.

A few moments pass before I go to the roof and disassemble the device I'd previously installed. I finish, trot down the steps, and have barely left the stairwell when the elevator in front of me sounds with a *ding*. My brain yells *Run* but my feet are stuck. Who would come up here at this time on a summer night? Another farewell party?

The door opens. I stand face to face with Dr. Slompka. At one-thirty in the morning this can't be good. I consider dropping the tools and cable and hightailing it down the hallway. Instead, I go with the surprised look that's already on my face. "Sir! This is unexpected. I hope my abrupt announcement this afternoon isn't the reason for your visit." It's not a good opening, but it's better than shouting, "Bifurcation!" again. I begin coiling the stiff coax in my hands.

He gives me a long look, but doesn't say anything. If he thinks I'm going to fill the silence and possibly incriminate myself, then he doesn't know my skill level. I gather the cable into perfect circles as though it's the most important thing in the world.

His hands go to his hips. Another not-good sign. "I didn't expect you to be working tonight," he says. "What do you have there?"

I consider telling him I'd amped the radio station beyond FCC regulations, but only when *I* broadcast so it wouldn't interfere with many other stations. I shrug. "Replaced some cable. I'll be leaving in the morning, so I'm finishing off things I never got around to doing."

"I couldn't sleep tonight. I've been thinking about what you said this afternoon."

"Sorry to cause a problem." I hope I look apologetic, because I'm *not* sorry to light a fire under them.

"I'm going to speak to you confidentially and honestly." He waits until I nod before going on. "What possessed you to ask Fred Klein to be on your dissertation committee? What were you thinking?"

My lips flatline. I look down the hallway, choosing my words carefully. "Honestly, I really like him as an instructor. He's eclectic in his approach. Allows discussions to veer outside the text. In Particle Astrophysics and Cosmology he didn't even follow the syllabus. He—"

"Wait. He didn't follow any part of it?" Dr. Slompka's eyebrows pinch together. "There are salient learning points that must be covered for accreditation. What did he teach?"

"We were tested on the syllabus material, but he didn't cover it. We had to teach ourselves." Dr. Slompka's stare becomes more intense. "I'm not trying to get him in trouble. I'm explaining why I wanted him on my committee. I thought the class was great. I learned double the information because he covered so many topics, and I retained more information because I had to research it for myself. He's a wild card, willing to experiment with different approaches. Doesn't follow the rules. I thought he'd be an asset to critical thinking."

"Well, yes, there's that." Dr. Slompka's shoulders relax. He heaves a sigh and rubs his face. "So now you're discovering that highly creative individuals are difficult to constrain. They create their own tenets. And one of Dr. Klein's personal rules is that any dissertation fewer than four hundred pages is lacking in research effort. Period."

I grimaced. "By the time I heard that rumor, it was too late to un-ask him to be on my committee. However, you're my chairman and advisor. I figured your opinion was the only one that truly counted. When I talked to you about minimum length, you said it needed to be long enough to sufficiently justify the thesis experiment. I assumed you'd have the final word."

"I know what I said, but he doesn't consider you ready."

"Ready? What more? Twice I've added resources just to 'puff up' the related-literature section. Actually, I thought one hundred pages would've been sufficient."

"You will be our youngest PhD and you've done it in three years, which is phenomenal. Dr. Klein argues that greater experience will lead you to more complex work and conclusions."

"That may true of social sciences, but math doesn't change simply because humans age. Wouldn't that be like adding post-doc work on top of the dissertation requirements? I've met the residency conditions. You and I have consulted regularly, ensuring procedures are solid. Are you saying the research is slipshod?"

"No. No, I'm saying Dr. Klein, for all his willingness to try new methods, is very narrow when it comes to the requirements of a doctorate. It took him five years to complete his work. That's normative."

"You're saying he's jealous?"

Dr. Slompka's face looks as though he's been caught throwing a colleague under a bus.

"Well, that's just crappy. I never suspected his problem was with me personally. I thought the riff was between you two. He wanted your job and was acting like a stag challenging you."

"I will admit he can be a challenge." He rubs his brow, massaging his forehead. "He feels your willingness to walk away when you're so close to completion is evidence of ... uh ... your youthfulness."

"So you're saying he thinks I should hang around, take more classes, and age—like wine or cheese?" My voice rises. I'm trying to keep the anger out, but not succeeding. "I'm twenty-six and I suppose it's irritating that I'm also a woman."

"I believe you're taking this too far."

"If you say so." I stare at the elevator, tapping the coiled cable against my leg. "May I tell you something?"

"Please." He points to a hallway bench and we both sit down.

"When I was eight, I really wanted a life-size doll. Every time we were in Eugene and drove by Sears and Roebuck, I'd moon over her. She was three-feet tall and looked like a real kid with shiny blond hair. I even named her Melinda and talked about her a lot. Being a weird, mathy kid, I didn't have many friends.

"It took Mama two years because we were paying off debt, but somehow she scraped together enough money to get me that doll. It didn't take long for the wonderfulness of Melinda to wear off. She smelled like a plastic swimming pool. Her legs didn't bend so she sat splay-legged and fell off every chair. Her arms either stayed at her side or stuck forward like The Mummy. I hauled her up a tree one time and got paddled because "she's too expensive to drag through the woods." So really, all I could do with Melinda was brush her hair, and I didn't even bother combing my own rat-nest most mornings.

"I let her watch me do homework, only so Mama wouldn't feel like she'd wasted money. But Melinda taught me one thing: what a person wants with all her heart can suddenly change.

"So now ... fast forward ... I'm at my oral defense, listening to Dr. Klein and you debate natural width, and I have a Melinda moment. I realize the time I was happiest was when I was in Amsterdam, working with others on real projects and actual space problems.

"I'm not saying the doctorate isn't important. I do want it because it'll open doors, but what I really want has changed. Or maybe it was what I always wanted and didn't realize it. I desperately need to use what I've learned. I want to solve problems and help others in the quest. It's time for me to go to work."

Dr Slompka nods, a tired look washing over his face. He stares at the floor tiles. I stare at them, too. After a while, he interrupts our thoughts. "Academia certainly feels different than the real world."

"Yep."

"So what will you do?"

I hesitate, weighing how much truth I should share. "I'll say goodbye to my family, then I'm off to find a job and make new discoveries."

"You can use my name for references."

"Thanks. That means a lot. And thanks for chairing my committee—no matter how it turns out." The conversation stalls. We stare at the floor again. Equations and theories are much easier to discuss than expectations. "Hey!" I say in a more upbeat tone. "I made some of the revisions Dr. Klein requested. I'll put it on your desk before I leave."

He seems genuinely pleased. "Thank you. I look forward to reviewing it." He stands. "Well, it's late. I need to get going, but one more thing is bothering me. It's the actual reason I came tonight."

I stand too, gripping the coax with both hands.

"As I said, I couldn't sleep. I poured a bourbon and sat on my back porch. The moon's up, a waxing crescent. Have you seen it?" I shake my head. "You should get out and look. It's a gorgeous night.

"I was thinking about your dissertation problem and I agree, you've spent enough time on this project. But there are politics at work here. As head of the department I may be able to influence Dr. Klein concerning the solid foundation of your research and that a degree should be granted. The only successful argument he could use is if he had evidence that you lacked moral integrity and maturity as a candidate of our university."

My stomach clutches. I squeeze the coax harder. I've never considered myself very moral.

"So," he continues, "I sipped my drink and switched on the radio." He looks at me.

I look at the stairwell, calculating the number of steps to get to the bottom floor.

"Imagine my surprise when I heard your voice interrupting Garth Brooks."

"You listen to country music?"

"How many times have you done a broadcast?"

"I've made a few public service announcements to the community."

"And you did it because ...?"

I let out a long sigh. "Because it was there. Because what good are mistakes if you can't learn from them and keep others from making the same blunders? I hope my stories helped someone, but honestly, no one listens to our station. With riveting afternoon programming like 'Campus Crime' or 'Elope with Stephanie,' I doubt that anyone but you noticed the all-night boot music was interrupted."

"It's very hard to constrain creative types. They tend to make up their own rules, don't they?" He stares at me.

I meet his gaze adding a shrug. "My mama always said so."

"Well, the Physics Department only maintains the equipment. The Communications Department handles programming, so I don't consider it my problem. But let's hope Dr. Klein wasn't listening—or he thinks you'd gotten permission—instead of hijacking the radio station. That was your last broadcast, right?"

I nod, a smile tickling the corner of my mouth.

"What's so funny?" He punches the elevator button. The doors immediately open. He holds them as he listens to me.

"When I was overseas, I went to the Physics Club but was always the outsider. Then one night, they asked me to go to a country-western bar. They wanted me to translate and explain songs like 'Your Cheatin' Heart,' 'Crazy,' and 'Waltz Across Texas.' I can honestly say cowboy music changed my international social life."

He smiles and steps inside. "Don't stay late. You've done enough." The door begins closing as he adds, "Whatever happened to Melinda?"

"I gave her to my kid-sister who loved to braid hair."

He's laughing as he calls through the narrowing gap, "It's been a pleasure, Sophia Bolton. Go change the world."

The doors close. I stand facing my reflection in the polished steel. Once again silence settles over the hallway. I'm not sure what just happened. Had events tipped in my favor? I so prefer equations over social interactions.

By now it's two a.m. With cleaning duties and revisions finished, I empty the custodian's closet, carrying my belongings to

Buckminster, my Cortina, so I'll be ready to leave early tomorrow.

In one last trip to the roof, I settle in a lounge chair. Many times, I've been up here to clear my head. The anemometer spins slowly, but the hummingbird feeder is gone. The experiment must be over—end of the school year.

Above, the crescent moon glows. The campus and town are softly lit by yellow sodium lights, giving the landscape a dreamy quality. All is quiet. All is in its place. Now I can think about Mama.

Now I can cry.

Bird trill awakens me. I stretch and blink at the pink dawn. Lights are switching off in the eastern part of town. I hadn't meant to fall asleep on the roof, but it seems fitting.

Downstairs, I leave the department keys, my forwarding address, and my revised dissertation on Dr. Slompka's desk. In the faculty lounge, I grab the last stale donut.

Buckminster sits in the parking lot, covered with dew. I breathe in cool air.

It's cozy behind the wheel with boxes surrounding me. The engine starts on the second crank. The sky is coral-gray, the sun at nautical twilight, and there's no traffic.

I tell the waking world, "This is the story of how I get on with my life."

## 41. 1999

THE BROWN ENVELOPE finds me after twenty-one months of riding people's desks, postal trucks, and airplanes.

The exterior is plastered with labels and inked messages: Return to Sender—Addressee has moved—Please forward.

Inside there's a letter from the university informing me I'd received a doctorate. I already knew because Dr. Slompka had emailed me, and I'd used him for references.

There's an old note from Mina: *Someone from communication brought this to the department. I thought you'd like to see it. Call more often. Hugs!*

A letter written in blocky print is inside.

*Dear Navigator,*

*I used to listen to your program. You said some good stuff. A kid named Clyde picked on me all the time. I never knew when he was gonna get at me. The bathroom was a bad place. I told the teacher, but she can't be everywhere. So I did what your dad told you to do. When Clyde tried to knock my lunch tray out of my hands again, I kicked him in the nards. My lunch went all over the floor, but I didn't care. Clyde cried and held his crotch.*

*I got thrown out of school for a week. But Clyde doesn't bother me anymore. Nobody does.*

*Please come back. Mom lets me listen to the radio at night. She thinks I won't hear her and dad argue that way. I could sure use some advice about girls that keep talking to me and won't leave me alone.*

*Your friend*
*Joel Macwinger*

Dear Joel,

Sorry to be late getting back to you. It's taken a while for your letter to catch up with me. I've been in California, Amsterdam, and now I'm in Maryland. I'm part of a team working to monitor neutron stars. That's what's left behind when a star explodes. The spinning, glowing cinder puts out a light sweeping through the darkness. It looks like it's pulsing. Someday we might be able to use these pulsars to navigate anywhere in our solar system. It takes a lot of people to do this project.

Of course, you're older now than when you asked for advice, but what I'll tell you should still be useful. If you remember, on that radio broadcast, I said my mother had a different way to get along with bullies. She said to try to avoid them, and if I couldn't, then try to talk to them.

Let me tell you something. I've used her talking method a whole lot more than my Dad's punch-them advice. You sound like a smart kid, so I know you understand when I say that often in kid-world another kid won't listen when you tell him to stop. You can tell him over and over, and he still won't stop. It's frustrating—but I'm sure you understand why you were suspended.

My mother once told me if a person is happy, they don't need to bully others ... so neither your Clyde nor my Eden were happy kids. It sounds like you discovered there will be times you have to stand your ground or the bully will keep running over you. It gets better as you get older. You'll keep finding better ways to deal with jerks.

Here's why you need to learn it. I work with many smart people. We don't always agree. Sometimes we argue. But we're clever enough to work together and solve our problems.

That's important because our project will be on the International Space Station (ISS). What we're doing might help space travel.

So when you look at the sky, the ISS could be passing over. It circles every ninety-two minutes. Our pulsar equipment may be in it, operating right over your head. It involves thousands of people from sixteen countries to keep the ISS orbiting.

You can be one of the smart people. You can figure out how to get along with others and how to keep space stations going. We need you because there's so much to explore in our world and in the Universe.

I'm sorry I won't be back at the radio station, but you can write to me. I travel a lot, but wherever I am, please know—I'm rooting for you.

Remember—take a risk and talk to girls. Be kind and you'll discover they have smart brains, too. And they make great friends.

Keep moving toward your dreams—no matter how small or large your steps. I've discovered that dreams are sort of like the stars; you can only see them part of the time, but rest assured they're out there—waiting for you.

Risk and compassion, Joel, every day.

Your friend, The Navigator,

Sophia Bolton, PhD
Astrophysicist
NASA Space-Flight Center

## 42. Thanks to ...

Rarely do we reach our dreams by ourselves. It's the people along the way that make any accomplishment a memorable journey. The dream of creating this story was supported by:

The folks at East Texas Oil Museum, Kilgore—offering great info and hospitality.

K.K. for telling me enough oil stories to fill two books.

Pat Stillwell—on how to paint tall, tall water towers.

Kimberly of Randy Roy's Redlight Tours—Amsterdam. I'd never have made the contacts and found the secret places without you.

Artur Nemeth, Hungary—for the gift of sharing what it was like living behind the Iron Curtain.

The Beautiful Amalie-for your candid info about working in Amsterdam.

David Lloyd-for doing the math calculations and explaining why "physics doesn't work that way." You know, I only understood about half of what you were saying. Thanks for keeping me on track.

NASA's team working on SEXTANT. The seed of inspiration for Sophia's goal. I used a different timeline, but congratulations on your first successful step toward deep space navigation.

Pat Lichen-for your gracious suggestions and razor-sharp mind in keeping the story on track.

Etta Place and Ken Walters—green pens, grammar guides, sharp eyes, patience, and a sense of humor.

The women of Chrysalis—their astute insight in helping craft Sophia Bolton's story.

My family—what a great, tireless sounding board. And thanks for enduring the barrage of questions I asked on every vacation. I'm so blessed that I get to make my trips around the sun with you!

Finally, a hug to my readers. Thank you for your kind words and encouragement. You'll never know how much they mean, especially during late-night writing sessions when self-doubt likes to sit on the edge of my desk, making comments.

My sincere thanks for your support.

**If you enjoyed this reading, check out these other books.**

barbarakayfroman.com

or

**Please consider leaving a review** at the site where you purchased this book.

Thanks for joining me on the journey.

Take a risk.
Show compassion—every day.

Good day (or good night) and good life, my friends.

## Thanks for reading!